The Magic of Meatloaf

Midlife Magic on the Menu, Book 1

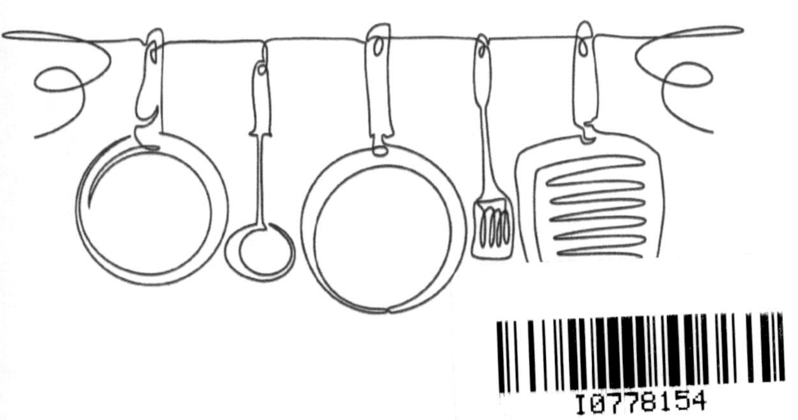

by Jessica Rosenberg

Published by Blue Octopus Press

www.BlueOctopusPress.com

(831) 471-7028

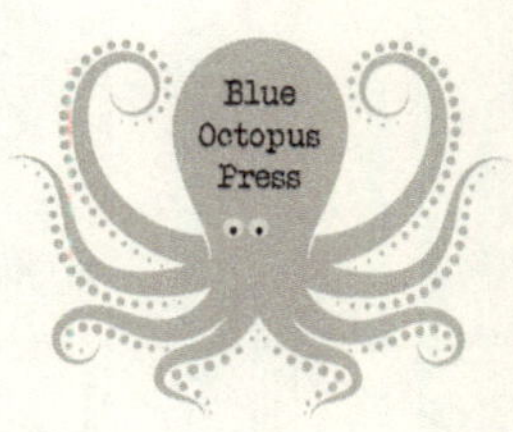

Rosenberg, Jessica

The Magid of Meatloaf: Midlife Magic on the Menu, book 1

Copyright © 2024 by Jessica Rosenberg

Cover design by Karen Dimmick/Arcane Covers

The Midlife Magic on the Menu Series is a work of fiction. Its characters, scenes, and locales are the product of the author's imagination or are used fictitiously. Any similarity of fictional characters to people living or dead is purely coincidental. All rights reserved. Printed in the United States of America. No portion of this book may be reproduced in any form without written permission from the publisher or author, except as permitted by U.S. copyright law. No portion of this book may be used for AI training. If you did not download this book from Amazon.com, you are reading a pirated copy.

I dedicate this book to the family and friends who showed up for me in my darkest hour, held my hand as I fell apart, and loved me when I was at my least lovable. I would not have survived the last six months without you, and this book would most assuredly not exist. *(Y'all know who you are.)*

You are proof of what we all already suspected: Friendship is the purest form of magic.

In the midst of winter, I found there was,
within me, an invincible summer.
~Albert Camus

ONE

"**M**elly, honey, I'm feeling a little under the weather. Would you be a dear and close up for me?" Aggie asked as I brushed past her to slide a stack of dirty plates into the large plastic bin behind the counter.

"Of course." Her face, never all that ruddy to begin with, was paler than usual, and she looked every one of her 82 years. "Is everything okay? Do you need to sit down for a minute?"

Her wan smile wasn't reassuring. "You're so sweet. Always worrying about me. Just a touch of a headache. Nothing a good night's sleep won't fix."

A good night's sleep was my boss's answer to everything. It didn't matter what was ailing you—heartache, headache, or existential angst—she always suggested a large glass of water and what she called a "hard reset," aka a good night's sleep. Annoyingly, she was right often enough that I'd stopped questioning the wisdom.

A glance around the diner revealed three tables that seemed almost ready to check out, and one lingering over coffee and pie.

"How about I run you home? It won't kill Momo to keep an eye on the customers for a minute."

"Might," Momo muttered from the kitchen.

While the main purpose of the opening in the wall was to pass food from the kitchen to the restaurant, it also allowed Momo to keep tabs on everything happening in the diner without ever having to leave his griddle.

When I'd first met the burly short-order cook, I'd assumed he was a cranky, middle-aged guy whose hard life had left him with little love for anything or anyone, and opted to steer as clear of him as the job allowed. I'd expected my usual cheery disposition to rub him the wrong way, but if it did, he never let on. I was starting to suspect that his gruff exterior, crew cut presumably held over from his Navy days, and late-night club bouncer physique hid something deeper than a general disdain for people and life. He certainly never missed an opportunity to weigh in on conversations we had behind the counter.

"Jus' like being included," he'd say when I told him he didn't have to give his two cents on every single interaction.

I couldn't entirely fault him. Spending every shift alone in front of a steaming griddle sounded like absolute torture to me.

"No, no, love. That's very sweet of you, but I think I can drive myself two short blocks." Aggie untied her apron and tucked it under the counter. Her bright smile only partially masked the pained wince that flashed across her face when she straightened up. "Really, I'm fine. I need to take care of a few things in the office before I go. And you have work to do."

She winked, a saucy twinkle glinting in her eye, and just like that, the tough-as-nails diner owner was back. The fist that had wrapped itself around my belly when I'd spied the frail old lady inside her indomitable armor loosened.

Of course she was fine. She was Aggie, the woman who'd opened up her heart and life to the downtrodden, broken woman who'd shown up one afternoon, reeling from loss and with nowhere to go. She was the diner owner who single-handedly kept the quaint beach town of Portney, Massachusetts supplied with world-class, comforting, home-cooked meals served in an eclectically decorated diner pulled right out of the 1950s. I'd half expected that the job she'd offered as she served me a steaming plate of meatloaf and mashed potatoes would require me to brush off my dusty roller-skating skills.

She hadn't missed a day of work since I'd joined her team. No matter how early I made my way to the diner, I knew I'd find her bustling around. Most days, she left long after I stumbled home at the end of a grueling day of waiting tables and keeping people hydrated and caffeinated.

"Table nine looks like they need more water. Offer them a slice of pie on the house to make up for the wait."

Whatever weakness I'd detected was nowhere to be seen as she issued a few more directives about what I needed to do before locking up. Notably, that I shouldn't forget to turn off the train.

Even though this diner wasn't a converted train wagon, Aggie's husband, Mitch, had built a model version of the train that had inspired its design. The little dining car even had a tiny Aggie in it, and a conductor who looked like Mitch hung from the locomotive, waving to the people eating in the restaurant below as the train looped around and around. Over the years, Mitch had added trees and buildings around the track that ran along the walls close to the ceiling and above the windows, creating a miniature Portney that delighted visitors and locals alike.

By the time the swinging doors that led to her tiny office and then to the employee entrance at the back of the diner had stilled, I'd almost convinced myself I'd imagined the shaky old lady I'd glimpsed. It wasn't like this was the first time Aggie had asked me to lock up. Maybe she was finally ready to hand off the workload she'd allegedly hired me to take on.

The rhythmic rasping of Momo's metal spatula scraping up the day's residue on the large steel griddle in the kitchen followed me as I made my way to the other side of the counter to top off waters and check on the stragglers lingering over their coffees.

"All set?" I asked the couple I suspected were on a first date that appeared to be going well. They hadn't stopped chatting all evening, sneaking covert looks and shy smiles. Their tentative awkwardness shouldn't have been endearing, but it triggered an unexpected pang of longing that caught me off guard. Despite being closer to 40 than 30, I'd somehow never been on a real first date. It was probably time to accept that I'd long passed that stage of life.

It wasn't like I'd had a choice. And even if I had, I would have made the same one every single time. An awkward first date or two would have ranked far below being there for my mother when she'd most needed me. Even if she'd ended up requiring help for far longer than either of us had expected when I'd left school to care for her through her mysterious illness.

"Oh, yes. I'm sorry, were you hoping to close up?" the young man asked, looking around him as though he hadn't noticed how much time had passed. His date looked equally dazed.

"No rush at all!" I replied, not bothering to suppress my grin. "Can I get you a slice of pie? Or maybe some more coffee?"

Glancing at each other, they chuckled awkwardly.

"We'd better not. I have an early day tomorrow," the young woman replied, scrunching up her nose apologetically. "It's already way past my bedtime."

I swallowed a laugh as her date's ears turned red, and he studiously looked anywhere but in her direction. "Whenever y'all are ready. No rush," I said, dropping the check on the table between them. "We'll be here a while."

The women in the last booth were gathering their things when I approached. A stack of bills that more than covered their tab rested at the edge of the table.

"All set?" I asked anyway.

"All set," Cassie replied with a grin. "Sorry to cut and run."

I laughed. The Brewhahas, as everyone in town referred to the close friend group, never bolted their food. Nor did they ever leave until just before closing. Since Aggie adored them and never rushed them, I didn't, either. It helped that they tipped generously and made me feel equally welcome when I stopped by their stores.

"Thank you, Melly. The meatloaf was as perfect as ever." Cassie's cousin Juliette beamed at me as she maneuvered herself out of the bench seat. "I have to run. I promised Tybalt that I'd relieve him of babysitting duty hours ago. Whoops!" She arched her eyebrows and turned her mouth down into a comical grimace.

"As if you won't find him passed out on the couch, dead to the world," teased Hattie, the owner of the quirky pet shop up the road.

"Or maybe somewhere other than the couch?" Crystal, Cassie's barista and business partner, waggled her eyebrows suggestively. "Ow!" she cried out when her girlfriend, Amy, elbowed her in the ribs with a glare. "What? Don't pretend I'm not the only one who's noticed that he occasionally shows up to work wearing the same clothing as the day before!"

The flushed ears of the young man on the first date had nothing on the blush that turned Juliette's face an alarming shade of pink. As far as I knew, Tybalt was simply the business partner who managed their rare book business. He typically spent a lot of time out of state, hunting down rare manuscripts they'd been hired to locate, but he had been in town more frequently since Juliette had adopted her daughter.

A familiar longing washed over me as the friendly banter and teasing flowed back and forth. The last time I'd been part of such a close-knit group, I'd been a fresh-faced college student. Some days, I missed that girl almost as much as I missed her friends. But she was so far removed from who I'd become, she may as well have lived on a different planet.

The rest of the Brewhahas followed Juliette and the shy couple out of the diner, and I slid the lock home as I turned the bright pink neon *open* sign off with a grateful sigh. My mother had hated waitressing so much, I'd been surprised to find that I enjoyed working at Aggie's more than I'd expected to when I'd accepted her job offer. Still, at the end of a long day, nothing beat taking off my clogs, slipping out of my work clothes, and getting into bed with a hot cup of tea.

My feet throbbed as I pocketed the generous tip the Brewhahas had left me. I couldn't be sure without counting, but I had a hunch that I'd finally accumulated enough one- and five-dollar bills to pay for the paint and materials needed to refinish another section of the ancient Airstream I lived in behind the diner.

Basking in the post-meatloaf night calm, I moved from booth to booth, collecting the salt and pepper shakers, the sugar containers, and the other condiments. As much as I longed for my bed, I knew better than to put off refilling everything until the morning. It always seemed like a good idea until half a dozen breakfast diners clamored for more ketchup while I was trying to pour coffee as fast as our regulars inhaled it.

I'd just finished topping off the salt shakers when the sound of a revving motor broke the stillness. During the summer, it wasn't unusual to hear the occasional car roaring through town long after most people had turned in for the night. This far into the offseason, Portney tended to be peaceful after dark.

Twin lights blinded me as I turned to the window, trying to make sense of the incongruous noise. Before I could put two and two together, a massive shape exploded through the steel and glass front of the diner, sending booths and benches shooting left and right as though they weighed nothing more than their dollhouse counterparts. The force of the impact picked me up like a child's toy and threw me across the room into the jukebox. The air in my lungs whooshed from me as I slid to the ground in a heap.

The world stood still, as if everything had been sucked away, leaving me disoriented and desperately sucking in a breath that wouldn't come. When reality flooded back in, it did so with a *POP* that reminded me of being on a plane. Sound erupted around me as the vise gripping my chest finally relented enough for a trickle of air to enter my screaming lungs. A strident ringing drowned out all other noise, and dark pulsating splotches obscured my vision. Through the dancing black dots, I thought I recognized the wood-paneled station wagon Aggie'd been driving since her daughter was in grade school. Nauseated, I squeezed my eyes shut, willing the world to stop spinning long enough for me to get my bearings.

"Melly! Melly! Are you okay?" Momo's frantic voice cut through the persistent high-pitched shriek, but when I tried to lift my hand to wave him over, pain exploded out of my left shoulder. I lowered my arm with a groan.

"Don't move!" Momo's horrified voice filtered through the fuzziness in my brain in a way that the noise and pain hadn't managed, and terror flamed to life in my chest.

"What happened?" I asked between panicked breaths.

Every bone and muscle in my body protested loudly when I tried to pull myself upright. I relented with a moan and sank back to the floor.

I didn't even have it in me to protest as Momo pried my eyes open one at a time and ran sure hands over me, though I cried out when he hit a tender spot on my head.

"Sorry," he muttered, not sounding sorry at all. "You took a nasty knock to the head. Possible concussion, but nothing seems broken. Can't be sure you didn't injure your neck, so no more moving 'til the paramedics arrive." He rested his hand on my uninjured shoulder in a surprisingly gentle pat.

"Don't go!" Terror clawed at my throat when he pulled back to get to his feet. I fumbled for his sleeve and grabbed it before he could get away.

"You're okay. I'm not going far. I just need to check on Aggie," Momo said, glancing back at the massive car resting in the unrecognizable remains of what, a minute ago, had been a familiar space.

Guilt washed over me. I'd been so caught up in my own pain that I hadn't spared even a thought for our boss. Momo swore under his breath.

"What is it? What's wrong?" I croaked out. The urge to rush over to help slammed up against Momo's warning about my neck. I could feel my toes and wiggle them, which I suspected meant that my spine was fine. But what did I know? I was an almost middle-aged diner waitress with a fondness for medical TV dramas. Last I'd checked, that didn't translate to a medical degree.

I stayed put, settling for opening my eyes to watch Momo pick his way through the debris. When he got to the car, the relentless noise finally made sense. My ears weren't ringing from the explosion. The sound echoing around the diner was the never-ending howl of someone leaning on a car horn. My stomach bottomed out.

"Melly! Melly! Are you okay?" Cassie's concerned face floated into near focus as other familiar forms rushed to Momo's aid.

I winced, jerking away from a sudden, sharp pain when she touched my head.

"Sorry! Sorry!" Cassie yanked her hand back, and I blinked at the red on her fingers.

I fumbled for my head with the hand that didn't make my shoulder shriek. Cassie reached out to stop me.

"Don't touch it. Your hands are a mess," she said, handing me a folded napkin to press against my head where she pointed.

The pain that shot through my head made me whimper. I mustered what I hoped was a reassuring smile when Cassie's forehead crumpled with worry.

"I think I'm okay," I mumbled.

Her attempt at a reassuring smile was about as successful as mine. "Don't move, okay? The paramedics are almost here."

I glanced over her at the car, but the windshield was too dusty for me to see more than Aggie's concerningly still form slumped over the steering wheel. She didn't move when Momo yanked the driver's side door open with a screech. My heart crawled into my throat.

"Is she... Is she...okay?" I whispered hoarsely as Momo leaned into the car. The sudden relief of hearing her groan made my head spin, and I squeezed my eyes shut until I was sure I wouldn't throw up.

"I don't know," Cassie replied. "We'll know more in a moment or two. How are you feeling?"

I grimaced. "A lot like I just got hit by a car."

The soothing sound Cassie made instead of chuckling brought home the enormity of the situation. This had to be a dream, a nightmare. People didn't just drive into diners.

With their sirens adding to the already unbearable cacophony, a bevy of emergency vehicles pulled into the diner parking lot, and time sped up.

Silence settled on the diner like a heavy blanket when a firefighter placed a cervical collar around Aggie's neck and maneuvered her out of the car and onto a gurney. A different medic eased one around my neck despite my protests that I felt fine.

"It's just a precaution, ma'am. Better to be safe than sorry," the kind-faced young man said, likely not intending to sound patronizing. He was too busy straightening my legs and preparing to roll me onto a backboard to notice my exasperated eye roll.

His slightly older partner winked at me. "He means well. Don't you, Pacey?"

"What?" the young paramedic asked, glancing up from examining my head wound.

"Maybe just don't call anyone 'ma'am,' his partner replied with a teasing grin that made him blush and turn back to his work.

"I'm Amber, and this is my very green partner, Pacey. We are going to take good care of you. Okay? What's your name, love?" the more senior paramedic asked, distracting me from her junior partner's fumbling attempts to wrap my head in gauze without lifting it from the backboard.

Wincing, I answered, "Mel. Melly to some."

"You the owner of this place?" she asked.

"No. She is." I rolled my eyes toward the car. "Is she okay?"

"I can't say for sure. My colleagues are examining her. But she's in excellent hands. How about you? Does anything other than your head hurt?"

I grimaced. "My left shoulder doesn't feel right. I think it's what hit the jukebox the hardest."

"That's possible," she said, nodding before pinching each finger on my left hand. "Can you feel this?" She smiled when I grunted in reply. "That's good. Let one of us know if those fingers go numb or feel weird. In the meantime, I'm going to pin your arm to your chest so that you don't damage your shoulder further, then we'll get you over to County General to have them give you a once-over. Okay?"

Since she was already strapping my arm to my chest with a thick bandage before the words had left her mouth, I wasn't sure why she'd bothered to ask.

Faster than I could have topped up a round of coffees, my arm was pinned in place, my head thickly bandaged, and the two paramedics had hoisted my backboard onto a gurney, strapped me down, and loaded me into a second ambulance.

"Is there anyone who should come with us?" The paramedic asked, making sure I was strapped in as comfortably as possible.

Spying Cassie and her friends huddled a few feet away, I swallowed down the lump that formed in my throat to answer, "No. It's just me."

If she noticed my eyes getting glassy, the spike of pain that shot through my head when the ambulance slammed shut made me miss it.

I'd never thought I could feel as alone as the day I'd lost my mother and found myself entirely on my own. I'd been wrong.

TWO

After running my head through a CT scan, X-raying my shoulder in multiple positions, and monitoring my vitals for a few hours, the hospital agreed to release me with one caveat. I couldn't go home alone.

"It's a minor concussion, but it's still a concussion, and we just can't take the risk. You understand, don't you?" The busy nurse who'd been checking in on me every half hour barely looked up from my chart to ask the question.

To my utter mortification, my eyes filled with hot tears that burned as they rolled down my face. I hadn't cried when I'd been thrown against the jukebox, when I'd been loaded into the ambulance, or even during the excruciating X-ray. Apparently, a banged-up shoulder, concussion, and a pounding headache that echoed the machines beeping all around me were nothing compared to being told I couldn't go home to take a warm shower, put on my comfiest pajamas, and sink into my own bed, where all I wanted to do was pull the covers over my head and never emerge.

Misunderstanding, the nurse frowned when she looked up and saw my tears. "Oh, honey, are you in pain? I can get you something a little stronger if the acetaminophen isn't doing the trick." All business now that her skills were required, the nurse checked my IV and took advantage of the moment to shine her small penlight into my eyes.

When she was done, I shook my head, but when I opened my mouth to explain, the only thing that came out was a sob. *Get it together, Mel. You're tougher than this.* Except I wasn't. At least not in a hospital. Despite my best efforts to suppress them, the constant noise, nurses calling out to each other, and buzzing halogen lights triggered an avalanche of memories I wasn't ready to process. Memories of endless hours spent at my mother's bedside as her health progressively failed that I doubted I'd ever be ready to process.

Nothing drives home that orphaned feeling quite like being alone in a hospital bed with no one to call.

I snorted a wet, self-deprecating laugh at myself. Could I claim the title of orphan if my last living parent had died when I was an adult?

Beating back the specter of that other hospital, I forced my focus back to the current one and smiled wanly at the nurse.

"No, it's not the pain. I'm fine. It's just that I don't have anyone to call." I did my best to suppress the sob working its way up my tight throat.

Her disbelieving glance didn't make me feel any better about my pitiful circumstance. "Really? Not even a coworker? Imagine having no one to call."

Her judgmental tone didn't match her compassionate expression, and I hesitated, unsure how to answer. She stared at me, waiting for a reply, so I opted to ignore her somewhat harsh judgment and answer her question.

"Well, my boss is the reason I'm here. Even if she hadn't crashed her car, she doesn't look like she's in any condition to drive me anywhere."

I gestured toward the other side of the large ER, where Aggie lay in a matching hospital bed. The large rectangular bandage hiding half her head made her look like a shrunken, frail version of herself. Wrinkles and gnarled hands aside, she'd never struck me as, well, *old* before tonight. She was the life of the diner. All hustle and bustle, with a memory that would give Ken Jennings a run for his money. She only needed to meet a customer once to remember them and their usual order. When I'd settled myself at her counter, at a complete loss for where to go or what to do with my life, she'd poured me a cup of coffee, handed me a slice of the best apple pie I'd ever tasted, and in no time at all, teased out of me the reason I looked so lost. Moments later, I had a job and a place to live.

That was Aggie. Not the shell of a woman lying painfully still in a bed that looked three sizes too big for her. I'd begged the nurses for information about her condition, but, as I wasn't family, all I'd gotten were some half-hearted pats on the arm and the assurances that they were taking good care of her.

A few hours after we'd been brought in, a tall, thin woman with perfect hair and makeup wearing a pantsuit that looked like it cost more than what I earned in a month had blown into the ER, aggressively cornering anyone in scrubs. I hadn't fully believed that this complete antithesis to Aggie had been her daughter until she'd plumped up her mother's pillows and tugged the bedding into place before sitting down to type furiously on her phone. Her frequent frustrated sighs were audible even over the constant ER hubbub.

"It's just the two of you there?" the nurse asked, as though she couldn't fathom any business run by a tiny old lady and a lone, frazzled employee.

"No, there's also a short-order cook."

The nurse perked up. "That's something," she said peevishly before continuing in the calm, even tone she'd been using. "Great! If you give me his number, I'll call him for you."

I blinked silently at her, drawing a complete blank when I tried to picture Momo outside the diner kitchen.

"Melody?" she prompted when I didn't answer. "Can I have his number?"

The alternative to calling Momo at midnight was spending the rest of the night in the ER, where the lights and constant noise would make it impossible to get any sleep. Reluctantly, I nodded and pulled my phone out of my pocket.

Twenty missed texts.

My stomach clenched as I stared at the screen, trying to understand. I didn't know enough people to justify that number. With my heart in my throat, I unlocked the phone and thumbed open the text app.

One from Cassie said they were thinking of me, and to let them know if I needed anything.

Nineteen from Momo.

My mouth dried up as guilt washed over me. It hadn't even occurred to me that he'd be worried. What was wrong with me?

Uh...you have a concussion?

Ignoring my rational brain, I opened the thread and groaned at the progressively worried texts, the last of which made me feel sheepish. Scrunching up my nose into an embarrassed grimace, I met the nurse's gaze.

"You don't need to call him. He's in the waiting room. He's not family, so they won't let him back here."

The nurse brightened and clapped her hands. "Fantastic! I'll go get him right now."

She bustled off before I could protest. When she returned a moment later with Momo trailing behind her, his forehead uncharacteristically creased in concern, my guilt only intensified. I could have spared him hours of worry if I'd just checked my phone.

"You okay?" His surprisingly comforting gruff voice triggered a fresh wave of tears, and his eyes widened in alarm as they overflowed and cascaded down my face. "It's bad?"

The small grunt of pain that escaped when I shook my head only deepened his worried frown. The nurse smiled when he turned to her for confirmation.

"Nothing a little rest and a few good meals won't fix. The two of you can be on your way just as soon as you sign these discharge papers. That shoulder is just bruised, but she's really going to feel it tomorrow, so I recommend keeping it in the sling and resting it as much as possible." I winced. Throbbing pain already radiated from my shoulder, down my back, and up my neck. It was hard to fathom how it could hurt more. "She does have a concussion, but you don't need to wake Melody up every hour. Just let her sleep and rest her brain. However, if she throws up, feels weak, dizzy, or disoriented, or if she starts bleeding from her ears or nose, then you need to get her back here immediately."

"Bleeding from her ears or nose?" Momo echoed, arching an eyebrow at the nurse.

She waved her hand dismissively. "It would be a sign of a more serious head injury. But there's no indication of one on her CT scan, so no need to worry. I'm just obligated to mention it. That said, you don't want to take a concussion lightly. No screens for two days. No working. No standing for too long. Rest. Rest. Rest. Drink lots of nonalcoholic fluids, and if you can stand it, no caffeine for a day or two. Got it?"

As she dispensed orders with the speed and cadence of a machine gun, she bustled around the bed, removing my IV, bandaging my arm, and checking that my shoulder sling fit properly.

"It should feel better in a few days, but don't push it. And if it's not getting better by the end of the week, give your PCP a call. And you're all set!" She helped me swing my legs over the side of the bed, slipped my shoes onto my feet, and helped me stand up with a bright smile. "Off you go!"

Momo and I eyed each other warily, and I voiced the question we were both thinking. "How long do I need to be supervised?"

The nurse chuckled like I'd told a joke. "Just tonight. You should be fine to sleep on your own by tomorrow evening. But remember, rest!" She shook an admonishing finger at me as though I looked like I was about to suggest we head straight to a nightclub instead of the bed I was so desperate to sink into.

As she darted away, I glanced over at Aggie's bed. Momo followed my gaze. When his eyes landed on our boss, they narrowed.

"That's Heather." The way he said her name told me everything I needed to know about what he thought of Aggie's daughter, but he didn't stop there. "She's gonna make her sell the diner. Been threatening it for years. Now she's gonna get 'xactly what she wants. Her momma nearby in some sterile home, where she can keep an eye on her without having to travel. Cryin' shame."

He turned his back on the two women, shoulders and eyes tight with anger.

"Wait, do you really think so?" I turned to glance at Aggie and her daughter over my shoulder, but he pushed me toward the exit with a firm hand on my back.

Ignoring my question, he shifted gears. "Can't take you to your place. You gotta come to mine. That okay with you?"

"Uh." I grappled for the words that would get me out of sleeping on a strange couch. "I'm sure it's fine for me to go home alone. They're just covering their behinds. I don't want to put you out. I already feel terrible that you spent half the night here." The steely look he leveled on me was hard to interpret. "You don't really have to watch over me all night. I have my phone. I can always call or text you if I don't feel well."

Momo squared his jaw and flattened his lips into the expression he usually reserved for unreasonable customers who insisted he'd cooked something wrong.

"Told 'em I'd watch over you. Gonna watch over you. At my place. Stop fussing."

He lengthened his stride, and I scurried to catch up. "Okay, but why at your place?"

Slowing slightly in response to my pained breathing, he glanced down at me. "Cuz of my brother. And cuz you live in a tin can."

I stopped dead in my tracks. "You have a brother?" Without answering, he reached back and grabbed my good arm, tugging me forward. "You've never mentioned him!"

Momo shrugged. "Never came up."

Without another word, he helped me into his car with unexpected gentleness and fastened the seatbelt around my sling before even letting me try doing it on my own. He pointedly ignored every question I lobbed at him as he drove through the sleepy streets.

I fell silent when we passed the diner. Aggie's car had somehow been pulled from the wreckage, and someone had boarded up the hole it had left with a large piece of plywood that did nothing to mask the extent of the destruction.

It was going to take more than a spot of tidying up to get the place open again. And if Aggie's daughter didn't let her come back to work, where did that leave Momo and me?

THREE

Momo's place was nicer than the rundown apartment building on the edge of the rougher part of town had led me to expect. The lobby and hallways hadn't seen a fresh coat of paint since the Reagan era, and I didn't even want to contemplate when the carpet had been installed or what color it had been on that day. But Momo's front door opened onto a tidy space with clean white walls decorated with classic jazz posters. The main living area was separated from an open-plan kitchenette with a breakfast counter. The only sign that anyone lived there was the large bookshelf overflowing with books.

I was ashamed to admit that I'd never imagined Momo to be much of a reader, let alone one who hoarded books.

As if being in his pristine space made him realize how grimy I was, Momo pointed me to the bathroom, handing me a towel and a clean T-shirt before I could get a closer look.

My entire body hurt, and I tried not to cry as the soap found every tiny cut and scratch on my arms and face. I wanted nothing more than to put my head under the shower stream and let the water wash away the day, but that would mean getting the bandage on my head wet. Then Momo would have to fix that, and he'd already gone far above and beyond for me.

Putting on the comically large T-shirt that Momo had lent me was easier than getting out of my clothes. The shower had relaxed some of the battered muscles in my shoulder and back and I was moving a little more freely.

When I stepped out of the bathroom, there was no sign of my coworker, but the couch had been turned into a comfortable-looking bed that I slipped into with a grateful groan.

I fell asleep the instant my head touched the pillow and would have stayed asleep all morning if the rising sun shining through the window hadn't landed on my face. My shoulder screamed in protest when I attempted to roll away from the light, and the events of the previous evening came rushing back.

Aggie crashed her car into the diner.

Aggie crashed her car into the diner, and I might no longer have a job or a place to live. Familiar dread pooled in my gut as I repeated the words silently to myself. It hearkened back to losing my mother and finding myself walking the disconcerting line of being able to go anywhere but having nowhere to go. I'd stared endlessly into the abyss of the complete unknown, terrified to take the first step into a world where I knew no one and no one knew me.

The grief counselor from my mother's hospice center had explained that too many options had thrown me into decision paralysis. I was like one of those chickens placed on a white line that can't decide whether to go right or left, so it stands still until the line is erased.

"Pick a place at random and just go," the counselor had suggested. "Or don't go anywhere. Stay here and see how that feels."

I couldn't bear the thought of staying in the town where I'd watched my mother transform from a woman brimming with life and laughter to a wilted shell of herself. So, I'd traded in the junker I'd learned to drive in for a memory-free, equally beat-up Subaru and hit the road. For the first time in my life, I'd let my gut call the shots, following whichever branch of the highway felt right until I'd landed at the counter of a retro diner in a quaint beach town.

A diner with a car-shaped hole in it and an owner who was probably still in the hospital. I glared at the abyss lurking in the back of my head. The time to move on might be coming, but my gut didn't seem in any hurry to leave.

If anything, it was telling me to stay put and see things through.

Until someone says otherwise, you still have a job. So, get out of bed and get on with it.

Aggie had given me a place to call home and a purpose when I'd been desperate for both. The least I could do was be there for her when she faced the destruction of the dream she'd built with her husband.

Convincing my body was harder. It took the scent of the coffee brewing in Momo's kitchen and the lure of a hot shower in my bathroom to get me to scooch my sorry pile of tortured muscles to the edge of the bed.

A shockingly long time later, I was up and had pulled on my grimy jeans, opting to keep the shirt Momo had lent me to sleep in rather than attempting to shake the last of the glass and debris out of mine. When I emerged from the bathroom, hair mostly smoothed back and arm snuggly in my sling, Momo was waiting for me, travel mug of coffee in one hand and the barest hint of a snarky grin on his face. It was possible that getting up and dressed had resulted in some colorful swearing and groaning. I was beyond grateful that he'd ignored the nurse's recommendation to steer clear of caffeine.

"Wait! I haven't met your brother!" I protested, accepting the proffered cup with my free hand.

He hitched his right shoulder as he opened the front door. "He's sleeping. Won't be up at least for another two hours."

He seemed relieved when the door closed behind us.

Halfway to the elevator, Momo paused to knock three times on the neighbor's door before following me the rest of the way down the hall.

"Aren't you going to wait until they come to the door?" My head was still pounding, and my throbbing shoulder made thinking about anything challenging, but he'd never struck me as the kind of person to ding-dong-ditch anyone.

For a moment, he looked confused, but when he shook his head, his usual neutral expression fell back into place. "She listens out for him. I knock when I leave."

"Why does your brother need someone to listen out for him?"

He didn't answer until after we'd entered the elevator and it lurched into motion.

"Accident when we were kids left him special," he said, making air quotes around the last word.

As we rode to the ground floor, I sipped my coffee to keep myself from filling the silence that followed his bare-bones explanation with anxious chatter. I'd learned more about my only coworker in the last few hours than I had in the six months I'd worked with him. He'd offered no commentary as he pointed out the bathroom, where he kept the glasses in the kitchen, and where I'd be sleeping, but he hadn't seemed disturbed about having me in his apartment.

In the light of day, he seemed more rattled to have me in his personal space. Or maybe I was reading too much into it. After all, the previous day had been unsettling, and there was no reason to think the next few would be any better.

"Thanks for taking me home with you last night. I appreciate it," I said as I awkwardly attempted to buckle myself in, grunting in pain when I stretched my shoulder too far.

With a sound that could have meant anything from "happy to help" to "give me that" or even both at once, Momo reached over and tugged the buckle out of my hand. Without a word, he clicked it into place and started the car.

The weight of the silence in the car grew as we neared the diner, and when Momo pulled into his usual spot, we sat as though getting out of the car and facing the reality that awaited us was more than either of us could handle.

"I almost convinced myself it hadn't happened," he said.

I nodded. Despite my injuries and where I'd spent the night, I had also somehow expected to find Aggie bustling around behind the counter and the coffee machines percolating happily.

Finally, he turned the car off and let out a deep sigh. "Ain't gonna clean itself up."

I froze with my hand on the door handle, unable to take my eyes off the plywood covering the gaping hole. I could still hear Aggie's car revving. Could still feel the impact of the car hitting the diner.

It was a freak accident. It won't happen again.

My rational brain had to be right. How often did people crash into stores? Plus, people would be extra cautious in this parking lot for months to come. If anything, this was the safest day to be inside the diner.

Still, my hand refused to move as my heart rate sped up.

Sensing something was wrong, Momo glanced down at me and hesitated. Out of the corner of my eye, I saw his expression soften into something too close to pity for my liking. But not even that unfroze my hand.

"No cleaning for you. You heard the nurse. Go home. Get yourself together," he said, tilting his head at the path leading from the parking lot around the diner to the small yard that housed my camper. "I'll see what needs doing." I narrowed my eyes at him, but there wasn't a trace of snark or judgment on his face. "'S gonna be okay," he added, though it was unclear if he was trying to reassure himself or me.

Relief that I didn't have to go into the diner just yet, and possibly the concussion, made my legs shaky as I made my way to the vintage camper I'd been living in since the day I'd arrived in Portney. Vintage made it sound much classier than warranted. When Aggie had offered to let me live in it rent-free in exchange for fixing it up, along with a job in the diner if I was interested, I'd accepted sight unseen.

When she'd shown me the trailer in question, I'd only mildly regretted my haste. Even in its sorry state, the silvery outer shell of the small camper had tugged at my romantic soul. I'd fallen in love instantly with the aging hunk of metal sitting in the tiny overgrown clearing behind the diner. The smell lingering from decades of her husband's fishing excursions had been a little harder to overcome.

Weeks of scouring every nook and cranny had downgraded the stench from "rank all the time" to "mildly unpleasant when it rained." I was still working on changing the man-cave décor to something slightly more aligned with my aesthetic and true to the vintage gem hidden under all the grime.

My first order of business had been to sanitize the tiny bathroom so I wouldn't need showers to recover from my showers. Next, I had big plans to replace the ancient laminate kitchen counter with wood countertops salvaged from a junkyard.

Vintage Airstream purists would turn their noses up at the small espresso machine I'd scored at a thrift store, taken apart, fixed up, and installed in my teensy kitchen. I didn't care. Its cherry-red and chrome finish made me smile almost as much as the liquid gold it produced at the touch of a button.

While the coffee machine hissed and gurgled, I turned on the shower and gingerly pulled my arm out of my sling, groaning as the battered muscles protested every move. Removing the rest of my clothing was no less painful and took far longer than anticipated. By the time I stepped into the tiny bathroom at the far end of the Airstream, the air was thick with steam that delightfully wrapped itself around me. I lowered myself into the micro-bathtub and pulled the hand-held shower to my chest as I rested my head against the cool fiberglass wall behind me. The hot water felt as wonderful on my bruised and battered body as I'd hoped.

The night had turned my aching muscles to rocks, which made washing my hair challenging. I gave it a half-hearted attempt, then settled for letting the hardest setting on the shower head wash out the last of the conditioner before letting the jets needle the tightness out of my shoulders. The fancy showerhead was no more vintage than the coffee machine, but it had been well worth the splurge. Some luxuries were more like necessities.

Sending a grateful thought toward Aggie for letting me hook the Airstream to the diner's endless supply of hot water, I sat in the tub until my fingers and toes turned pruney. At some point, Momo was going to barge in to see if I was still alive. I owed it to him to spare him the sight of me folded up like a pretzel in my minuscule bathtub.

I had railed about the shower situation when I'd first moved in. But like everything in the cozy camper, it had grown on me. I'd miss it if Aggie decided it wasn't worth rebuilding the diner. Who knew where I'd end up next.

There's always... I yanked my brain off that train of thought. *Not an option, and you know it.*

Shaking off the tense knot that formed between my shoulder blades whenever I even came close to thinking about the thing I wouldn't let myself think about, I busied myself with toweling off. Easier said than done in the cramped space with a shoulder that howled each time I forgot it was injured and moved too fast.

Feeling a lot more like myself in my clothes, and with my hair smelling of mangoes and mint again rather than Momo's woodsy shower gel, I pulled the sling off my bed and maneuvered my arm back into it and let out a long sigh of relief as the strain of holding up my throbbing shoulder eased.

By the time I'd poured myself a cup of coffee and lowered myself into the Airstream's doorway and dangled my legs out of the camper, I regretted getting out of the shower, but no amount of tantalizing hot water would convince me to get undressed again. Instead, I closed my eyes and tipped my head back. With the warm fall sun caressing my face and surrounded by the nature sounds of my little yard, I could almost forget the previous day. Not entirely. Not even the happy *caws* of the local crows reporting on the neighborhood's happenings drowned out the endless looping sound of Aggie's car speeding up and crashing into the diner.

It had all happened so fast. One moment, I'd been humming to myself, and the next, everything had changed. If I'd been watching it on TV, I would have rewound the show to see what I'd missed.

A soft *plink* drew my attention back to the yard. A large crow stared at me from a safe distance, head cocked to the side questioningly.

I resisted the urge to shrink away. I'd once read that crows were far smarter than most animals, which I'd somehow interpreted to mean they took offense if they felt slighted. For someone with a horrible bird phobia, nothing sounded worse than an angry, vindictive flock of crows.

Forcing my mouth into a semblance of a smile, I fought down the panic bubbling up in my gut. *He won't hurt you. He's just curious. Birds aren't evil. They're just small animals. Small animals with sharp beaks and talons. Small animals with hollow bones that defy the laws of physics and biology. And wings that flutter and beat against the air.* I shuddered at the thought of wings brushing against me. The crow cocked his head further and hopped a step closer.

I scooted back into the camper, hoisted my feet up, and held my hands out. "Hi. Hey. Hi, little guy. Please don't be offended. I just... I'm just a little nervous."

The crow froze, then hopped back two steps.

I sucked in a shaky breath. *You are ridiculous. Who has a bird phobia?* It wasn't the first time I'd berated myself for having the most absurd of all phobias. The blame fell squarely on Daphne du Maurier's and Alfred Hitchcock's shoulders, which didn't help me in the least when I found myself face to face with a flock of pigeons or witnessed a flight of crows taking off over my head. I'd read the book once and only ever seen the movie poster, but no matter what anyone said, *The Shining* had nothing on *The Birds* when it came to horror fiction. The scene where the woman crunched her way over a bed of stunned birds to escape had haunted me for years, and I somehow doubted it would ever leave me.

Sensing that my unease had only slightly waned, the crow hopped a little farther away before staring pointedly back and forth between my feet and my face a few times. I followed his gaze to a shiny green rock about the size of a quarter.

When I hesitated, the bird jerked his head pointedly at the rock and rolled his beady eyes at me.

"Is this...for me?" I asked. Despite knowing how much it would hurt, I still leaned over to pick up the shiny stone. "It's very pretty. Thank you." The rock was a deep greenish gray with shiny flecks that shimmered in the light as I turned it over in my hand. It reminded me of the bathroom tiles in the house my mother and I had lived in until she passed away.

Happy that I'd accepted his gift, the crow lowered his head to fluff his feathers. Then he fixed his gaze on the apple I'd intended to eat for my breakfast.

I picked it up and held it out. "You want my apple," I guessed. My stomach growled in protest. I hadn't eaten anything since lunch the previous day, and the apple was the only thing I'd found in my kitchen other than a few packages of pasta and rice.

The crow straightened, and for some inexplicable reason, I got the sense that he was proud of me for understanding.

"Hold on a second. I think we can compromise."

Getting up without putting all of my weight on my shoulder was challenging, but I managed it without swearing too loudly. When I returned with a paring knife, the crow hadn't moved.

I showed him the tool and gestured at the apple. "How about we share?"

Maybe it was the accident, maybe it was the warm sun and the idyllic setting, or maybe it was just the uncertainty lurking in the shadows, but somehow, sharing an apple with a crow who'd just given me a present didn't seem half as strange as it might have a day or two earlier.

FOUR

Even though Aggie's car had been removed from the center of the diner, the mess it had created was still there. She'd plowed through the front of the restaurant into a booth, sending one of the vinyl bench seats halfway across the room and smashing the other into bits. Amazingly, the table didn't look damaged, just tipped over onto its side a few feet from where it usually stood. The booths around the crash site had shifted, but they didn't appear damaged, and I didn't think putting them back into place would be all that hard.

The diner itself was another story. Two of the large plate windows had been obliterated by the impact, and the rest were all at least cracked. Glass shards glinted everywhere I looked, and drywall dust covered every surface I could see. The metal frame of the restaurant was twisted on itself like a piece of fancy abstract art. I had no idea who we'd call to replace it or the mangled stainless-steel siding lying where the booth had been.

Most devastating of all, a long section of the model train track hung in front of the plywood used to board up the gaping hole made by Aggie's car. Tiny trees and houses were scattered among the glass shards and drywall dust, and the train itself lay in multiple pieces right where the car had been, as though Mitch had crashed along with his wife.

My heart sank as I took in the extent of the damage and sifted through the debris to find tiny Aggie and Tom. I wasn't sure what would hurt more: that her husband's beloved train had run its last loop, or that she was the one who'd broken it. Either way, no matter how well we fixed up the diner, it would never be the same.

"Knock, knock! Can we come in?"

I whirled to the entrance, my best customer service smile hopefully masking the ache in my heart, ready to send the misguided customer on their way with a firm but apologetic "We won't be open for business for a while," and faltered when I saw who was at the door.

Cassie smiled warmly at me as she pushed open the makeshift door and stepped into the diner. Juliette followed her in and froze. Her eyes widened with dismay, and one hand flew up to cover her mouth as she looked around the diner.

"We thought you could use a hand cleaning up," Cassie explained, brandishing a broom and a box of heavy-duty trash bags.

The casual act of kindness tipped me over the edge I'd been teetering on as I took in the destruction. Blinking back tears, I smiled at the two women. Even though I was drawn to their boisterous friend group, we'd never progressed much beyond casual banter and knowing their meal preferences. Juliette's order never wavered. Meatloaf, mashed potatoes, steamed carrots, and gravy on the side. She didn't complain if anything came out a little different than she liked, but her distress was so palpable, I always made sure her meal was perfect before bringing it over. Cassie was more of a wildcard. Her passion for food meant she didn't have a "usual." Momo got a kick out of surprising her with new creations.

"No cleaning," Momo grunted, popping into view through the opening to the kitchen. "Heather called. No touching anything 'til the insurance people come."

I shrugged apologetically and grimaced at the mess. "Guess that's a no. I'm sorry you came all this way for nothing. We appreciate the offer, though."

"That whole long block," Cassie teased. "No worries, holler when you're ready to clean. Anything we can do to help you reopen faster. Can't leave this town without meatloaf! People might riot."

"If we open up again," Momo muttered in the kitchen, low enough that I wasn't sure I'd heard him right.

"Did you say something?" I called back.

His head popped back into view. "What?"

"Did you say something?" I repeated.

"Yeah. Heather said no cleaning." His frown looked more concerned than annoyed.

I frowned back. "No, you said something about maybe not opening again."

Momo's eyebrows crawled up his forehead as his mouth turned down at the corners. He shook his head slowly, eyeing me with concern.

Cassie and Juliette wore the same baffled expression.

"I didn't hear him say anything," Cassie said, hitching her shoulder in a small shrug.

"Big knock to the head," Juliette murmured.

"I'm fine. It's just a mild concussion," I replied, even though she hadn't technically asked a question. Her concerned expression shifted to confusion, then back to concern when I explained my comment. "You said something about the knock on my head?"

An anxious knot settled in my chest when she shook her head. Had I hit my head harder than the doctors thought?

Plastering what I hoped was a reassuring smile on my face, I waved their concern away. "I'm fine. I'll text if I need help later!"

They half-heartedly protested when I insisted they didn't need to stick around and finally retreated to their combination bakery/bookshop a block up the street, promising to come check on me during their afternoon lull.

I was debating whether it was wise to run home for another cup of coffee when a silver Mercedes turning into the parking lot made me flinch. I chuckled awkwardly.

Getting my central nervous system to believe that not every car would drive into the building was going to take a hot minute.

Aggie's daughter, Heather, emerged from the driver's side, dressed like she'd walked out of a fashion magazine, if fashion magazines catered to the wives of Fortune 500 CEOs. She tugged her navy blazer into place and wiped her hands over nonexistent wrinkles on white bellbottoms that would have made me look like a clown. She appeared to have been born to wear couture clothing. After pulling her shoulders back and plastering a determined look on her face, she walked around the car to help her mother get out.

It was a relief to see Aggie in her usual flowy tunic and cropped jeans rather than her hospital gown, less so to see the cast encasing the entirety of her right arm. Even more distressing were the bright white sneakers in place of her beloved ancient Birkenstocks.

By the time Heather walked in, dragging her mother with a death grip on her left arm, her face scrunched up like the smell in the diner offended her, I was already predisposed to hate her. The first words out of her mouth cemented the feeling.

"Hateful place. Can't wait to see it razed to the ground."

My friendly greeting to Aggie died on my lips.

"Excuse me?" I couldn't believe she'd said that out loud, standing where her mother had nearly died less than twenty-four hours earlier.

Heather looked me up and down disdainfully. "I didn't say anything." She shook her head. "Typical."

"I'm sorry, typical of what?"

My head throbbed, and I fervently wished I'd stayed in the camper rather than coming out to see how I could help.

Heather's eyebrows narrowed in what might have been a frown if Botox hadn't frozen half her face, shaking her head as if she couldn't believe she had to talk to me. "Milly? Dilly? Gilly? What did she call the new waitress? Never could keep them straight."

I opened and shut my mouth, unsure how to answer.

"Heather, this is Melly," Aggie said in a subdued voice I barely recognized. "Melly, this is my daughter, Heather."

Swaying alarmingly, my usually spry boss looked like she'd aged ten years.

"Mom!" Heather barked before letting out an exasperated huff. "Sit down already. You're making me dizzy. The stuff I have to put up with. Seriously."

I jerked back, horrified by the resentment lacing her words. In the few months that I'd worked for her, Aggie had been active, with it, and completely independent. She ran a diner on her own and volunteered at her church thrift store whenever she had a free moment. Heather made it sound like she'd been saddled with an unbearable burden.

Take a breath, Mel. You don't know the entire story, Mel. Aggie is not your responsibility. No one asked for your help. Stay out of it. She's just your boss.

I plastered a smile on my face as Aggie lowered herself onto the nearest bench, shoulders slumped with exhaustion, and did my best to ignore the small voice protesting that "just" a boss wouldn't have housed me and gone out of her way to make sure I always had everything I needed. "Just" a boss wouldn't have kept an eye out at the thrift store for things I'd love. "Just" a boss wouldn't have consistently, casually dropped off leftovers she swore she couldn't finish on her own when she thought I was a little tight on cash.

"I'm afraid we got off on the wrong foot." I held out my hand. "Hi. I'm Melly. You must be Heather. I've heard so many wonderful things about you."

"I bet you have," Heather said. Her snide tone clashed with the tight smile she turned on me. "Hi. Sorry. It's been a day." Glancing at the small butterfly bandage on my forehead, she added, "Which I guess you know." A sudden flicker of panic widened her eyes. "What if she sues?"

I gaped at her, unsure how to answer. Talking to Heather was giving me a worse headache than being hit by her mother's car.

"What if who sues? I have no intention of suing anyone, if that's what you meant."

Heather tried to frown again. "I didn't say anything about suing."

"You just..."

She interrupted me with an impatient wave of her hand before I could protest further.

"Never mind. We're just here to get a few things from my mother's office before we hit the road." Glancing at her watch, she sucked in a sharp breath. "Traffic's going to be awful. He's going to be furious."

Rubbing the back of my neck, I focused on the only thing that made sense and directed my question at Aggie. "When will you be back? What should we do with all this in the meantime?" I waved helplessly at the chaos surrounding us.

Aggie didn't even register that I'd asked her a question. My heart twinged painfully when I followed her gaze to the broken train and caught the glint of tears in her eyes.

Heather shrugged dismissively and answered for her mother. "The insurance people will be here in the morning. The real estate agent is coming at noon. Do whatever she tells you to do."

"Real estate agent?" Mo asked, suddenly appearing at the pass-through window. He'd made himself noticeably scarce as soon as Heather and Aggie had stepped into the diner.

Heather nodded firmly. "Yes. Long overdue, if you ask me. Actually..." She looked around as if finally noticing the debris from the accident. "After the insurance guy comes, could you clean up a little? That would be super helpful. We need every penny we can wring from this hole."

I dragged in a deep breath through my nose and willed the buzzing in my head to stop long enough for the world to stop spinning. "Can we please slow down for a minute? I'm not sure I follow." I rubbed my forehead and bit back an exhausted sigh. "Let me get this straight. You're taking Aggie...somewhere?" I arched an eyebrow at Heather. When she didn't elaborate, I kept going. "A real estate agent is coming because you're... selling?" I gestured helplessly at the mess. "And you think we can clean all this up by noon tomorrow?"

"Oh, good. You're smarter than you look," Heather said.

"Heather!" Aggie gasped, jerking up her head to shoot me an apologetic look.

Maybe Aggie was more injured than I realized. Heather had said far worse since she'd walked in.

"I'm sorry. My head is killing me. If I understand correctly, even though you're essentially firing us, you want Momo and me to clean up this place so that it'll sell for more money?"

"Wasn't going to say it out loud." Heather's saccharine smile made my teeth hurt. In a completely different tone of voice, she added, "If you wouldn't mind. We would so appreciate it. I mean, my poor mother…" She let her voice trail away, sparing her mother a concerned glance as forced as her smile.

Aggie ignored her as she glanced around the diner, visually taking stock of everything she and her husband had accumulated over the years. Aside from his train, his pride and joy had been the vintage jukebox that was the reason my head was throbbing so painfully. It was defective, so he'd won it for pennies at an auction. It had taken him all of five minutes to find the record gumming up the works. He'd been gone for a decade, but Aggie still relished telling the story to anyone who showed even a modicum of interest in the behemoth hogging the entire back wall of the diner.

After a moment of awkward silence, Heather straightened up and clapped her hands together. "Great. That's settled, then. I'll go get the papers, Mom. We have a long drive ahead of us, and Greg and the kids are expecting us for dinner. Expecting me to come make dinner," she corrected with a barely suppressed sigh. "Worst timing ever."

"For you? Or for us?" I couldn't help asking.

This time, her frown almost made a dent in her frozen forehead. "What on earth are you talking about?" she asked before throwing her hands in the air with a dramatic sigh. "I do not have time for this."

Momo came out of the kitchen, wiping his hands on a dishtowel as Heather vanished into the office, muttering under her breath. Aggie brightened a smidge as soon as she was out of sight.

"I am so sorry, sweetheart. Are you okay?" she asked, looking me over with worried eyes and waving me over so she could cup my face in her free hand.

"I'm fine, really," I replied, placing my hand on hers and giving it a gentle squeeze. "Are you okay? They wouldn't tell us anything at the hospital."

"About as good as an old woman who drove her car into her diner because she fell asleep at the wheel and broke her arm in four places can be," she replied with a rueful grimace. "Everything else is fine, but I'm useless without my arm." She sighed and released my face to grab Momo's hand. "I'm sorry. This isn't how I wanted things to play out. You both deserve better."

"I don't understand. You don't want this?" I asked.

Aggie's answering smile was so sad that my heart ached. "I'm an old woman, Melly. I've had a beautiful life filled with amazing people and incredible opportunities. The love of my life and I built this place and ran it for over forty magical years. And I kept right on going after he passed away. There was nowhere else I wanted to be." She looked sadly at the surrounding wreckage. "I don't want to rebuild without him. It wouldn't be the same. It's time for this place to become someone else's dream. Plus, I think that one needs me," she said, tipping her head toward the office with a little worried frown. "Something's up with her and that husband of hers." She shook her head. "Good-for-nothing lowlife, that one."

The hint of a mischievous twinkle glinted in her eye. "I'll be okay. Don't you worry. I have big plans to start a chapter of the Cougar & Claws book club there. Plus, I hear those homes are hotbeds of activity, if you know what I mean." She wiggled her eyebrows suggestively and laughed at my horrified expression. The Cougars & Claws were a group of septa and octogenarians that met weekly at Wyrd Words, Juliette's bookshop, to discuss the shifter romances they devoured. I'd never seen them in action, but from what I'd heard, they liked their books far spicier than their food. "Hey! I said I was old, not dead! And I've been a widow for nearly a decade. It's about time for these hips to see a little action again." She shimmied in place and laughed again when I grabbed her good arm to keep her from tumbling out of her seat.

"You do whatever you need to do to take care of that sweet brother of yours, you hear me?" she said, turning to face Momo, her expression serious again. "But don't forget to live. He might be important, but so are you." She reached for his face, and he met her halfway, bending over to accommodate her seated frame. Her gnarled hand gripped the back of his head with unexpected force, and she pulled his forehead to hers. The contrast of his much larger, dark head against her wrinkled, pale one was as striking as the moment was tender.

Momo jumped out of Aggie's grip when the office door opened. He kissed her gently on her forehead before vanishing back into the kitchen. Heather emerged from the office clutching a folder of papers.

"Let's go, Mom. Can't get caught in rush hour traffic."

"Oh, I had hoped to collect a few things," Aggie said in the same subdued voice she'd used around Heather before.

Heather glanced at her watch and sniffed. "We just don't have time, Mom. Greg..." She let her voice trail away.

"Of course, dear. Whatever you say," Aggie said with a last sad look around the diner.

"I'll box your things up as if they were mine and bring everything to you," I whispered in her ear as I pulled her into a tight hug and slipped the model versions of her husband and her into her pocket.

She pulled back to look me in the eye and pat my cheek one last time. "I wish we'd had more time," she murmured. "But you're going to be okay. Remember how I always say caterpillars melt into goo before they become butterflies? Well, I've caught glimpses of the Melly who will emerge from her cocoon, and she is a sight to behold. Don't forget to take care of yourself the way you take care of others, and you'll be better than fine."

"Mother," Heather huffed impatiently. "The traffic?"

"Yes, dear," Aggie said demurely, pulling away from me with a wink. "We mustn't forget the traffic."

FIVE

"I guess that's that," Momo said morosely, coming out of the kitchen again as the silver car pulled out of the parking lot. He let out a sigh that seemed to travel all the way from his toes and slumped against the doorjamb. "Hate to ask, but my neighbor is busy, and I have a job interview this evening. Could you watch my brother?"

Multiple questions jumped into my head at once. I settled on the most relevant. "You want me to watch your brother?" I asked, glancing dubiously at my sling.

"Just need someone to sit on the couch and watch movies with him for a couple hours. Won't need your arm."

"Sure. I can manage that. How do you already have a job interview?"

Momo shrugged. "Saw the writing on the wall. Put out some feelers. Caught a nibble. No big deal."

I frowned. "If you say so."

It hadn't occurred to me that I might need a job. Or a new place to live, for that matter. The weight of everything that had happened over the last twenty-four hours settled on me like an anvil, and the throbbing behind my eyes gave way to a jackhammer that seemed determined to crack open my skull.

I grabbed the back of a bar stool and rubbed my eyes. "Happy to watch your brother this evening, but I'm going to need to lie down for a few hours so I can be somewhat helpful."

Momo chuckled. "He's easy. I'll order pizza and you can doze on the couch while he watches movies. He gets spooked when it's dark out. Just don't want him to be alone."

"That, I can do," I said. "But I still need to nap."

Even though I'd spent the previous night there, it was still disconcerting to walk up to Momo's door. It swung open a minute later, and I found myself face to face with what I could only describe as a softer version of my tough-as-nails co-worker. I'd never thought of Momo as hardened by life, but the man beaming at me had none of the lines and creases his brother had earned throughout what I presumed had been tough years.

"Hi! I'm Remi! You're Melly. Our names rhyme!" His delight was infectious, and I couldn't help grinning back at him, even as I stood awkwardly in the hall wondering how I was supposed to come in while he blocked the entrance.

"Let her in, Rem. She can't watch TV with you from out there," Momo said in a gentler tone than I'd ever heard from him. He stepped into sight behind his brother, drying a bowl with a bright yellow dishcloth.

"Oh, yeah!" Remi said, jumping back, the floor reverberating slightly with the shock of his landing. "We're going to watch *The Muppet Movie*! Momo said so!" His bright smile dimmed a bit, and his forehead wrinkled into a worried frown. "But only if you want to. Momo said I had to ask. Do you like the Muppets?" His eyes widened as he waited to see if I'd dash his hopes.

I smiled reassuringly. "I love the Muppets. And I haven't seen a Muppets movie in years, so that sounds perfect."

Momo shot me a grateful smile as Remi lumbered to the couch and dropped into his clearly preferred spot.

"Thanks for that," Momo murmured as he brushed past me to grab his coat. "There's pizza in the kitchen. He's already eaten. I made popcorn. It's on the kitchen counter. Don't let him hold the bowl even if he begs."

He hesitated at the door, clearly reluctant to leave. "I'll only be gone an hour. Two tops. If the movie ends, he'll probably want to watch it again. He likes doing that. But if he doesn't..."

"Go. I've got this. I babysat my way through high school."

Momo frowned. "He's not a baby. He's only three years younger than me."

I rolled my eyes. "I just meant that I'm hard to rattle. Go. It's rude to be late for an interview."

Momo hesitated again, then, with a deep exhale, let himself out.

When the door closed behind him, I took a deep breath of my own before turning to grin at Remi. "Popcorn, eh? Does your brother always spoil you like that?"

The next two hours flew by. I quickly discovered why Remi wasn't supposed to hold the popcorn. He made an even bigger mess helping me pick up the spilled snack until I tasked him with lining up the pieces that had landed on the coffee table. For a few minutes, Remi hummed along to the movie as he carefully pushed each piece of popcorn into one long, sinuous line. When he got bored with the job, he climbed back onto the couch and hugged a cushion to his chest and lost himself in the movie until the credits started rolling.

His eyes filled with tears, and his bottom lip wobbled alarmingly.

"What's wrong, bud?" I asked, grinning at him around my second slice of pizza. "Don't you want to watch it again?"

Seeing his eyes light up almost made my lingering headache go away.

We were halfway through the second showing when Momo let himself back into the apartment. He'd only been gone a few hours, but he looked like he'd worked two back-to-back meatloaf nights. The exhaustion and strain melted off his face when his eyes landed on his brother.

"Momo! Momo! Come quick! Miss Piggy!" Remi cried, bouncing up and down on the couch, jabbing a finger at the TV.

"What? She's in this movie? Who knew?" Momo teased, taking off his jacket and hanging it up.

"You did!" Remi cried, laughing like his brother had just told the best joke he'd ever heard.

"I'll come watch it with you in a minute. We probably should let Mel get home."

Remi swung his head back and forth, looking at us with a mix of incredulity and bewilderment. "But movie's not over."

"Isn't this the second time you're watching it?" A hint of Momo's weariness bled into his tone.

Remi's frown deepened, and his lip wobbled again. "Movie's not over," he repeated, the words a little higher pitched and more strained.

"It's okay! I can stay!" I hurried to say. It wasn't like I had anywhere pressing to be or any reason to get up early the next day. "I like this part."

A wide grin wiped every sign of stress off Remi's face. "Yeah!" he crowed, throwing himself against the couch's backrest. Liking the sensation, he did it again and again until the front legs of the couch lifted off the ground and dropped back down with a crash. That only seemed to amuse him even more.

My stomach lurched in time with the couch, and my fingers closed reflexively on the armrest as I focused on keeping down that second slice of pizza.

"Hey, buddy. I think you're scaring Mel," Momo said without a hint of reproach or anger from the armchair he'd settled himself into with a cold beer he'd grabbed from the fridge.

Remi stopped abruptly, his hands flying up to cover his face. "Sorry. Sorry!" he mumbled.

"It's okay! I'm fine!" I reassured him.

When he lowered his hands, his eyebrows were raised comically high. "I rock again?" he asked, the words shaking with suppressed laughter.

I chuckled. "Let's not."

Remi shrugged as if the answer didn't bother him one way or another and turned his attention back to the movie.

When I glanced back at the TV, I caught Momo's eyes lingering on his brother, a fleeting smile heavy with exasperation and love on his face.

"How did the interview go?" I whispered. Remi had settled back into the couch, his chin resting on the cushion he clutched tightly in his arms.

"Eh." Momo shrugged. "There'll be other jobs." He looked away, but not quickly enough for me to miss the worry pinching his eyes.

Other restaurant jobs that let him get home before ten every night? Other jobs close to home? Doubtful on both counts. Portney was a small town. We only had a handful of restaurants, and I doubted any of them were hiring in the offseason. Everything else was at least an hour away, and the new guy on the line would undoubtedly get the worst shifts.

A pit formed in my stomach as I glanced back and forth between the two brothers, one whose biggest concern was watching a movie to the end, and the other who seemed to carry the weight of the world on his shoulders. The urge to step in and fix everything hit me hard, but Aggie's words about taking care of myself echoed in my head.

I had to take care of myself. Momo and Remi had been on their own for a long time. They didn't need me to play the hero. Even if I had the answer to his problems.

A solution that made me sick to my stomach to consider.

SIX

The insurance agent was a young man barely old enough to shave regularly, dressed in a white, short-sleeved button-down shirt emblazoned with the company's logo. He walked around the diner, poking at piles of debris and peering into the cracks Aggie's car had left in the walls, muttering under his breath as he jotted down notes.

A scant half-hour after arriving, he'd snapped his portfolio closed and handed me his card. He'd announced that he'd call Heather with his findings in a few days, but that we were cleared to clean up, as he hadn't noticed enough structural damage to warrant sending out an engineer.

"These old diners aren't built like modern buildings. Because they're modeled on old-school trains, they're designed to take a hit and keep on chugging. The slab didn't sustain any damage, and the steel frame of the building is sound. You'll only have to replace this section, and you'll be good to go."

With a curt nod, he hurried out to a white pickup truck that made him look even younger and smaller and pulled out of the parking lot just as a beige Lexus SUV pulled in.

A real estate agent straight out of central casting had taken his place in the diner. She'd poked at the same piles and looked in the same cracks, but she'd also inspected the undamaged parts of the diner, making little *tsk* sounds as she took notes.

"This place is a real slice of history, isn't it?" Her disdain made her comment sound like a condemnation rather than the accolade it should have been.

"It really is," I'd replied with what I hoped was enough awe and appreciation to make her see the true value of the vintage diner.

"I wonder if someone from Starbucks or Dunkin' might be interested in the location," she murmured, tapping her chin with her pen thoughtfully.

I somehow kept the revulsion from my face. Portney was one of the few places along the Eastern Seaboard that had yet to give in to the corporatization sweeping the nation. It would only take one major chain to transform the quaint town into one of the countless interchangeable tourist destinations up and down the coast.

Out of morbid curiosity, and partly to fill the heavy silence of her mental calculations, I asked about the going rate for a small diner in a quaint beach town. I'd expected her to quote something around a half a million dollars. The sound of Momo's teeth grinding had been audible over her amused laughter.

Ignoring the daggers he was shooting at her from his eyes, she'd given my arm a patronizing pat and trilled, "Aren't you a doll? I wish!" Her laughter had made my scalp prickle, but I'd kept my irritation off my face. "Selling restaurants is hard enough on a good day. At the start of the offseason, it's nearly hopeless. I'll be listing this for one-thirty and crossing my fingers that we get over a hundred." She'd laughed again at my flabbergasted expression, entirely misreading the shock on my face. "For a big corporation, that'd be petty cash!"

Gritting my teeth, I'd resolutely ignored the little voice in my head repeating *You can keep it from happening,* in a loop. I could. But at what cost? Just because I had the money didn't mean it was mine to use.

The door to the safe swung shut behind the earnest bank attendant, cutting me off from the hushed hubbub of the bank. The silence wrapped itself around my throat like a noose. My vision blurred as I fought to take a breath.

I'd never been a fan of small, enclosed places. The fact that the vault was hermetically sealed didn't help; neither did feeling like I was committing a crime.

It's not a crime. You didn't steal it. You found it. That's different.

I could leave. Tell the woman I'd changed my mind. Walk right back into the bank and pretend I'd never stashed anything in this vault in the first place.

You could help preserve Portney's soul. You could help Momo and his brother.

That thought was harder to ignore.

"Ready?" the bank attendant asked, pulling a long silver key from her pocket. She slid it into the left slot of the small rectangular panel numbered 498 and paused, giving me a moment to collect myself.

"Yes," I replied with a smile that faltered as I struggled to pull mine out of the depths of the coin section in my wallet. Stashing important things in the compartment that never actually held any coins was a good idea until the item in question was long and skinny enough to get wedged in the lining.

Her patient expression didn't change when I finally grasped the key and pulled it out triumphantly, or when I pushed it into the slot next to hers. Once we'd both turned our keys, she opened the small door. She pulled out the long, thin metal drawer and placed it on the table in the center of the vault, then excused herself, murmuring that she'd be right outside if I needed her.

Not unless you know what I'm supposed to do, I thought to myself as she pulled the door closed behind her and left me alone with my conscience.

I held my breath as I lifted the lid of the box. I'd put them there, but the five rows of neatly stacked and bound bills still startled me. There were just so many of them. Enough to hide the small velvet pouch I'd tucked under the back row of bills.

My hand shook as I ran my fingers over the bills I'd found hidden in an old warehouse-store-sized tampon box tucked in the back of my mother's closet shortly after she passed away. Cleaning out her things while reeling from grief, shock, and exhaustion had been harder than I could ever have imagined. I'd spent over fifteen years waiting for the inevitable, only to find that when it happened, I wasn't ready to let her go.

The grief counselor sent by the hospice program explained that my denial stemmed from our brain's tendency to seek the familiar and resist change. Safety lies in familiarity, so we reframe reality to fit what we know will keep us safe. I couldn't envision a life where I was on my own, so, like the frog that doesn't realize the cold water in the pot he jumped into is slowly heating up, I rationalized every setback and downturn in my mother's health. She could barely eat, drink, or lift her head at the end, yet I'd somehow convinced myself we had more time.

It didn't help that the day she took her final breath, she'd woken up brimming with energy. I'd found her sitting up in bed, alert and smiling, eager for a good chat. All day she'd dispensed advice, most of which she'd already drummed into my head, speaking faster and faster as if she knew she was running out of time.

"Take a breath, Mom, you're going to tire yourself out speaking that fast," I'd cautioned, holding out a glass of water that she waved away impatiently. "What's the rush?"

"There's no time. How did we run out of time?" she'd answered, grabbing my hand in a surprisingly powerful grip for her feeble hands.

The contrast of her skeletal hand in my healthy one had been striking. I'd seen them close up every week when I painted her nails, but I'd never registered just how much of her had been erased over the years.

"Are you listening, Melody?"

"Yes, Mama. I'm listening," I'd replied, looking up from our hands into her glittering eyes.

"Good. This one is important." Her hand had tightened around mine, and she'd sat up a bit straighter. "Trust the little voice inside you. She sees and knows more than you give her credit for. That little voice is the best friend you'll ever have. Don't ignore her."

"Don't ignore the voices in my head. Got it." She'd taken no notice of my amused smile.

"It's my fault you're going to be alone. I'm so sorry, my beautiful Melody. Find people who make you feel like you belong exactly as you are. You deserve people who feed your soul, not your insecurities. And don't mistake being needed for being loved. One drains you, the other fills you up. Oh! And don't forget that sometimes, people you think of as friends don't value you as much as you value them. Your gut will know who they are. Just like it'll know your true friends."

"I'll be fine, Mom. But that won't be for a long while. Look at how well you're doing today!" I'd pulled my hand out of her grasp to straighten her pillow, but she'd batted me away.

"Don't settle. Not for a man. Not for a job. Not for anything. I raised you better than that. Don't you forget it. I know you'll do great things if you put your mind to it."

"Of course, Mama. I always do my best to make you proud." I smothered a flicker of defensiveness under a bright smile. A school counselor I'd briefly met with at the start of high school had helped me see that my mother's high expectations of me were less about me than about her. All of her pushing, nagging, and nitpicking came from a place of love, not disappointment, even if "how come you didn't do better on your bio test" sounded a lot more like criticism than encouragement to me. Just once, it would have been nice to hear that I was doing a great job, and that she was proud of how hard I worked.

Her eyes narrowed, and she grabbed my arm, squeezing harder than her feeble muscles should have allowed.

"Melody, I have to tell you something important."

"Oh, yeah? Is it that I should take up all the space I need? Or that I shouldn't dim my light to make someone else comfortable in their darkness? Maybe you want to remind me that 'No' is a complete sentence?" I'd teased, repeating some of her favorite adages as I perched myself on the edge of her bed to take her hand in mine. "I've listened, Mom. You did a good job. I'll be fine when you leave me...in a very long time." I'd leaned forward to add extra emphasis to the last three words.

"Yes. Yes. But I have to tell you. I did something."

"What did you do?" I'd asked, trying to stay in the moment and not let my mind wander to the million things I needed to do. Maybe the little voice in my head had known I'd needed to pay attention.

She'd hesitated, then blown out a frustrated breath as she shook her head as if to clear a pesky thought. "It doesn't matter. This is what matters," she'd said, fumbling with the front of her nightshirt.

With my help, she'd pulled out a pendant about the size of my thumb. Until her gnarled hand closed over it, I'd recoiled instinctively from the roughly cut blood-red stone glinting ominously from within its black wire cage, my stomach threatening to empty itself all over her bed.

"He asked me to keep this safe until he could come back to get it. He never came, but I kept it hidden." Her voice had quivered alarmingly as she grabbed my forearm with her free hand.

"Who, Mama? Who asked you to keep it safe?"

She ignored my question. "Bury me with it. Never, ever touch it." Gripping my arm tighter, she'd pulled herself almost upright with a strength she hadn't had in months. "Promise me, Melody," she rasped, her alarmingly wide eyes pinning me in place.

A hoarsely whispered, "I promise I'll never touch it," was the best I'd managed. The instant the words were out, she'd fallen into my arms, limp like a rag doll.

Spooked, my hands shook as I settled her back against her pillows and pulled the blankets up to cover her emaciated frame. She'd breathed her last words into my ear when I leaned over to brush the hair out of her eyes.

"Love you, my favorite Melody."

A lump formed in my throat as I remembered her calling me that. It had been our favorite inside joke, born from a funny misunderstanding in a music class. *I miss you, Mom. I wish you were here so you could tell me what to do.*

I'd been suitably horrified when the funeral attendant handed me the little velvet bag containing the red pendant after the funeral. His half-hearted, apologetic shrug was the only response I received to my protest that it should have been buried with my mother.

For a while, I'd been able to convince myself that the pendant repulsed me because she'd been wearing it when she died. I'd only contemplated putting it on once. Even though I hadn't actually seen it before the day she died, I'd often noticed its shape under a sweater or through the opening of a blouse. My romantic side had almost convinced me that wearing something so important to her would keep her close to my heart. But when I'd opened the bag, my stomach had rebelled as I pictured her begging me to never, ever touch it.

I'd put it away, but no matter where I stashed it, I couldn't shake the feeling that I was constantly being watched. It was the primary reason I'd rented the safety deposit box. The secondary reason had been the $250,000 in cash tucked with the pendant behind my winter clothes in the cabinet that served as the base for my bed in the camper.

What were you hoping coming here would do, Mel? I wondered, staring down at the neatly bound stacks of hundred-dollar bills. *Nothing's changed.*

I still had no idea where the money had come from, or why it had been hidden on the highest shelf in the back of my mother's closet. The weight that settled on my chest when I'd pulled it down and peeked inside to see why it was so heavy had felt an awful lot like resentment.

While her mysterious illness had changed the trajectory of my life, I genuinely didn't regret that I'd left school when her health had taken such a drastic turn. She'd had me young and raised me on her own, so she'd been more a friend than a mother. I hadn't hesitated to show up for her the way she'd always showed up for me, even if I had only just struck out on my own.

It had taken me three years of working while attending community college to amass enough credits and money to transfer to a four-year school as a junior. I'd still been struggling to make real connections and find my place when I'd gotten the call telling me that my mother had fainted and was in the hospital.

I'd been almost home before it occurred to me that loading up my car with the entire contents of my dorm room and asking the school for an emergency leave of absence had been an overreaction. She'd only been in the hospital for a few days that time, but her health had fluctuated for a decade from dire to mostly fine. There'd been no denying her slow and steady decline.

Taking care of her had quickly become my life. I squeezed community college classes in between endless doctors' appointments and the occasional shift at a nearby diner. All my downtime was spent paying medical bills and submitting insurance appeals. Her disability aid and my infrequent paychecks had barely covered her medication and our expenses, so I'd learned to stretch dollars in creative ways. Her gratitude and appreciation had more than made up for any occasional longing for an easier path.

I truly hadn't minded the hardship, but the money stashed in her closet would have paved the road for a much smoother ride and might have given us access to medical care we hadn't been able to afford.

My resentment had vanished as soon as I remembered how guilty she'd felt over my constant sacrifice and struggle. She would have told me about the money if it had been hers to use. And if she hadn't used it...

A wave of grief washed over me and threatened to take me down with it. My legs wobbled until I grabbed the edge of the table to steady myself.

I miss you so much, Mom. I'm so lost without you.

I choked back a strangled sob. If I started crying, I'd never stop. My mother had been my best friend. We'd shared everything, even clothes. I could count on her to know whether I needed advice or a laugh. She'd heard more of my teen secrets and woes than my friends. I always assumed she'd confided all of her secrets to me. But if she'd taken this monumental one to her grave, what else had she kept from me?

I hated not knowing how she'd ended up with the money, or why she'd hidden it instead of putting it in a bank or using it. Finding out that there were things I'd never know about her hurt almost as much as losing her.

I jerked my thoughts back to the present with a deep breath. The attendant probably had better things to do than sit around while I pulled myself out of a grief vortex.

My fingers hovered over the last row of bills until I gave in to the urge to make sure the necklace was still there. I plucked the stack resting on top of the little velvet bag and put it aside. It was exactly where I'd left it. The velvet had molded itself to the pendant, and before I even realized what I was doing, my fingers were almost touching it.

I yanked my hand back. My heart thundered as I dropped the stack of bills back onto the bag, hiding it from view.

Forcing my attention away from the hidden pendant, I rested my shaky hand on the stack of bills closest to me. Without knowing why my mother had this money or why she hadn't used it, there was no way to fathom what I was supposed to do with it. Had she saved it for me to use? Had she been stashing it for someone? What right did I have to use it without knowing?

I groaned.

What good was the cash doing anyone sitting in this vault?

The real estate agent's voice telling us the valuation of the diner layered itself over the image of Momo fretting about his brother's care. With less than half the cash in the box, I could save his job and make his worries vanish.

Half of the cash that wasn't mine.

"Arg!" I cried, dropping my head into my free hand to rub my forehead. Closing my eyes had zero impact on the headache that had plagued me on and off since the crash. As Aggie would have predicted, a good night of sleep had helped. I'd felt better until the back-to-back visits of the insurance adjuster and real estate agent had set off the jackhammer again.

You should have followed the nurse's recommendation, my mother's voice noted in my head.

"She didn't have a diner disaster on her hands and people counting on her to help them," I snapped back silently.

Oh? People asked you to help?

I hesitated. No. Not in so many words. But Aggie was hurt, and her daughter was taking advantage of the situation to bulldoze her dreams. And Momo hadn't said a word as the insurance adjuster and the real estate agents decided the fate of the diner he loved, but his face had spoken volumes.

While learning how little Aggie's life work amounted to had made my heart ache, it had infuriated Momo. He'd stormed off to the kitchen, where he'd banged around loudly until the real estate agent took the hint and excused herself with a promise to be in touch in the morning.

While technically, he hadn't asked for help, his distress had left a tight ball of nerves in the pit of my belly. He'd taken the job with Aggie immediately after being honorably discharged from the Navy so he could take care of his little brother. After a life of service to others, didn't he deserve to have someone take care of him for once?

The cash in the metal box taunted me. Half would buy the diner outright. With a quarter, I could offer Aggie a down payment and pay off the rest month by month.

Half or a quarter of the money that wasn't rightfully mine to spend.

"Ugh," I groaned again, dropping my head onto the cool metal table and wrapping my arms around it.

I had almost talked myself into taking the cash and dealing with the fallout later when my phone buzzed in my pocket.

Dinner? Remi insists.
I'm cooking. Not him. In case that wasn't clear.

Momo had never invited me for dinner before. No one in Portney had.

Be right there.

My reply text had barely left my phone before I slammed the box shut and shoved it back into the wall.

Things would be clearer in the morning. The real estate agent hadn't mentioned when she was going to list the diner for sale, but surely one evening wouldn't make a difference.

SEVEN

"I might have a solution," I said, focusing on an errant garlic bread crumb near the center of the table.

We'd made a serious dent in the massive lasagna Momo had pulled out of the oven, muttering, "None of that gourmet foam BS here." It made me wonder just what they'd made him do during his interview. Whatever it was, he hadn't been a fan.

The garlic bread and salad hadn't been as mind-blowing as the pasta, but I'd still eaten more than my fair share. As we devoured the feast, laughing at Remi's antics and sharing stories about our pasts, the easy banter and friendship filled a hollow I had never noticed in my heart, and a decision came to me. I was sure it was the right one as I turned to Momo and met his questioning gaze.

"If I buy the diner, you can keep your job, and nothing has to change for Remi."

Momo barked a laugh that made his brother jump. He arched an eyebrow at me and smirked. "With your wages? Unless you're getting more tips than what you share with me."

I smirked back at him. "Maybe if you cooked a little faster, we'd get better tips." The snort I got in response definitely counted as a second laugh. "I have some money set aside. Enough to buy the diner if Heather agrees to sell it to me." I kept my tone light, as though saying the words out loud didn't make me want to throw up all that yummy lasagna. While my heart and my mind were fully made up, my stomach and the voice howling that the money wasn't mine to spend weren't entirely on board.

For an uncomfortably long time, Momo stared at me with an unreadable expression on his face.

"Why?" he finally asked. The word hung heavy between us, far more loaded than it should have been.

Uncomfortable and unused to having my offers of help questioned, I shrugged as if I regularly offered to spend over a hundred thousand dollars to help a friend. "Why not?"

Momo's stare didn't waver. Neither did his impassive expression. A tornado of feelings swirling around my pounding heart churned up the lasagna in my belly. To keep the food where it belonged, I jumped to my feet and paced until the emotions cleared enough to reveal the fear lurking beneath them. Gripping the back of my chair, I gave in to his silent demand to elaborate.

"Fine. If you must know, I don't have a good reason." I threw my hands in the air and walked away from the table.

Momo followed me to the sitting area and lowered himself into his armchair as I threw myself onto the couch next to Remi, who was once again engrossed in *The Muppet Movie*. He stared at me with the same infuriating expression that gave nothing away as I gathered my thoughts and tried to rein in my out-of-control emotions.

"How about, because I can? Because it's the right thing to do? Because what happened isn't fair to Remi or you? Because I want to?" The truth of the last statement slammed into me so hard, I thought Remi was rocking the couch again. I leaned forward, resting my elbows on my knees, and met Momo's gaze. "I want to. I love that place. It was supposed to be a temporary stop on my way to figuring out where I wanted to settle, but it's grown on me. I'm happy there. I've spent my whole life doing things for others, and I want to do this for myself."

Momo arched an eyebrow and glanced pointedly at Remi before looking back at me.

"Okay, fine, I'm doing it for you two, but mostly for me. Really."

He chuckled and shook his head. "Baby girl, you tell yourself that all day and all night if it helps, but we both know if you do this, it ain't for you."

I squirmed in my seat, unused to being seen so clearly. "Can't both be true? Can't I do it for all three of us?"

The original goal might have been helping them, but the idea had wrapped itself around my heart and grabbed hold. A flutter of excitement I hadn't felt since I'd first left for college rippled through me. I could make it mine as we did the repairs. And we could tweak the menu, maybe bring it into the twenty-first century. My fingers itched for a pen and paper to jot down the ideas blooming in my head faster than I could track.

"I want half," Momo said, disrupting my silent brainstorm session.

"Half?" My eyebrows jumped halfway up my forehead. "Have *you* been holding tips back from me?"

"Funny girl," he deadpanned, sounding so much like his brother, it made me do a double-take.

"Your brother said that to me yesterday."

Momo cocked his head and frowned thoughtfully at his brother. "He did?"

I shrugged. "I heard him say it." At least, I thought I had. No need to mention that I hadn't noticed his lips move as he spoke. Or that it had been when I'd cursed a blue streak as the popcorn went flying.

Bringing the conversation back on track, I asked, "You heard the real estate agent say what she was listing the place for, right?"

Momo paled a little and gulped before nodding resolutely. "I did." He squared his jaw and glanced at his brother. "Worth it if it means I never get the rug pulled out from under me like that again."

"I have the money. I promise I'd never do that to you," I said softly.

He shook his head, lips pressed tightly closed. "I want a part of this."

"Fine, how about a third? I'll pay the rest. One third for the diner, one third for the back lot and trailer. Plus, I'll cover whatever the insurance doesn't for the renovations."

He stared at me for a long moment without blinking and finally nodded slowly. "One third, two thirds. Partners. I like the sound of that." Scooching forward in his seat, he held his hand out. I leaned in and grasped it, surprised at how much softer it was than I'd expected.

"Partners," I said.

Remi's meaty hand landed on top of ours. "Partners!" he crowed, then threw himself backward onto the couch in an avalanche of giggles, muttering "partners" over and over to himself between gales of laughter.

Momo's serious expression cracked as he let out a booming laugh of his own.

"Popcorn!" cried Remi, clapping his large hands together as his brother passed him on his way to clear the table.

"No!" I cried just as loudly, covering my face. It had taken three rounds of shampoo to get all the popcorn bits out of my hair the night before.

Momo laughed again. "Told you not to let him hold the bowl."

"Funny guy," I replied, tossing a couch cushion in his direction. He darted out of reach faster than his big frame should have allowed.

EIGHT

Somehow, almost a week after the crash, the damage to the diner looked worse than ever. Possibly because cleanup was officially my responsibility. Well, our responsibility.

I caught Momo's eye and grimaced as Heather peeled out of the parking lot. I'd hoped Aggie would be present for the sale, but according to her daughter, she was still settling into her new home and had opted to stay put. Something about Heather's behavior had felt a little off, but she hadn't given us a moment to quibble, insisting she only had a half hour to spare for the transaction. A flash of fear that she might back out of the incredible deal she'd offered us on behalf of her mother had silenced any misgivings her baffling behavior had triggered.

"Where do we even start?" I asked, already overwhelmed with everything that needed to be done.

"Beats me," he replied with a shrug. "Lunch?"

My stomach rumbled loudly in response, and our laughter eased some of the uncomfortable tension that had formed between us as we finalized the purchase of the diner. Caught up in Heather's urgency and the excitement of the moment, we'd been almost giddy as we signed a thick stack of papers under the eagle eye of the notary public. But something had shifted when I handed Heather the cash.

Neither of us had said a word as she opened the crisp manila envelope to glance at the twelve stacks of hundred-dollar bills. Personally, I would have counted every last bill to make sure none of the $ 120,000 was missing, but she'd snapped the envelope closed, stuffed it into her purse, and left with a curt goodbye.

"That was weird, right?" I asked as Momo vanished into the kitchen.

"So weird," he replied, popping up to make eye contact. "Almost backed out."

"What?" He'd seemed so confident as we negotiated the terms. Heather had agreed so fast, it made me wonder if our opening bid should have been smaller.

He popped up again. "I agreed with you. It was weird. Why was she in such a hurry?"

"No, the other thing. About almost backing out?"

"I didn't say that," he replied from inside the kitchen. "You hearing voices?" He glanced through the opening with the closest thing to a grin I'd ever seen on his face. "Or are you projecting? Grab some napkins, would you?"

"Funny."

I grabbed a stack of napkins and gave the counter a half-hearted swipe to remove the worst of the grime.

"Nuh-uh," Momo said, coming out of the kitchen with two heaping plates of food and a bottle tucked under his arm. "We can do better than that." He led the way to the booth with the least debris at the far end of the diner and put the plates down. "Sit. I'll grab glasses. We're celebrating." He pulled the bottle from under his arm and set it on the table with a flourish. "Sparkling apple juice…because concussion."

"Fine, but we're doing it properly with sparkling wine next week," I grumbled.

My phone pinged before he returned with the cups, and I frowned as I read the email Heather had forwarded.

"Well, there goes that." I dropped my phone on the table and ran my hands through my hair with a sigh.

"What?" Momo asked, sliding into the booth across the table from me.

"The adjuster got back to Heather. It'll take at least a month to get the money for repairs." I slumped against the backrest. "What are we supposed to do? Wait to reopen?" Had we made a mistake of epic proportions?

Anxiety gripped my stomach as I looked around the diner, taking stock of everything that needed to be done before we could reopen. The gnawing pit in my belly grew in time with the list of necessary repairs.

I could take more money out of the vault.

The thought sat in my head, glittering enticingly, but giving in to that temptation was a slippery slope. If I went back and pulled a little more money for the repairs, what would stop me from doing it the next time we needed a new coffee machine, or the booths needed reupholstering, or the oven died? The goal was to put all the money back not use more, even if it was for my diner.

My diner.

What had we done? The weight of the responsibility suddenly felt very real. What did we know about running a diner? A few business management classes at a third-rate community college hardly made me a business mogul. Momo had assured me he'd picked up everything there was to know about running the place from working alongside Aggie for so long. But what if he'd overestimated his abilities? At least he was already the point person for the food and drink suppliers. I'd need to comb through Aggie's files when we needed to restock paper goods and everything else.

How long could we afford to stay closed? Momo had sunk all his savings into the diner. And I had all of thirty-six dollars in my checking account. If we didn't open soon, we'd both be in serious trouble. Not to mention the food that would go to waste if we didn't use it soon. The diner had already been closed for a week.

But even if we swept up all the glass and dust and moved the booths and benches back into place, at the very least, we were still short three windows, a door, and two large sections of siding. The plywood that had been hastily put up in their place and in place of a door was ugly but functional. A coat of paint would pretty it up, but it wouldn't hide that the place looked like it was mid-construction. Hardly something I wanted diners to mention in online reviews.

"Mel!" Momo's voice cut through the panic, and I realized it wasn't the first time he'd called my name.

"Sorry, I was…"

"Panicking. Yes. I saw," he said calmly. "Eat. You'll feel better. People don't appreciate good food."

My anxiety jumped up another notch when I looked at my plate.

"Pork chops? You made us pork chops? We can't afford that! We can't afford anything!" I cried, shaking my hands in frustration.

"First, they'd have gone bad before we could serve them. Second, we're gonna be fine. Eat." With infuriating calmness, he cut into his pork chop and took a bite.

My mouth watered. They looked so good.

"Just eat already," Momo groused, his words clear despite the food in his mouth.

I put a bite of pork chop in my mouth and groaned with delight. "You are a food magician, you know that?"

"Yes. I know. That's why we're going to be fine."

"But the repairs! There's so much to do, and we have no money!"

"Eat!" Momo barked. "We have hands, don't we? We'll figure it out. Stop fretting."

The scent of pork chops and mashed potatoes tickled my nose. If I was going to expend so much energy worrying, I might as well fuel up.

I was considering licking my plate clean when a timid knock on the partially open plywood door brought me to my senses.

"Hi! Hello! Anyone there?" a familiar voice called out over the sound of the plywood door opening further a little more. "We're here to help."

"Oh! Hi!" I replied, bouncing to my feet to greet them. Annoyingly, Momo had been right, and I felt better with food in my belly. He stood up and stacked our plates as I hurried to greet Cassie and the people behind her. "What are you doing here?"

"Like I said, we're here to help," Cassie replied, stepping aside to reveal pretty much every shop owner on the street and a few people I didn't recognize. "We figured the insurance adjuster had come through, and you'd be ready to clean."

"But..." I protested.

"Wow." Crystal pushed past Juliette to get a better look at the mess.

"It's pretty bad. I know." How had three shattered windows generated so many tiny pieces of broken glass? The shards glittered under the diner lights like shimmering diamonds.

A puckish grin lit up Crystal's face, and her bright eyes glimmered with amusement. "I don't know. It's kind of pretty. Not exactly safe, but pretty."

"Unfortunately, safe is a prerequisite to reopening." I let out a sigh as the weight of what we'd done hit me again.

"Probably a good idea," Juliette said, looking as anxious about the mess as I felt. "Does Aggie have a reopening date?"

"Well..." I said, glancing at Momo for help. He arched an eyebrow and tipped his chin in my direction. I rubbed the back of my neck. "Funny story, but we bought the diner from Aggie this morning. It's ours, lock, stock, and broken glass." My statement was met with a variety of smiles and looks of dismay that I hoped had more to do with the extent of the repairs than disappointment in the new ownership. "We're itching to get started, but we've hit a snag."

"Already?" Hattie remarked from the back of the crowd. The owner of the fabulous pet shop just beyond Cassie and Juliette's bakery/bookshop wasn't known for her tact.

"Insurance blah blah," I explained with a wry grimace. "We won't get the funds for the repairs for at least a month."

"Then I guess it's a good thing we came prepared." Deputy Sheriff Sam Griffin, Cassie's boyfriend, gestured to a trio of pickup trucks piled high with an assortment of construction materials. "That expression. Best feeling in the world."

I flushed hard, wondering what expression I'd been making.

"What is happening?" I whispered to Momo, who'd left the kitchen to investigate the chaos.

"It's a Portney thing," Cassie said.

"When one of ours needs help, we show up," the deputy sheriff finished.

The motley crew crowding the makeshift entrance cheered in agreement.

"Where would you like us to start?" he added, pushing his way to the front of the crowd.

NINE

"Do you have everything you need?" I asked, peering into the kitchen for the sixth time that morning.

"I said yes, and I meant yes. If you don't get out and let me do my job, I walk." Momo glanced at the ceiling, muttering Spanish curse words under his breath.

"Can't walk out when you own the place," I teased, backing out to the relative safety of the other side of the swinging door separating the kitchen from the restaurant. "We've got this, right?" I asked, momentarily giving in to the anxiety clawing its way up my throat.

"Only if you go do your part," Momo replied with an exasperated sigh mitigated by the affectionate look he threw me. "We've got this. Stop worrying so much. Gonna make your headache worse."

I shot him a grateful smile and rubbed my forehead. While my shoulder had mostly healed over the last couple of days, the headaches were coming and going with alarming frequency and intensity. It was my fault. Instead of resting, like the nurse had recommended, I'd jumped into the diner renovations with two feet and zero regard for my health.

It had been my bright idea to reopen on meatloaf night, figuring that it would bring in the crowds. In hindsight, I understood why Momo had pushed for a nice, quiet Monday lunch service. Unfortunately for me, I'd won that argument.

"For Pete's sake. Stop fretting and open the door already before they break it," Momo grumbled from the kitchen.

"Right. Right." I straightened one last napkin dispenser and turned on the new neon LCD *open* sign.

Thanks to the Portney Main Street Merchants' Association, which I was pretty sure had been formed on the spot, I had an actual door to unlock rather than a makeshift plywood stand-in. My neighbors had moved the booths back to where they belonged, and every stray piece of glass and speck of dust had been swept up. Even the black-and-white floor tiles had been polished until they gleamed under the bright overhead lights. If it weren't for the three large sheets of plywood lining the front of the restaurant, the accident could have been a figment of the town's collective imagination.

If the regulars had turned out to gawk at the scene of the incident, they were in for a disappointment. Maybe the new décor would distract them. Some people would probably disagree, but I thought that my eclectic collection of upcycled art scavenged from the dump and various thrift stores gave the diner a quirky, retro-modern feel.

"Melly! The place looks amazing!" Cassie cried as she followed Crystal and Amy in. "Probably wouldn't have put up that purple monstrosity, but it kinda works," she added, her smile not wavering even as she criticized my decorating skills.

I glanced over my shoulder at the "purple monstrosity" and frowned. The cute shelves with scalloped edges had been stained and cracked when I'd pulled them from a thrift store volunteer's hands as he headed to the trash. It had taken me forever to sand off the old paint, but once I had, I'd been rewarded with a set of gorgeous maple wall shelves perfect for the area behind the cash register. Granted, because of a headache flare, I'd grabbed the wrong stain, but the purple made me smile, and I was proud of the work I'd done.

"I don't know, I think I did a pretty good job," I replied, with a shrug.

Cassie's eyes widened as her eyebrows jumped. "Did I say that out loud?" she asked before slapping her hand across her mouth.

"Say what out loud?" Crystal asked, frowning at her.

Ears bright pink and eyes open wide in horror, Cassie glanced at her friend, then back at me. "Uh, nothing. I was just commenting on the uniqueness of those shelves."

Crystal looked over my shoulder at the piece of furniture in question and smiled appreciatively. "Cute! Where did you find those?"

Mollified by Crystal's apparent appreciation of my work, I explained as I led the trio to their favorite booth. "I refurbished them."

"Oh, yeah?" Amy asked, popping up between the two women to get a better look.

"Yeah," I replied, smiling sheepishly. "I enjoy breathing new life into discarded items."

"I love that!" Amy said, sliding into the booth and taking the menu I handed her. "That's so creative! I'd love to see some other pieces you've made."

Suddenly uncomfortable with all the attention, I smiled at her in response and changed the subject. "I'm afraid it's just a short menu tonight. We're easing into things."

"Hey, as long as you're serving meatloaf and mashed potatoes. I'm happy." Hattie scooted into the booth next to Cassie. "Sorry I'm late," she said. "Bunnies got out of their enclosure. Chaos ensued." She let out an exasperated sigh. "Some people need to learn how to latch cages," she added, glancing at Cassie, who ignored the pointed comment.

By the time the diner was packed with regulars happily enjoying their meatloaf as if they'd been deprived for months and not just two weeks, my head was pounding.

"Shouldn't the plywood be absorbing some of the noise?" I asked Momo as I grabbed two more plates of meatloaf from under the heat lamps we'd installed above the pass-through window.

"What?" he asked, already glancing at the next order ticket.

"Never mind." Maybe I should have listened when the nurse had ordered me to take it easy. In my defense, not being able to afford groceries wouldn't be great for my concussion, either.

I was seriously regretting not taking her advice as I cashed out the last table. Between my throbbing feet and pounding head, I was ready for a long soak and a three-day nap so I could forget the endless grumbles about the lack of pie. When Aggie had been in charge, the diners hadn't been so critical. Or it just hadn't stung when it hadn't been my name on the deed.

"That was amazing, Melly. I'm so glad you've taken over this place. It would have been a shame to see it go to a stranger. I'm so sorry about what I said earlier. I can't believe I let that comment slip out," Cassie said, her ears growing pink again. "It was so uncalled for. Your shelves are beautiful."

"It's okay, really," I replied a little tersely. No matter how much I wanted to brush it off, her criticism had stung. "Everyone is entitled to their tastes."

"Well, if there's anything I can do to make up for my rudeness, please let me know," she said before turning away.

"Actually, you might be able to help me," I said, grabbing her arm as a solution to my pie problem materialized. "Aggie was our resident pie expert. Momo is busy with the savory stuff, and I shouldn't even be allowed into a kitchen. Do you think we could set up a regular order? Say, three pies on weekdays and five on the weekends to start? We'll put your name on the menu!"

She nodded enthusiastically. "I'd love that! How about a few classic flavors and a special offering every day? Mocha Monday? Triple Berry Tuesday?" She tapped her chin thoughtfully as she ran through ideas in her head. "Watermelon Wednesday?"

I made a face. "Not so sure about watermelon pie," I said, laughing. "But I like where your head is."

Cassie blinked a few times and rubbed her forehead. "I must be more tired than I realized. I could have sworn I kept that last one to myself. It sounds a little iffy. Better get some sleep! I'll send Christina around ten. The morning rush will be over by then."

"I'll be here!"

I heaved a sigh of relief as I closed the door behind them and flipped the lock closed. Just in case, I turned off the outside lights and the *open* sign. Outsourcing the pies was a stroke of genius. One less thing on my plate meant one less way to let Momo down.

TEN

"Mel, Christina's at the back door with a stack of boxes. Says they're pies," Momo called from the kitchen.

"Be right there," I muttered, keeping my focus on the few remaining breakfast diners.

The morning crowd had thinned. Only four tables were still occupied. At one of them, someone had uttered the word "kidnap" as I passed. The first time, I had assumed someone was discussing a book or movie. But I'd caught a few more snippets of the conversation as I puttered around, putting away menus, wiping down cleared tables, and reorganizing sugar packets. Unless a novel or film featuring Portney had come out recently, it had to be a real kidnapping. I just couldn't figure out who was discussing it. All I knew was that one person was excited about the plan, and the other thought it was a terrible idea. The sheriff would laugh me out the door if I went to him without something a little more tangible.

Behind me, Cassie's bread baker and general assistant, Christina, slid a stack of white cake boxes onto the counter, pointedly clearing her throat as I ran my eyes over the remaining diners one more time. None of them looked like potential kidnappers. Two women in their mid-thirties were taking their sweet time finishing their coffee as they gabbed about a hot sale. A sweet old couple who shared the eggs and bacon platter at least once a week spoke quietly to each other, as they always did. A lone guy in a phone company coverall sitting in the booth closest to the door mopped up the last of his eggs with a piece of toast. And a young couple with twin toddlers who were trashing the booth at the far end of the diner kept shooting me apologetic smiles. I suspected they'd be leaving me a nice tip to make up for the entire meal's worth of food scattered over the floor and the benches.

"Do any of these people look capable of a crime?" I whispered to Christina.

Cassie's assistant frowned as she shot me a side glance. "What?"

"I swear, I heard one of them planning a kidnapping. I just can't tell who, almost like the voice I heard doesn't quite match the ones I hear now."

"Wow. Someone forgot to take her meds this morning," Christina replied.

Snapping my head around, I gaped at her. "What...?"

"I didn't say anything."

"Yes, you did. You said something about me forgetting to take my meds."

Christina managed to look both horrified and embarrassed. The tips of her ears and nose turned a pretty shade of pink as she stammered, "I didn't say that out loud, did I?"

"You must have. How else would I have heard you?" Had everyone lost their minds when I'd hit my head? "And no, I didn't forget to take my meds. I never forget to take them."

Christina blanched. "Can you hear this?"

"Of course I can hear that. Why wouldn't I hear you? You're three feet away."

"Because I said it in my head and not out loud," Christina replied, fixing me with her gaze.

"What are you talking about? Is this your idea of a joke?" A flash of anger warmed my face as a vivid memory popped into my head of everyone in the middle school cafeteria pointing and laughing at the massive red stain on the back of my pants. The popular girls had distracted me so that I wouldn't see the puddle of ketchup on the only free chair at their table. In a split second, I'd gone from floating on

Cloud 9 over being invited to join them, to wishing the earth would swallow me up. It had taken me years to live down the embarrassingly unimaginative nickname one of their jock friends had coined on the spot: "P.P.", short for Period Pants. The whole thing had turned me off pranks. "I seriously don't have time for that," I bristled. When I turned to grab the boxes off the counter, she placed a hand on my arm to stop me.

"I haven't said a thing out loud since you told me you never forget to take your meds. Look at my mouth if you don't believe me."

Rolling my eyes, I rounded on her. "Fine, say something else."

"Okay. Don't freak out. But have you ever heard of telepathy?"

I blinked at her immobile lips, trying to make sense of what I was seeing.

"Are you one of those... what are they called?" I scrambled for the word. "A ventriloquist!" I cried, jabbing an accusing finger at her, relieved to have figured it out.

She shook her head slowly. "I'm not the one doing this. You are," she replied.

My legs wobbled, and I kept my eyes glued to her immobile lips as I grabbed the edge of the counter to keep from falling over.

This is not happening. This is reality, not some low-budget sci-fi channel show. I got a nasty bump to the head. Maybe I got knocked out, and I haven't woken up yet. That's it. I'm dreaming. It would explain a lot. Like, why I agreed to buy half of a diner. And why everyone suddenly seems to be saying the quiet parts out loud.

The panic gripping my chest must have shown on my face, because Christina's eyes filled with concern as she reached over to put her hand on mine.

"You're not imagining things. You're hearing my thoughts. I know, it's trippy. But I think I can explain."

My answering laugh bordered on hysterical, and my voice came out higher pitched than usual. "You can explain? You think I can hear thoughts, and you can explain?"

"Mel? You okay out there?" Momo asked, leaning back to glance at me through the pass-through window.

"I'm fine. Everything is fine," I said a little louder than strictly necessary, widening my eyes at Christina. *What if she's right? I'll be the most hated person in town. I'll be shunned. Who wants to hang around someone who can hear their thoughts?*

A sob worked its way up my throat, and I slapped my hands over my mouth to keep it from escaping. The instant I let go of the counter, my legs gave out, and I sank to the ground with a *whoomph*.

Christina grimaced down at me. "Stay there for a second while I wrap up your last two tables. I'll be right back."

She patted my shoulder and got up. A moment later, I heard her speak softly to the remaining diners. Suddenly drained, I dropped my head onto my knees. Pushing through the repairs so we could reopen sooner had been a mistake. If I'd stayed in bed for a few days, relaxed, and let my brain heal, maybe I wouldn't be hallucinating. What if buying the diner had been a concussion-fueled mistake?

My flight reflex flared to life, and if I hadn't been too exhausted to stand up, I would have been halfway to the airport by the time Christina returned after ushering out the last customer and locking the door behind them.

"We don't close after breakfast," I said as she sat on the floor across from me, leaning against the wall and resting her forearms on her knees. "The lunch crowd will be in soon."

"The lunch crowd can wait a moment. This is more important."

She stared me down with one eyebrow quirked until I snapped my mouth shut. After a long silence, she took a deep breath.

"Do you believe in magic?" The matter-of-fact look on her face would have been the same if she'd asked me if I liked tomato soup or wore pants.

"Did you just ask me if I believe in magic?" I asked, my voice bordering on hysteria. "That feels like an absurd non sequitur."

"Yes. Do you believe in magic?" she repeated.

I stared back at her without blinking for a moment, sorting through the half-dozen answers that popped into my head before settling on "No, Christina, I do not believe in magic. I am a grown-up who knows the difference between fantasy and reality."

Christina winced and ran her hands through her hair. "Then you're going to hate everything I'm about to tell you. I'm sorry."

I laughed darkly. "You're going to tell me magic is real?"

Christina groaned and glanced toward the door as if judging how quickly she could escape. But instead of jumping to her feet, she took a deep breath and squared her shoulders. Holding out her hands defensively, she said, "I'm not the best person for this. Crystal would do a much better job, but I'll do my best. Okay?"

She peered at me as if waiting for an answer, so I resigned myself to the ridiculousness unfolding and waved my hand at her. "Sure. Whatever you say."

Christina nodded once, then launched into her explanation. "Long story short, magic is real, witches are real, and if you're hearing thoughts, odds are that you have witch blood in your veins."

I stared at her, unblinking, waiting for her to admit she was punking me, but when her anxious expression didn't crack, I smiled awkwardly. She really believed what she was saying. The grown woman sitting across from me in the cramped space behind the diner counter one hundred percent believed what she was saying.

"You mean, like Wicca?" I asked, grasping at rational straws.

Christina shook her head. "No. Wicca is very real, but I mean *magic,* magic. Floating fireballs, spells, and all that jazz."

I stared wordlessly at her.

"I'm not kidding," Christina said with a frustrated sigh.

"Can you prove it?" I asked, raising an eyebrow.

Christina's ears turned pink, and she glanced away. "Unfortunately, my magic can't really be demonstrated."

"That's convenient," I said, shaking my head. "Look, I'm not sure what your end game is here, but I'm exhausted. My head is pounding. And whatever this is," I waved my hand vaguely in her direction, "I just don't have it in me today."

"Well, you can't say I didn't try. I have to run. I'll send Cassie or Crystal by later. Maybe they'll do a better job," she said, awkwardly getting to her feet and brushing herself off. "Stupid jerk and that stupid fight. Men are so...ugh."

"They're not all bad," I said when she finally ran out of steam.

"What?" Christina's momentary confusion gave way to anger. "Hey! Stay out of my head!"

"Whoa!" I protested, holding my hands up defensively. "I have no idea how I'm even doing this. Trust me, if I could turn it off, I would!"

"At least you're admitting you're hearing thoughts. Maybe that's progress." Christina rubbed her eyes wearily. "Sorry. I'm not myself today. Rough night."

"Stupid jerk?" I asked, peering up at her.

She chuckled sadly. "Stupid jerk. My boyfriend. If you can call a guy I've had more fights with than dates that." I grimaced sympathetically at her as she shrugged helplessly. "Don't worry about me. I'll figure it out. You have enough on your plate."

Exhaustion settled on me again. My head was pounding, and black dots swirled in front of my eyes. Christina's expression shifted from mildly frustrated to alarmed when I swayed in place hard enough to almost tip over. I rested one hand on the floor to steady myself and rubbed my face with my other one. "I think I need to lie down. Thank Cassie for the pies, would you?"

With her help, I got to my feet with only one pained grunt when I twisted my shoulder too far.

"Mo? I need to lie down for a bit. What do you say we close for lunch and open for dinner in a few hours?"

"You okay?" he asked, peering at me from the other side of the pass-through and frowning when he caught sight of my face. "You look like something the cat dragged in. Get some sleep. I'll make a sign for the door."

Christina followed me out through the employee entrance and turned as we approached the path leading to my camper. "Are you good with the whole 'magic is real' thing? I might have botched the explanation."

"Honestly, I don't know what I think. Maybe it'll all make sense after I've slept a little." Without waiting for a response, I turned away and headed around the diner to the camper. Hearing thoughts was already a stretch. But magic? No way that was real.

ELEVEN

Magic is real. Have you ever heard of telepathy?
Magic is real. Heard of telepathy?
Magic. Telepathy?
Telepathy. Magpathy. Telemag. Magic.
Telema.

Christina's words looped around in my head as I tossed and turned on my bed until they turned into a series of nonsensical sounds. I grabbed a pillow and pulled it over my face with a groan to block out the light spilling in from the Airstream's many windows and attempt to muffle the sound of Christina's voice.

Since the voice was in my head, the pillow proved useless in that regard. It wasn't much more effective at blocking out the light. For what essentially amounted to a tin can on wheels, the camper was surprisingly bright during the day. I gave up on napping after twenty minutes of trying to find a position that didn't hurt my shoulder and kept my face out of the sun.

Flinging the pillow to the side, I flopped onto my back with a sigh. I was physically exhausted, but I'd never get any rest if I didn't quiet my brain. Unfortunately for me, I usually calmed my mind by moving my body.

The next best thing sat right outside my front door.

I rolled myself out of bed and into the kitchen in search of a snack and something to drink. Most of what I'd inherited from Aggie's husband had ended up at the dump, but I'd kept the two ancient deck chairs that had sat outside the camper for decades and would probably be there long after I left. The discolored woven vinyl ribbons were cracking in spots, but the chairs were surprisingly comfortable and sturdy despite their age. I lowered myself gingerly onto the one closest to the door and set my glass of iced tea onto the little mosaic table I'd found at a tag sale and fixed up.

Outside, the sun warming my face was far more pleasant than it had been inside. I closed my eyes to savor the heat and the calm. Other than birds bickering off to my right and the faint clinks and clangs coming from the open diner kitchen window, it was quiet. Enough to make me realize just how loud it had been in the diner all morning.

It was getting harder and harder to pretend that Christina hadn't been joking around. For starters, we didn't have enough of a relationship for her to prank me, nor had she appeared to be enjoying herself. Then there was the undeniable fact that she'd been talking without moving her lips. Or that people had been saying really strange things to me for days. But telepathy? Really? I shook my head. Hearing people's *thoughts*? Even as dread pooled in my stomach, a flicker of excitement and awe took hold of me.

I can hear thoughts.

I can hear *thoughts.*

I can hear thoughts.

It still sounded absurd. My whole life, I'd thought telepathy was a made-up gimmick used by authors and TV producers to move their plot along. If it were real, wouldn't people know? If ghosts were real, people would know! Same with magic!

I tried to laugh, but it came out flat.

If magic were real, people would know, right?

Unbidden, the image of Cassie's bakery with its tongue-in-cheek pastry names popped into my mind. Truth Cake. Confidence Muffins. Cheer-up Croissants. Gimmicks. Right? Except that the croissants cheered me up when I was down. But how could anyone be sad when eating buttery, flaky pastry?

Juliette's bookshop, Wyrd Words, also had a magic-inspired name. And every single book I'd ever bought from her had been exactly what I needed to read right then. Was there more to it than Juliette knowing her stock that well?

Soft footfalls pulled me from my thoughts. The sun had gone from pleasantly warm to bright enough to force me to blink to clear my vision so I could see who'd arrived. I'd only been outside a few minutes, but everything seemed a little *more* than it had when I'd closed my eyes.

"It's the magic." Cassie stood in front of me. "You can't see it until that part of you awakens."

When I raised a skeptical eyebrow in her direction, she gestured around the small yard where faint trails of colorful light filaments connected to everything around me danced in the wind. I glanced at her for an explanation, and when I looked back, the strands of light had vanished, leaving the yard the way it usually looked.

"Magic is inconsistent when it first awakens. Eventually, you'll learn to control when you see it." She lowered herself cautiously onto my rickety old chair's twin.

Propping my elbow on my knee, I dropped my head into my hand and rubbed my forehead.

"Magic isn't real, Cassie." I looked up at her.

"I know exactly how you feel," she said with a kind smile.

"Somehow, I doubt that," I replied drily. How could she possibly know what it was like to wake up one day and find yourself tossed into a world where nothing made sense anymore?

"No, I really do." She grinned at my dubious expression. "I was in your shoes not all that long ago. Well, not your exact shoes," she added when my frown deepened. "Imagine finding out that everything you bake does more than just taste good."

"So, the pastry names?..." I asked, as some of my skepticism gave way to curiosity.

Cassie shrugged and laughed. "Some of them. Most of them are just for show. But there is a whole secret menu for those in the know." She tapped the side of her nose and winked mischievously, then laughed again when my eyes widened. "But I fought it hard, too. My pride and ego didn't want to hear that magic made me a better baker. But then there were fireballs."

My head snapped up. "Fireballs?"

Cassie grinned. "Yeah. When I point-blank accused her of drugging my coffee, Crystal threw a few fireballs at me."

"Crystal threw fireballs at you?" I echoed weakly as terror grabbed my stomach in its fist and twisted. If I conjured a fireball in my sleep, the Airstream would go up like kindling around me.

Not noticing my worried glance at my hands, Cassie clarified. "Okay, maybe she didn't exactly throw them at me. But she floated a few over my head the day she told me I was a witch."

Letting that go for a moment, I stayed with the fireballs. "Actual fire? Floating in the air?" When she nodded, I asked what I really wanted to know. "And you..." I gulped. "You can do that, too?"

Her mouth turned down in disappointment. "Nah. Air's my thing, not fire."

The tension holding me upright vanished in a poof of relief, and I sagged back in my chair. "Ha!" I laughed. "Now I know you're all messing with me. What I don't get is why."

"We're not messing with you." Cassie frowned. "Why would we do that?"

"That's what I'd like to know!" I cried, throwing my hands in the air. "Magic isn't real, Cassie. It's all parlor tricks. I saw a documentary once. It's all illusion and sleight of hand."

Cassie's frown melted away as she chuckled to herself. "I see the confusion. The magic of redirection and making people see what they want to see is different. This is the magic I'm talking about."

I followed her gaze to the dirt at my feet, where the wind stirred up the dust. As I watched, a tornado-like funnel of dirt just a few inches tall formed and danced between my feet before settling where it had started, scattering into a pretty, circular pattern.

Open-mouthed, I stared at the spot, then looked up at Cassie, who shrugged apologetically. "Sorry, I know it's not as cool as a fireball."

It took me three tries before I managed to say something. "That...that's not possible."

Apparently convinced that the chair wouldn't collapse under her, Cassie settled herself against the backrest. Taking a deep breath, she lifted her right ankle to her left knee.

"Let's see if I can do a better job of explaining this to you than I did to Amy." She paused for a moment and stared out into the woods as she considered her words. "Would you agree that there's a lot about this world that we neither know nor understand?" When I half shrugged in response, she continued. "For instance, humans have only explored about eighty percent of the ocean. Right?"

I tipped my head in agreement. "What does that have to do with magic?"

"Gimme a second. I'm getting there," she replied with a small laugh. "What happens in the other twenty percent is a mystery, but we can make educated assumptions based on what we know."

She glanced at me to see if I was following her logic, so I nodded, still unclear about where her analogy was heading but intrigued enough to see it through to the end.

"Imagine, if you will, that it's hundreds of years ago. People believe the sun is the center of the universe, apples fall out of trees for no reason at all, and people think spirits and humors make them get sick and kill them." She grimaced. "Sorry. Aurie is learning about the Enlightenment. I was helping her study last night."

Blowing out a sigh, I nodded slowly. Cassie's daughter, Aurie, was a spitfire who occasionally came into the diner with her mom for milkshakes after school. Helping her study would probably also make me grimace.

"You're saying that just because people didn't believe in science doesn't mean it didn't exist."

"Exactly!" she cried, beaming at me like I was a child who'd done well on a quiz. "Magic, like science back then, is a force in the universe that hasn't been studied and analyzed. It was always there. Apples fell from trees before gravity was theorized. People got sick and died long before germs and viruses were discovered."

"But science didn't become real because people understood or noticed it. There are no dancing fireballs for people to dismiss as quirks of nature!"

"You've got me there." She pursed her lips and tapped her chin, looking off into the distance at the squabbling birds. Her eyes brightened as an idea came to her. "Light. Color."

I frowned. "You've lost me."

"Aurie's also learning about eyes and, you know, cones and all that." She gestured vaguely at her face. "Our eyes have a certain number of cones that allow us to see a portion of the colors in a prism. Birds have more cones, so they see more colors. To us, female birds look drab and boring. To them, they're gorgeous. And there's that shrimp in the ocean that sees more colors than any other animal on earth."

"Are you saying that some humans have more or different receptors that let them see magic when others can't?"

"Yes!" she cried. "Exactly!" Her energy dipped. "Well, kinda. Most people can see the effects of magic, like my little dust tornado. And they can feel the result of magic, like when they eat some of my bespelled pastries. Witches can see the magic and manipulate it."

"If you say so," I replied, not entirely convinced, but losing interest in the metaphor. "So, what does that have to do with me?"

"Well, Christina says you're hearing thoughts. And I suspect you saw the magic filaments earlier."

"The what?"

"Oh, those tiny strands of light that connect everything. Pure elemental magic."

"And?"

"We could be wrong, but Christina seemed pretty certain, and she's been a witch much longer than I have. Telepathy is a witch ability. We think you're a witch, Melly. Like me. And Christina, and Crystal, and, well, the rest of the Brewhahas, along with about half of the people in this town. You're special, Melly. Like us."

A flash of anger propelled me to my feet. "That is ridiculous," I cried, barely resisting the urge to stomp my foot.

"It is?" Cassie looked baffled at my reaction.

"Yes! You think that I'm a witch. And you're a witch. And Crystal, Christina, Hattie, and Juliette are witches." Shaking my head, I ran my hand through my hair, carefully avoiding my stitches. "It's the most absurd thing I've ever heard. I'm not a witch. I'm just a woman who works at a diner." I paused. "Who owns a diner. Whatever. I am a nobody. I didn't even finish college."

"I'm not sure what that has to do with anything," Cassie replied. "But you are not a nobody. You're far more than that."

"No, I'm not. I'm not special. I'm not anything." Hot tears flooded my eyes as I choked down the ball of grief pushing its way up into my throat. "I was someone when my mother was alive and needed me. Now that she's gone, I'm no one."

I sat back down on the chair with a thump that caused an ominous creak and glanced away from Cassie, staring at the trees through my tears until I had the grief compressed back into its usual manageable shape and I could trust myself to speak without venting more mortifying self-reflections.

Cassie sat quietly as I composed myself, and I delayed looking over at her as long as I could. If there was one thing I hated more than crying, it was losing it in front of someone else. Especially a virtual stranger.

"I'm sorry," I muttered, looking down at my hands.

I was so lost in my misery, I didn't notice Cassie move, so I jumped when her hand settled on my knee.

"I'm sorry anyone has ever made you feel like your only worth lies in what you bring to others. That your only value is your ability to help. I may not know you very well, but even I know that's not true. It wasn't true before, and it's certainly not true now that your magic is awakening."

"Well, phew." I threw my hands in the air. "Glad to know magic will finally make me noticeable," I said, putting air quotes around the word magic.

Instead of irritating me, Cassie's laughter at my overly dramatic response pulled me out of my tailspin.

"As I said earlier, I know exactly how you feel. You cannot imagine the tantrum I threw when I thought people were telling me magic was the secret ingredient that made my baking great. I was so mad!" She laughed again as she shook her head.

"Then what happened?"

Cassie chuckled and rubbed her forehead. "Oh, I tried to pretend none of it was true and whammied the entire town with a coffee cake that made them all tell me things about my great aunt that I never, ever wanted to know."

I couldn't help laughing. "Like what?"

"Trust me, you also don't want to know. Suffice it to say that one too many people told me about her 'clothing optional' sunbathing habits." Cassie shuddered, but her eyes danced with delight.

"So... like more than two people?" I offered with a teasing grin.

"Exactly!" Cassie cried, burying her face in her hands. "It was horrible."

"Wait. I can't hear your thoughts." I sat up and looked over at Cassie.

"Oh, so you admit you can hear thoughts?" Cassie asked, raising one eyebrow suggestively. "Does that mean my lesson about magic did the trick?"

I sighed and gestured at the neat circle of dust left behind by her tornado. "Do I have a choice?"

She laughed again. "Not really, no. As your magic takes hold, the effects will become more noticeable."

"Meaning?" I asked, frowning.

"Meaning that right now, you probably only hear thoughts when you're worked up. Going forward, it'll happen increasingly frequently and consistently. And because magic isn't a fan of being ignored, if you try, it'll make you sit up and take notice."

"Fantastic," I drawled. So much for just pretending none of this was happening.

Cassie grinned. "As for why you can't hear my thoughts, like you, I have a secondary magical ability that forced me to learn how to shut my mind off from others. If you'd like, I can teach you. It's not fool-proof, but it helps."

TWELVE

"So, I close my eyes and envision a box?" I asked, tilting my head to the side in an unconscious imitation of my crow friend's uncertainty. "How does a box help? Wouldn't thoughts just flow over and around it?"

Cassie hesitated, then said, "That's how I started."

When she didn't elaborate, I gestured for her to keep going. "And now?"

She grimaced. "My magic is different than yours. When it first emerged, anything I was feeling when I baked seeped into what I made. Anyone who ate the pastry or cake would feel the same way, or their actions were influenced by those feelings. Does that make sense? It's hard to explain."

I nodded. "I think so. When you're feeling happy or confident, the person who eats the croissants you made cheers up or becomes more self-assured."

"Exactly!" Her grin dissolved into a wince. "Awesome when making feel-good snacks. Less so when I bake when I'm upset."

"Oh, no!" The implications of that were all too easy to grasp. My hands flew up to cover my horrified expression.

"It's as bad as you picture. I've been assured that nothing I bake will make anyone act out of character, but…" Her gaze turned inward, and she shuddered. She shook her head and smiled deprecatingly. "Eventually, my magic evolved to letting me taste the emotions people feel." She laughed at the look of disgust on my face. "It wasn't pretty, and it motivated me to find a solution."

"I can imagine!"

"I tried the box solution, but I found it to be hit or miss. Every time I felt or tasted a new emotion, I had to act fast to catch it. Since most emotions are fleeting, I missed a bunch. As it so happens, emotions are also messy and don't enjoy being chased down and shoved into a box."

The visual made me chuckle.

"After a few frustrating months, I noticed that if I looked inward, I could see the general area of my brain where the emotions lurk." She shrugged and opened her hands. "I built a mental wall around it. When I realized that made accessing my empath powers challenging, I built a little door into the wall."

"You built a wall. In your head." It was absurd, but she nodded emphatically.

"I know how it sounds. If I hadn't done it myself, I'd have the same look on my face. I think it might be a witch thing. But I promise it can help."

I shot her a look that would have made my mother send me to my room to think long and hard about my attitude. Cassie laughed.

"What's the worst that can happen? It doesn't work, and you feel a little silly?" she asked. I answered her with a rueful smile and a tiny shrug. "Good news: no one has ever died from ridicule."

Feeling silly about potentially feeling silly, I snorted a laugh. "You're right. I have nothing to lose by trying."

"That's the spirit!" she replied with a laugh. "It's not as hard as it sounds. Let's try something. Close your eyes." Shutting out the bright afternoon sun was a relief, and the throbbing in my head eased a little. Cassie shifted and continued in a low, soothing voice, "Can you turn your gaze inward? What do you see?"

"Whah..." I started saying in protest.

"Shhh. Humor me and try."

"Fine." Biting my lower lip, I brought my focus inward. It sounded ridiculous and hokey, but the thought of a lifetime of being bombarded by people's thoughts made me queasy. If I didn't figure this out, the dinner service was going to be untenable. My heart sped up as a clear image formed in my head.

"I knew you'd get it quickly!" Cassie gushed. "What do you see?"

"It's kinda dark, but it looks familiar. Like I've been here before."

"That makes sense. It's the inside of your head. Can you visualize some sort of light source?" she coached calmly.

A thin metal chain that looked suspiciously like the one that controlled the light in my mother's walk-in closet unfurled in front of me. Anxiety gripped my chest as I imagined tugging it on. The last time I'd been in my mother's closet, I'd discovered something I wish I hadn't found. What would I see when the light went on this time?

With a click, light bloomed, revealing the inside of a house my mother and I had lived in when I was little. I'd never forgotten the faded floral wallpaper.

"Can you see anything?" Cassie prompted.

"A living room. It's empty. No furniture. I don't see any windows." My heart rate spiked until I took a mental step back.

"You're okay, Melly. Stay with me. You're safe. I promise. You're inside your own head. All you have to do is open your eyes to come out. But don't do it yet!" she cried as my eyelids fluttered. Despite feeling the floral walls closing in on me and the panic rising, I kept my eyes closed tight. "Good. Good. Take a slow breath in through your nose and breathe it out even slower, as if you're blowing out a hundred birthday candles. Everything's okay." I followed her instructions until the panic receded. "You're doing great. What else can you see?"

"It's a large room with multiple doors and a spiral staircase off in the corner."

Cassie clapped her hands. "Amazing. It's so cool how everyone's mental space looks different."

"Oh yeah? What does yours look like?" The crisp visualization faded as I asked.

"No, no! Don't lose your focus. Stay with me. You're in the room. You see doors and a staircase. Can you tell where any of them lead?"

Frowning, I focused inwardly again. "I think the stairs lead to memories. Not climbing those." I shuddered. Just imagining what lurked up there made my stomach hurt. "One door is purple with a big yellow ducky painted on it. I loved that door. My mom painted it for my fourth birthday. There's a smudge under the duck from when I tried to help."

"You can open it. Or you can tell me about the next door," Cassie suggested softly.

"I don't think I want to go in there." I turned away from the purple door, feeling a little tug in my belly that I wasn't anxious about investigating. "The door next to it is my college dorm room. At least I think it is. My name's not on it." But, then again, my name hadn't been on my actual dorm room either, as if the school had known ahead of time that I wouldn't be there long. "The next one is the door to the Airstream."

"This is amazing," Cassie murmured. "They might be doors to the different parts of you that existed at those ages."

Tabling that thought for later, I faced the door all the way to the right and drew in a sharp breath. "I don't recognize this one," I whispered hoarsely, awed by its beauty. "It's smaller than the other three. More ornate. It's a shimmering green and is covered in intricate glittering designs that shift when I look too closely at them."

"Oh!" Cassie breathed. "What do you think is behind it? Is it open?"

"I think..." I paused, squirming uncomfortably in my chair.

"It's okay. Remember, you're safe. Just taking a little stroll inside your head. Nothing to worry about. Wait." Her voice sharpened. "Unless there's something back there that you don't want to tell me. I don't have to know everything!"

Even without opening my eyes, I could tell she'd turned a hot shade of pink. I laughed.

"Nothing like that," I assured her. "But I think it might be the door to my magic. Is that possible?"

"Anything is possible," Cassie said, having recovered her cool. "Is it open?"

"A little more than the others, but not so much that I can see inside it. The light coming out seems richer than regular light. Thicker, somehow."

"Wow," Cassie breathed.

"Should I close it?"

"Can you?" she asked, curiosity raising the timbre of her voice.

Even though the door was clear across the room in my head, once I thought about getting closer, I was. The door tingled slightly under my palm when I visualized placing my hand on it, and I held my breath. The urge to grab the doorknob and fling the door wide open gripped me hard as tendrils of the bright warmth from the other side licked at my hand and encircled my forearm, promising me wonders beyond my imagination. All I had to do was open the door all the way and step into the magic. A burst of panic and maybe a little self-preservation made me slam the door instead of pulling, instantly snuffing out the siren's call of the magic. I sagged against the now dull green door and shied away from wondering if I'd deprived myself of something marvelous or saved myself from something unspeakable.

"I closed it." I hated the way my voice shook as I shoved my shaky hands between my thighs.

"Amazing. Just amazing," Cassie sounded a little awed, but I didn't trust myself to not burst into tears if I opened my eyes, so I kept them pressed closed. "Let's test it out."

She fell silent for a moment, but I heard nothing other than the birds and the outrageously loud camper fridge.

"Did you hear that?"

I shook my head. "Not a word."

"Then I think it's safe to say that you have found your mental shield. Keeping that door closed should keep you from hearing anyone's thoughts."

Relief turned my bones to jelly, and I slumped down in my seat. Blinking back treacherous tears, I opened my eyes and let out a shaky breath.

"That is wonderful news. I am so glad I can put all this behind me and forget it ever happened."

"Oh." Cassie's smile fell. "Sorry. No. That's not how this works. Once your powers have awoken, you're stuck with them." She grimaced sympathetically.

"Can't I just keep the door shut? I'll block it or something." In my head, a massive couch popped into existence and slammed up against the door.

Her lips curled inward, and she shook her head apologetically. "It might work, but I doubt it. If I've learned anything about magic since I arrived in Portney, it's that there's no suppressing it for long. The older witches like to say, 'magic will out.' It'll find a way. But you should be good at least through dinner."

I dropped my head back and groaned. "I guess that's better than nothing."

As a kid, I'd fantasized about hearing people's thoughts so I wouldn't have to guess how they felt about me. I was fully cured of that dream. There was such a thing as knowing too much. If I never heard another stray judgment about my hair or the diner's décor, it would be too soon.

Maybe the fix would hold until I found a more permanent solution. Preferably before hearing people's thoughts drove me mad. Which hopefully wouldn't occur before I figured out where the money and the pendant had come from and returned the money I'd borrowed to buy the diner.

THIRTEEN

We were nearing the end of the breakfast service. My head wasn't pounding, and the only thoughts bouncing around my brain were mine. I silently thanked Cassie again for showing me how to block everyone out as I dropped a handful of silverware into the dirty dish bin. The previous evening's dinner service had been almost restful without two dozen thoughts battling for attention. Even now, with a handful of people finishing up their meals, my mind was delightfully quiet.

So quiet, I could almost pretend I'd imagined the whole thing.

Turning my back to the diner under the pretext of refilling the coffeepot, I closed my eyes and turned my gaze inward. Nothing had changed. The floral wallpaper, the stairs, and the two partly open doors were exactly where I'd first pictured them. The door to my magic was still dull green, with no light seeping around the edges, but the power it hid pulsed seductively in time with my thundering heart. Despite the fear gripping my throat, I couldn't resist reaching for the door. The deluge of thoughts that slammed into me when I turned the knob almost brought me to my knees.

> *Finish the story already. I swear he loves that phone more than me. First, the bank, then the cleaners, then the supermarket. Do I have time to stop at the library? Pie! Not with the frozen stuff in the car. I should start with the library. This better not be a waste of time. But that's two stops instead of one. Pie! Love pie. He's thinking about pie. The world could end, and he'd think about pie.*

I slammed the green door shut with a strangled gasp and pressed my trembling hands against the counter until a sharp female voice cut through my panic spiral.

"Excuse me, miss. Do you have a moment?"

"And some pie. Do you have some pie?"

Dragging a deep breath into my lungs, I plastered a smile on my face, wiped my shaky hands on my apron, and turned around, grabbing the freshly refilled coffee pot on the way.

"Hi! Welcome to, uh... our diner. How may I help you?" I asked the couple standing behind the counter.

The joy that bloomed on the guy's face more than made up for the painfully forced smile his gorgeous friend pointed in my direction. He had a cheeky, guy-next-door quality that made him surprisingly attractive and was completely at odds with her no-nonsense, pulled-together, couldn't-wait-to-be-anywhere-but-here attitude. Her bright red hair pulled back into a tight French twist was the only thing that hinted that there might be a little fire hiding under her ice queen armor.

"Did I mention I'd love some pie? Because I really would," the guy said, drawing my attention away from his companion.

I would have tumbled headfirst into the blue eyes he pointed at me if my gaze hadn't caught on the dimple that deepened as his smile grew. My belly tightened uncomfortably.

"Do you also maybe have a restroom?" he continued, graciously not mentioning my sudden resemblance to a tomato. "It was a long drive. It'll do wonders for her mood," he said, dropping his voice and leaning forward conspiratorially.

The glower she leveled on him should, by all rights, have burned him to a crisp, but he brushed it off with a wink and an impish grin that made her ears turn the same shade of red I suspected colored my face.

"You're in luck. We have pie and a restroom." I smiled. "Where are you two coming from? Please, sit," I said in my best customer service, diner owner voice as I gestured to the nearest counter stools with two of our chunky white coffee mugs. "Coffee?"

The woman's eyes softened noticeably in response. "Please. Light cream. No sugar."

"I'll take mine with all the sugar she's passing up," the guy drawled.

"You're going to give yourself diabetes," she snapped, rolling her eyes as she lowered herself onto a counter stool.

"You keep saying that, and yet..." He cocked finger guns at her playfully before heading toward the restroom I pointed out. "If you're not going, I will." Turning around, he flashed the full wattage of his smile at me. "You know what? I don't even want to know what kind of pie you have. Surprise me." Mortifyingly, my face flushed even hotter when he winked.

I busied myself filling their mugs, but the bemused look the woman shot me made it very clear she could tell how flustered he'd left me. Just to confirm why she looked like a cat savoring a canary, I cracked open the little green door in my head.

Either I was getting the hang of it, or focusing on a single person helped filter out other people's thoughts. Hers were the only ones I heard.

He's like a freaking golden retriever puppy. It would be infuriating if it weren't so helpful. Darn it. Why did he leave? She's got that I'm-going-to-make-small-talk look.

My question about how their travels were going died on my lips as I slammed both the door in my head and my mouth shut. If she was surprised when I turned away without saying a word, she hid it well.

We had three types of pie, and I hesitated, eyeing the tiered platter dubiously. Apple pie? Or the more sophisticated chili-chocolate silk? Then again, Cassie's cherry pie was a fan favorite around here...

"Don't overthink it. I guarantee he'll have ordered a slice of each before we go. Might as well start with the apple." The redhead's dry tone held more affection than I expected. I smothered a tiny pinprick of jealousy.

"Sounds like you know him well," I commented, plating a generous slice of apple pie and topping it with a dollop of the homemade whipped cream Momo prepared every morning.

She shrugged. "He's been my partner for five years."

"Oh."

She caught the subtext of my response and added, "Work partner." But the tips of her ears flamed red again as she glanced toward the restroom. When she looked back at me, she was all business once again.

"You said you needed a moment of my time," I prompted.

"Yes, but I'll wait until Agent Thorne returns."

"Agent?" I asked.

She took a long swallow of her coffee instead of answering me and let out an appreciative sigh. "Good. Thank you. You wouldn't believe how many terrible cups of coffee we endure on the road."

Before I could respond, a woman at the other end of the diner waved me over. "Excuse me a minute," I murmured.

"Of course. Don't worry about me. I have my coffee, and I certainly don't mind a moment of silence." She shot me a wry look before taking another swallow.

A second happy sigh reached me as I rounded the diner counter. It was gratifying to hear. Momo had fought me on the coffee order, claiming no one would know if I got the cheaper beans. I was glad I'd pushed back. Lack of experience notwithstanding, in my gut, I knew that quality would make or break this place faster than saving a few bucks every week.

"All set?" I asked, approaching the customer who'd called me over.

By the time I'd run her credit card and returned to my spot behind the counter, Agent Thorne had already inhaled his slice of pie and was eyeing the remaining two options with unabashed longing.

"You cannot have more pie," his partner said. "You're going to make yourself sick."

His face fell as he looked longingly at the pie stand. "But *you* haven't had *any*," he said, a glint of hope lighting his eyes.

"I don't want any pie," she snapped. "I never want pie. I don't even *like* pie."

"She just doesn't like to broadcast her love of sweets," he stage-whispered, leaning closer. "I usually have to order pie and pretend it's for me. It's exhausting, but what's a guy to do?"

I couldn't help laughing in reply. "It'll be our little secret," I whispered back just as loudly as he had.

He glanced at her and faked being stung by her exasperated expression. "Careful, we're going to be Penny-lized if we keep joking around. We're supposed to be working, don't you know?" he said sternly, the glint in his eye belying his officious tone.

"I'm sorry, penny-what?" Confused, I glanced over at the woman and back at him.

She rolled her eyes and huffed an annoyed sigh. "My name is Penelope. Agent Penelope Sterling. He thinks his cute nicknames for me are hilarious."

"Well, she likes to tell people I'm a thorn in her side because my name is Agent Thorne. Dashiell Thorne, to be specific." He held out his hand for me to shake, and, when I took it, he squeezed and leaned forward with a seductive smile. "But my friends call me Dash."

His impish grin sent a flurry of butterflies cavorting around my belly. How many years had it been since someone had flirted with me? Far too many to count if I even had to ask myself the question.

"If we're done kidding around, maybe we could get down to business?" Agent Sterling sniped, glancing at her watch.

"Of course. How can I help?"

Dash opened his mouth to reply and snapped it shut with a little grunt of pain, then leaned over to rub his shin. "I didn't even do anything!"

"You were going to, and we both know it. I'm sure Ms...." She tipped her head at me.

"Melly's fine," I replied.

"I'm sure Ms. Melly over here has better things to do than watch your one-man comedy routine."

"Just Melly," I corrected.

Dash propped his elbow on the counter and rested his chin in his hand like he had all the time in the world and fully intended to use it. "As we mentioned, we are Agents Thorne and Sterling. We're unfortunately here on official business."

My heart thudded in my chest. "Unfortunately? What agency did you say you were from?"

"We didn't," she said without elaborating further.

"Only unfortunately because I would love to be here just to get to know you better," Dash said, winking at me.

"Enough, already! Can't you focus for even a minute?" Agent Sterling said. "Could you please just give him more pie? It should keep him occupied long enough for me to get to the point."

"Two more slices, coming up," I said, grinning at Dash. Something told me that more pie had been his endgame all along.

When I returned, Agent Sterling held up a picture for me to see. The image was hand-drawn and fuzzy, but it still sent my heart into my stomach.

Of all the diners in all the towns... I gulped. What were the odds that two agents from a mysterious agency would coincidentally show up in my diner carrying around a picture of the pendant currently locked away in my safety deposit box?

I had a feeling they were even slimmer than our projected profit margins for the week.

FOURTEEN

"I'm sorry. What am I looking at here?" I asked, hoping the ball of fear lodged in my throat didn't make me sound different. I wiped my clammy palms on my apron and reached for the picture.

Agent Sterling hung on a moment longer than necessary, only letting go when I gave a little tug.

"Sorry, my eyes aren't what they used to be," I said, pulling it closer to my face. There was no doubt in my mind that the pendant in the picture was the one my mother had been wearing when she died, but I put on a show of peering at it closely.

"I'm sorry." I winced. Too much apologizing would make me sound insincere, wouldn't it? Hadn't I once heard something to that effect on a true crime drama? "I've never seen that necklace or even anything that looks remotely like it. It's pretty, though," I held out the paper. The corner of Agent Sterling's lip twitched, then her face settled into its usual impassive expression. I couldn't tell if it meant she suspected I wasn't telling her the truth or if the movement was involuntary.

The cavorting butterflies in my belly had given way to writhing snakes the instant I'd laid eyes on the picture. They grew more active as she held my gaze. I didn't dare look away for fear of appearing guilty, not that I had anything to feel guilty about. She couldn't read my mind, could she? My breath caught in my throat, and I slammed shut all the doors in my head. Cassie hadn't told me how to block other people, but it seemed like a good precaution, just in case.

Her gaze didn't waver as I locked down my mind. Maybe I was imagining things.

"Psst, Henny Penny, you're doing that thing where you stare creepily at people," Dash murmured, elbowing her in the arm as he shot me an apologetic smile. "She does that when she's thinking sometimes. It's one of her more endearing qualities."

Cheeks flaming, Agent Sterling snatched the picture out of my hand and shoved it into a manila folder labeled *A A* that I'd been too distracted to notice. When she caught me staring, her face settled back into its usual inscrutable expression.

She pulled a small notebook from her pocket and flipped through a few pages before landing on one and scanning the information on it.

"To be honest, Ms.... Melly, we're actually here to speak to a Mr. Cruz." She tilted the notebook and squinted as she tried to decipher her handwriting. "A Mr. Mauricio Cruz. We understand he works here?"

Already flustered by the photo of the amulet, it took me a moment to recognize Momo's given name. "Yes," I stammered. "Well, no, not really anymore."

"So, Mr. Cruz no longer works here?" She leaned forward, pen poised to jot down my reply.

"No! Yes! Sorry, I'm all turned around."

"Which is it? Is he or is he not an employee here?" Agent Sterling pinned me in place with a piercing gaze that only rattled me more.

Pressing my hands on the counter, I took a deep breath and smiled. "No, Mauricio Cruz isn't an employee. He's now part-owner. But yes, he is here," I explained. "I don't see what he has to do with this."

Agent Sterling's answering smile held no warmth. "I'm afraid I can't discuss that. Unless you've remembered something?" she prompted with a pointed look. "If you wouldn't mind telling Mr. Cruz that we'd like to talk to him, I'd appreciate it."

A glance at Agent Thorne told me he wasn't coming to my rescue. He was staring at his notebook, but he appeared to be listening intently to our conversation.

"There's nothing to remember," I said, keeping my voice steady. "Let me see if Momo can step away from the kitchen to talk to you for a minute." I gestured to the coffee machines behind me. "Can I get you some more coffee in the meantime?" I asked. "I can brew a fresh pot if you'd prefer."

"Yes, please," Agent Sterling replied in a slightly friendlier tone.

"Coming right up," I said through my stiff smile, and spun away.

"Momo?" I whisper-called through the window to the kitchen.

"Yep?" he replied, popping his head into view.

"These people are researching a missing necklace of some sort." I tipped my head toward the agents seated a few feet away. "They'd like to talk to you."

A series of uneasy emotions flew over his face too fast for me to label. "They ask for me by name?"

I grimaced. "Yeah."

He nodded sharply. "Be right out."

The agents stood to greet him, and the trio moved a few feet farther away. Refilling the coffee machine gave me a reason to stay close, but the low-key hubbub in the diner made eavesdropping nearly impossible. Frustrated, I overshot and missed the filter, pouring ground coffee all over the counter. What did Momo have to do with my mother's necklace? How did they have his name? He hadn't mentioned being in Rhode Island when I'd first arrived, even though I hadn't hidden where I'd come from.

Curiosity gnawed at my belly as I swept up the worst of my mess. Had he and Aggie known about the necklace somehow? Was that why she'd hired me on the spot? No matter how I twisted the facts and tried to make them fit together, nothing made any sense. He'd had plenty of opportunity over the last six months to bring up the necklace, but he'd never even mentioned any kind of jewelry. It had to be a coincidence.

The need to know overpowered my conscience, and, holding my breath, I cracked open the door to my magic. Thoughts assailed me from all around the diner. Maybe I needed to be closer to pinpoint just one or two people.

The machine burbled when I turned it on, and I grabbed a cleaning cloth to wipe down the counter and give myself a somewhat legitimate reason to approach.

Guilt twisted my stomach, but I pushed it aside and cracked the door to my magic open again.

He knows nothing useful.
Total waste of time.

"Just to confirm, Mr. Cruz, you were stationed at Newport ten years ago and haven't been back there since?"

"Yes, ma'am. Haven't been back since I was honorably discharged and came home to care for my brother," Momo said in a clipped, direct tone I'd never heard him use. He sounded like he belonged in a uniform with shiny buttons rather than a dirty chef's jacket.

Agent Sterling jotted something down in her notebook and nodded. "In that case, we're all set here. Thank you for your time, Mr. Cruz. We'll be in touch if we have any further questions."

Momo nodded once and turned away. When I met his eyes and raised my eyebrows questioningly, he shrugged and shook his head.

"Thank you again for the coffee, Ms.... Melly," Agent Sterling said, coming back to the counter, her face as inscrutable as it had been all morning. "I hope we haven't taken up too much of your time." Ignoring the dry, sarcastic undertones of her statement seemed wise.

"Not at all," I replied. A flutter of panic beat at my chest as they gathered their things and prepared to leave. "Would you like a little more before you head out?"

When I'd first found the pendant, I had done a thorough search for even a hint of it online and had come up completely blank. I'd resigned myself to possibly never finding out the truth. As unsettling as it was to have these two show up in the diner unannounced asking questions that shook me to my core, I was terrified that they'd walk away and leave me in the dark again.

Everything about Agents Thorne and Sterling was a mystery, even what agency they worked for. If they left, I would never find them again, and any hope I had of knowing where the pendant and money had come from would vanish along with them.

Without replying, she turned to Agent Thorne to confer quietly with him.

I took my time organizing things that didn't require organizing, doing my best to appear uninterested in their exchange as I sheepishly cracked the little green door open again.

We have got to solve this. I need a break from this guy before I push him off a cliff. Or smother him with his precious pie.

Shifting my focus to Agent Thorne, I almost laughed.

Would it be rude to ask for a fourth slice? Four is too many, right? Sounds like it. This lead was such a stretch. Anything could have triggered that alert. She never listens. No way these two are savvy enough to keep the artifact hidden. At least the pie was good.

Miffed, I changed my mind about packing him a to-go slice.

I was so focused on my internal grumbling that it took me a moment to realize he was smiling, his dimple almost twinkling at me.

"That was some of the best pie I've ever had, Melly," he said, putting a hand on the counter and leaning casually toward me. "Thank you so much for accommodating us. My compliments to the chef."

I forced a smile past the sharp retort I wanted to throw at him. "If you'd like to compliment her yourself, you can swing by her bakery. It's just down the road. *La Baguette Magique!* You'll love it. It's a magical place."

Agent Sterling's gaze narrowed, and Agent Thorne's eyebrow jumped, sending a flood of panic surging through me. What had I said? The two agents who'd been making moves to get up and leave settled back in their seats. Even Agent Thorne suddenly looked all business.

Maybe she does know something, Agent Sterling thought, reminding me that the door to my magic was still open.

Reluctantly, I slammed it shut. Listening to people's thoughts was a blatant invasion of privacy. Not something to be abused. Even so, I kept my hand on the doorknob far longer than was right. It was just so much easier to know what people were thinking, especially when someone had a poker face as good as hers.

"Ms...." Agent Sterling prompted again, as if hoping I'd finally reward her with my last name. I'd first offered my first name to be friendly. Deeply ingrained suspicion born of hours of watching fictional and real crime dramas on TV told me to keep it to myself.

I smiled as warmly as possible. "Melly's fine."

As Agent Sterling's mouth tightened, Agent Thorne's smile grew. No doubt who was the good cop and who was the bad cop.

"If you have a few more minutes to spare, we have some additional questions," he said, keeping his expression light. While his demeanor screamed, "friendly chat among friends," my gut told me not to trust him at all. As if he could sense my reticence, his smile grew wider. When a dimple appeared, my resolve melted into a pile of gooey teen girl swoon.

"What can I tell you?" I asked, doing my best not to simper. Even without looking, I knew Agent Sterling was rolling her eyes. But, honestly, if he kept his big blue eyes trained on me, she could do whatever she wanted.

"Rein it in a little, Thorne. You're going to make the poor woman spontaneously combust."

Agent Thorne pulled back with a wink as my face warmed.

"Melly, do you think we could take a seat in a booth? We'd all be more comfortable, and it would be easier for us to chat." Agent Thorne flashed his dimple at me again, and I almost tripped over my own two feet getting out from behind the counter. Almost as an afterthought, I grabbed the fresh coffee pot and a mug for myself on the way, eliciting the first genuine smile from the female agent since she'd walked in.

When their cups were topped off and I'd filled one for myself, I slid into the booth across the table from the two agents. Side by side, their differences were striking. Where she was pulled together and professional, he was scruffy and disheveled. She was as uptight as he was relaxed, but their eyes held the same sparks of sharp intelligence. I suspected people constantly underestimated him and paid the price for it. I equally doubted anyone ever made that mistake regarding Agent Sterling.

They didn't wait long before getting to the point.

"Ms.... Melly," Agent Sterling started. "We haven't been entirely forthright with you. Agent Thorne and I work for two agencies that police very...*different* populations. Do you understand what I'm saying?"

"I'm not sure I do," I said, frowning at her.

The two agents glanced at each other, then back at me.

Agent Thorne smiled reassuringly. "I have a hunch that you know that the world is more nuanced than most people realize." He held my gaze, his head cocked sideways, waiting for me to catch up. I blinked helplessly as I weighed my options. Was he talking about witches? Or was I jumping to that conclusion because it was all I could think about?

"If you won't get to the point, I will," Agent Sterling snapped, glancing at the clock above the pass-through window, then back at me. "Hidden among the regular humans of the world are people who are a little *more*."

My eyes widened. "More how?" Rolling her eyes, Agent Sterling waved a pretend magic wand in the air. I inhaled sharply. "You're talking about witches."

Their faces relaxed in tandem, and Agent Thorne grinned at me.

"I knew you were special the moment I laid eyes on you." His smile widened until he jumped and yelped. "I didn't even *do* anything!"

"Really?" Agent Sterling deadpanned.

"Okay. Maybe I did," he replied, looking sheepish.

"That you know about the paranormal element will make this conversation easier," Agent Sterling said, turning her attention back to me. "To clarify, I work with an agency tasked with policing the paranormal entities of our world. Agent Thorne works for a little-known sub-division of the FBI that I guarantee you've never heard of."

"Try me," I challenged. I somehow doubted there was an investigative government agency I'd never heard of in at least one of my documentaries.

"I work for the DAE," Agent Thorne said with a cheeky wink.

"The Drug Enforcement Agency? I've obviously heard of it." I frowned at them.

"No, the D *A E*, Division of Anomalous Events. It's a bit of a mouthful. Thus, the acronym. My office investigates crimes that baffle other agencies," Agent Thorne explained. "When crimes fall under both of our purviews, we work together to solve them."

"I said witches. You said paranormal entities. Are you implying there are other, uh, is species the right word?" My skin prickled. Witches were already a lot to swallow. If he said that vampires were real, I might hyperventilate. If the movie *The Birds* had left me with a paralyzing fear of birds, it was nothing compared to how much *The Lost Boys* had messed me up when I was a kid.

"Yes, there are many types of paranormal entities. No, vampires are not real. Or if they once were, they went extinct a long time ago." Agent Thorne's eyes gleamed with suppressed amusement.

I narrowed my eyes at him. "How did you know I was thinking about vampires? Can you read my mind?"

"No. Can you?" he joked, quirking an eyebrow.

I snapped my mouth shut and threw out the first thing that came to mind to redirect the conversation.

"So, you work together on mysterious crimes that have something to do with the paranormal? I'm not sure I understand what that has to do with me." I directed the comment at both of them, glancing back and forth between them.

"Oh, I think you do." The quirk of Agent Sterling's eyebrow made my insides quake in an entirely different way than when Agent Thorne smiled at me. "How about you stop pretending and tell us what you know about the amulet?"

"What's an amulet?" I asked, genuinely baffled.

"It's just a fancy word for a pendant," Agent Sterling explained, keeping her eyes fixed on my face, watching for a reaction.

My inner child squirmed under her pointed stare until I remembered that I was a grown-up not as easily intimidated by authority.

"Well, as I told you earlier, I've never seen that pendant or even one that vaguely resembles it." Her eyes narrowed, but I kept going. "If that's all you wanted to ask me, I need to get back to work." I lifted my chin and returned her stare.

Agent Thorne chuckled. "Uh oh, Penny-Lane, you might have found your match in this one." His partner broke her stare to roll her eyes and release an annoyed huff. He turned his charming smile on me. "Hear me out,

Melly. This amulet has been in the wind for a very long time. Thanks to methods I'm not at liberty to disclose, its magical signature was detected in Rhode Island six months ago. Much to our delight, faint traces of its magical signature were picked up here a few days ago."

Even though I schooled my face, I saw his eyes light up when he caught the shift in my expression.

"Are you from Rhode Island, Melly?" he asked, leaning forward. His easy grin did nothing to soften his piercing gaze.

"I... ah..." There was no point in lying, not when they probably had access to all sorts of government databases. "No, but I cared for my mother through a long illness there." *Until she died six months ago,* I thought to myself.

"Sorry for your loss," Agent Sterling murmured without appearing to mean it.

Agent Thorne's smile didn't waver. "It's a lovely place."

"Yes," I answered, not sure what he wanted me to say.

"We're hoping that someone in your position could help us identify anyone who might have headed down this way from Rhode Island during the last six months."

"Someone in my position?" I frowned.

He cocked his head and shrugged. "A diner this good and this centrally located, I bet you see most of the locals at least once a month, if not more often."

"Something like that," I replied with a little shrug of my own. "Meatloaf nights are very popular with the regulars."

"Mmmm. Meatloaf. My mother made the best meatloaf." His wistful sigh made his partner shake her head.

"According to you, your mother made the best everything," she said.

"What can I say? The woman had her faults, but she was a great cook."

"You should stop by on Tuesday if you're still in town." Even if they were my only link to the pendant and the cash, I secretly hoped they wouldn't be.

When I'd inadvertently ended up with the amulet, I'd also inherited the job of keeping it safe. Unfortunately, I had no idea who to protect it from. For all I knew, Agents Thorne and Sterling were the very people who weren't supposed to get their hands on the blood-red pendant. At the rate they were connecting dots, they'd drag my secret out of me in no time if they stuck around. But if they left, I had no other way to learn more about the mysterious necklace I sorely wished I'd never seen.

"Maybe," Agent Sterling replied noncommittally. "In the meantime, can you think of anyone who arrived in town within the last six months?"

It was hard to suppress a smirk. "Agent Sterling, this is a beach town. Half of the people here are passing through on their way up or down the coast."

"The person we're looking for is a witch," Agent Thorne interjected. "Possibly someone nomadic who doesn't stay in the same place long. That should narrow it down quite a bit, no?"

"Sorry," I said, doing my best to keep my expression blank. "Nobody comes to mind. Maybe Miss Bitsy, the librarian, could help. She knows everything about everyone in this town."

"Then she sounds like the perfect person for us to talk to next," Agent Thorne said, tipping an imaginary hat at me and dropping a handful of bills he didn't bother counting on the counter. Then, with a last longing look at the pie display, he ushered his partner out the door.

It was going to take Miss Bitsy about three minutes to tell them I'd only been in town six months. They'd be back before the lunch service got underway, which meant I didn't have much time to figure out what I wanted to tell them.

FIFTEEN

The bell over the door to Wyrd Words jangled as I pushed it open. I'd been wrong. The agents hadn't returned either during lunch or after, which I could only hope meant they'd headed out of town.

Just because they hadn't come back didn't mean I'd stopped obsessing about the amulet.

When my original search hadn't turned up anything online, I'd convinced myself that my mother's panicked deathbed plea had stemmed from being near-death. The gut-churning revulsion I felt when the pendant was nearby had been easily dismissible as a symptom of my overwhelming grief.

But if two government agencies had spent decades hunting down the amulet, my mother might have been less delusional than I wanted to believe. Maybe it was valuable. Or linked to a crime. The thought made my chest ache.

What were you doing with it, Mom? How did a missing object important enough to command countless resources from two agencies end up in your possession? Was it tied to a crime? And if it was, how did you get mixed up in it? I don't understand.

My mother had been a waitress with no social life to speak of. She never went on dates or attended classes of any sort. Her days consisted of puttering around her small apartment, taking care of her dozens of plants, going to work, and coming home to do it all over again.

Nothing about her life had screamed, "There's a shocking amount of cash hidden in my closet, and I have a mysterious amulet hanging around my neck." She simply wasn't the type. I couldn't even picture her reading a mystery or watching a thriller.

And yet...

The thoughts chased each other around and around my head until I wanted to scream.

Picking up on my jumpiness and distraction, Momo suggested I take myself on a walk between services. For once, I didn't argue that I had work to do. If I stayed in the diner a moment longer, I was going to jump right out of my skin.

Just in case the agents were still hanging around, I headed in the opposite direction from the library and let my feet lead me to the one other place where answers might be lurking.

If my online search hadn't turned up anything, it was unlikely that I'd find information about the amulet in a bookshop, but the cozy store was as good a place as any to start. Even if Wyrd Words didn't have what I needed, maybe the soothing presence of books would at least calm me down.

"Hi, Melly! What are you doing here?" Juliette flushed, and the welcoming smile melted off her face. "I mean, it's nice to see you. I wasn't implying that it's strange that you're here or anything like that!" She grabbed her dress in a gesture I recognized from the countless times I'd fisted my apron to wipe off my clammy palms.

I smiled as reassuringly as possible. "Don't worry, I didn't take it like that at all. I had a little free time and realized I've never stopped by to see the new store." When Juliette's old store had burned down in a freak fire accident, she'd promptly reopened in the space connected to her cousin's bakery/coffee shop. "This place is amazing. Wait, is that an actual tree? That's incredible! Did you build the shop around it?" Fresh shoots jutted from the branches of the beautiful, healthy, gnarled oak growing in the corner of the store. "And are those seats on the branches? How clever!"

Juliette grinned. Delight seemed to have replaced the anxiety my arrival had triggered, and she led the way to the beautiful tree, explaining how it had grown overnight in response to an unspoken desire of her daughter's.

"It's how we knew she really belonged here with us, you know?"

I didn't know, but I smiled and nodded anyway, too distracted by the sheer size and detail of the tree to question the strange details of her explanation. My body was far too big for the cozy upper branch nooks, but I'd never wanted anything more than to escape reality up there for a few hours.

"Did you come here to browse, or were you looking for something in particular?"

Tearing my gaze from a tempting spot nestled at the junction of two branches, I glanced over at her, flinching at the somewhat forced smile on her face. How many times had she asked before I heard her?

"Sorry. This place is just..." My sentence faltered as I noticed the intricate carving work decorating the shelves that lined the back of the shop.

Juliette laughed. "Don't worry. I still feel that way sometimes, and I own the place. So, just browsing?"

Shaking my head, I dragged my focus back to our conversation. "I'm not actually sure you can help me. It's a bit of a long shot."

She cocked her head, and a small frown formed between her eyes. "Is everything okay?"

"Oh, yes! Everything is fine." I hesitated, unsure how to continue.

Juliette smiled. "I was about to have a cup of tea. Would you like to join me? You can tell me a little more about what you need."

My face warmed. This was ridiculous. What was I going to say? "My mom had a strange amulet being hunted down by two mysterious government agents with unclear intentions. You've never seen it and barely know me, but I somehow need you to help me learn more about it." How was she supposed to do that? I didn't even have the amulet on me to show her, and it had never occurred to me to take a picture of it.

Juliette gave my arm a little squeeze. "Believe me, whatever it is, I've heard weirder. Let's sit down, and you can tell me what you need." She led the way to the red velour couch tucked under the large shop window and gestured for me to sit next to her. On the coffee table, a stack of delicate porcelain cups sat next to a teapot shaped like a rotund chicken. Steam billowed lazily from the chicken's bright yellow beak.

"Were you expecting company? I didn't mean to intrude!"

"No! No!" Juliette assured me. "I just like to have enough on hand in case anyone stops by." The gentle scent of jasmine and bergamot tickled my nose as she poured out two cups and handed me one. "So, how can I help?"

"I honestly doubt you can," I started, taking an appreciative sniff. "This smells amazing. Thank you."

"Thank you! It's from a little tea shop I adore."

"I have an object, something my mother left me, that I'd like to know more about." If I'd needed proof that I was barking up the wrong tree—literally—Juliette's perplexed expression did the trick. "This is silly. I'm wasting your time. I'm sorry."

"No! You really aren't!" she protested. "Tell me more. I might be able to help."

Her eyes darted to the opening that separated her bookshop from her cousin's bakery and back at me. "How much did Christina and Cassie tell you about..." Her voice faded as she arched an eyebrow questioningly and fluttered her hand.

I grimaced. "The gist of what I got is that magic is real, and I have the unfortunate ability to hear people's thoughts, which may or may not be related to having witch blood in my veins." Leaning forward, I lowered my voice. "Between you and me, I'm not sure what to believe."

Juliette frowned and also leaned in. Keeping her voice as low as mine, she asked, "So, you *don't* hear thoughts?"

"Oh, no. That's real. And Cassie's tips for blocking everyone out have been very helpful. But the rest?" I made a skeptical face and waved my hand helplessly. "Come on. Magic? Witches? Next, you're going to tell me ghosts are floating around everywhere in here."

Juliette's eyes darted to a spot a few feet over my left shoulder, then toward the shop counter. "Just two today. But, yes, sometimes there are more." When my eyes widened, she hurried to add, "But don't worry. They're harmless. One is the original owner of the shop. She says she's not leaving until she's read every book on every shelf. And, well, since I keep bringing in new stock, I think she's here for the duration. The other..." She narrowed her eyes, staring over my shoulder again. "I've never seen before. He's a tow-headed, lanky man with intense eyes. Does that ring any bells for you?" she asked, looking back at me.

"For me? Why would you think that might mean something to me?"

Juliette scrunched her nose up uncomfortably. "No reason other than I get the feeling he's somehow connected to you."

My eyes widened even further as my heart skipped a beat, then started racing. "I have a ghost attached to me?" My voice came out three octaves higher than usual. "Why would I have a ghost attached to me?"

"I didn't say he definitely was attached to you," she hurried to say, patting my hand comfortingly. "But he only apparated when you arrived. I could be wrong!"

"Can't you... I don't know... ask him or something?" I still sounded pitchy, even to me, and I forced myself to take a shaky breath.

Juliette's eyes lost their focus for a moment as she stared off to my side. She shook her head and looked back at me. "I'm sorry. He's not talking to me. I'm not even sure he sees me."

"Is that normal?" I whispered.

She shrugged her right shoulder. "Honestly, with ghosts, it's hard to say what is or isn't normal. They each come with their own rules. But you didn't come here for a crash course on ghosts and their habits." She grinned warmly at me. "Don't worry about the magic stuff. It's a lot to take in at first."

"You're a..." I grimaced, unsure how polite it was to ask. "A witch, too?"

Juliette nodded. "I have a few unusual powers. Obviously, I can see ghosts. But I also have the magical ability to reunite lost objects with their owners."

"Wait. What?" I asked, frowning. "People ask you to find things they've lost?"

She winced. "More the opposite. Lost objects call to me. My magic nags me until I return them to their owners."

My heart leaped. Could I really be that lucky?

"How about we start at the beginning," she suggested, correctly assessing my sudden excitement, setting her empty cup on the table. "Tell me more about this object your mother left you."

The overwhelming urge to leave the amulet in the safety deposit box and forget it ever existed washed over me. There was a reason two government agents were on its trail, and I doubted it was because it made puppies and candy fall from the sky. I was the only person in the world who knew where it was safely locked away. What if bringing Juliette into it attracted the agents' attention somehow? What if it put her and her adopted daughter in danger?

My next breath got stuck in my throat, and, suddenly lightheaded, I tried to pull more air into my lungs and failed. This was wrong. Who was I to potentially endanger these people?

"I'm sorry," I gasped, clutching my chest as I jerked to my feet.

Juliette looked at me, her eyes wide with surprise.

What did I say? Was it the ghost thing? I should never have mentioned the creepy one attached to her. I scared her. Maybe she's mad.

I hope not, or she'll never welcome us back to the diner and then...

I blinked, unsure how to respond. "Uh, I'm not mad. I just... I need to think things over."

Juliette froze, her face suddenly bright red and her eyes flashing with anger. "You just read my thoughts." My heart plummeted to the bottom of my stomach.

"I'm so sorry," I cried. My hands flew up to cover my mouth as I quickly checked that the green door in my head was firmly shut. It was, but the glow on the other side was bright enough to render parts of the door almost translucent. That couldn't be good. "I'm so sorry. I didn't mean to. It was an accident. I'm sorry. I have to go."

By the time I stumbled out to the sidewalk, the door in my mind was opaque again, but a painful buzz of anxiety had settled in my gut. Making friends had been hard enough before I could listen to everyone's innermost thoughts. Who would ever want to be near me once they found out what I could do?

SIXTEEN

Even though I had fully intended to head left toward home and the diner, I turned right. I didn't want to see the amulet. Certainly didn't want to touch it. And yet, when I arrived in front of the bank, I couldn't stop myself from opening the heavy glass door.

Maybe I was overreacting. Crushed with grief, my eyes swollen nearly shut, I'd taken the velvet pouch the funeral attendant had handed me and peered inside. Everything inside me had screamed at me to put it away, so I'd pulled the bag closed without getting a good look. And when I'd briefly considered wearing it, my stomach had rebelled before I could even open the little pouch. For all I knew, my memory was wrong, and the stone wasn't even red.

By the time the bank attendant left me staring at the safety deposit box in the vault, I'd almost convinced myself that the pendant hidden away inside was a perfectly ordinary piece of jewelry, one my overactive imagination had turned into an eerie, glowing, fantastical gem that would incinerate anyone who so much as looked at it too closely.

Reality landed somewhere in the middle of the two extremes.

The pendant I tipped out of the thick navy velvet bag onto the table was exactly the one in the drawing the agents had shown me. It was far too ornate for anyone to call it ordinary, but it wasn't glowing or oozing any kind of evil that I could sense. But when I hovered my fingers over the amulet itself, my skin crawled, and my entire body tensed. My hand twitched, and when my index finger grazed cool stone, static electricity shot from the amulet into my finger and up my arm.

I jerked back with hiss, shaking my hand to dispell the tingling sensation of the shock. My heart galopped in a thunderous pounding that resonated all the way to my toes, and my breathing remained shallow and stilted until I put the amulet back in its bag and returned it to its place deep in the depths of the safety deposit box.

My skin crawled until I made it to the camper. I only had a few minutes to spare for a quick shower before I had to be at work, but any hope of washing off the amulet's unsettling sensation vanished when I heard my name.

Biting back a groan, I spun around and rocked back in surprise when Juliette rounded the diner and stopped at the tiny plastic white picket fence separating the diner parking lot and my yard.

"Juliette? What are you doing here?" Still tense from handling the amulet, I didn't realize I'd snapped the question until she shied back.

Chill, Melly. She's just a friendly neighbor stopping by to say hi. It's a thing people do, remember?

I took a deep breath and forced my shoulders to relax. "Did I forget something at the bookshop?" I asked, less aggressively, patting my pockets. As usual, my keys were in the left front pocket of my pants and my phone was in the right one, so that couldn't be why she'd run after me.

She held up her hand as she took a shuddering breath. "I don't get nearly enough exercise these days. And you walk fast. I saw you walk past the bookshop, and I thought I could catch up with you before you got home."

I winced apologetically. "Sorry about that. I was kind of in a hurry."

Juliette's eyes widened, and her face paled. "Oh, no! I'm sorry! I'll come back later. It's okay!" Hugging herself, she rubbed her upper arms. "It's just..." Her eyes darted around the small yard, landing on the weatherworn teak table before moving on to the ancient hummingbird feeder hanging over the galvanized steel planter near the door. She smiled at the slightly beat-up garden gnome sitting forlornly in the mostly empty planter.

"Oh! He's cute. Have you had him long?"

There was no reason why, but I had the strong sensation that the casual way she squatted by the little cement statue was an act. Everything about her smile as she lifted her hand to pet the gnome's head felt fake. But the genuine disappointment that made her face fall when her hand came into contact with the chipped paint of the little guy's once-red hat sparked my curiosity.

"Is everything okay?"

The smile she shot my way was a little shakier than it had been a moment before. She took a deep breath and stood up, flicking her fingers to shake off imaginary dirt. When that didn't seem to help, she wiped her hands on her skirt with a grimace.

Rubbing her forehead, she scrunched her nose and shook her head. "Yes? Kinda? Not really."

Her confusion made me chuckle despite the turmoil raging inside me. "That covers all the bases," I said. "How about you elaborate over a cup of tea? It won't be as fancy as the one you served me, but it should be drinkable."

Her grateful smile softened her face. "I'd love that. If it's not an imposition. You said you were in a hurry... I could always come back later if it's too much trouble."

"No trouble at all. I have just enough time to give you the grand tour." I tipped my head at the camper.

She eyed my shiny home with a dubious frown. "Grand tour? Really?"

"Hey! Don't knock my palace!" I chided with an offended sniff that turned into a laugh when her eyes widened in horror. "Just kidding. I know you didn't mean it that way."

With an embarrassed chuckle, she followed me up the metal stairs and into the Airstream.

"Oh! This is nice!"

"You don't have to sound so surprised," I replied, chuckling again as I looked around, seeing the place through the eyes of a visitor for the first time.

The inside of the camper had come a long way since I'd moved in, but it was obvious it still had a long way to go.

"Welcome to my humble and somewhat rusty abode. Over here you have the living room slash dining area, which can double as an extra bed if needed," I said, gesturing to the front end of the trailer.

"Obviously, this is the kitchen." The countertop attached to the small range rang hollow when I patted it. I couldn't wait to replace the cracked laminate with a butcher block slab.

"My bedroom," I said, indicating the double bed separated from the kitchen by a thin sheet of plywood. "The bathroom is at the end over there. And... that's the tour!" Despite being one of the larger models of Airstreams built in the 1970s, it was still small.

"It's lovely," Juliette said, looking around.

"Make yourself comfortable," I said, gesturing to the square table at the front end of the camper flanked by two built-in benches. The original square table had been hopelessly stained by what I hoped were fish guts. I'd scrubbed at the pink, red, and gray splotches with an eraser sponge for over an hour before giving the table up as a lost cause.

For a hot minute, I'd toyed with the idea of simply covering it with thick shelf liner, but there was no way I'd have been able to forget the stains it hid. Instead, I'd scoured vintage Airstream parts websites and message boards until I found an affordable replacement. *That* was covered in 1970s vintage vinyl. I'd scored the kitschy aqua oilcloth covered in bright red cherries at an estate sale. The bench still needed some work, but at least the red cushions with white corded trim matched the table's bold design.

Juliette settled herself on the bench as I pulled a small pitcher of iced tea from my tiny fridge. "I'd offer you some cookies, but I'm all out." She was already leery of my mind-reading ability. She didn't also need to know I'd eaten the entire box in bed the night before.

"That's okay. Tea is perfect."

"Iced okay?" I asked, holding up the pitcher and two glasses.

When she nodded, I poured us both a cup before pulling my phone and keys out of my pockets so they wouldn't dig into my thighs when I squeezed onto the other bench.

"What's that?" Juliette asked.

I glanced where she was pointing and froze. "That... that shouldn't be there." *That* should be in the secure vault at the bank where I'd left it. I could see myself tucking the little velvet pouch into the safety deposit box, could hear the lid of the metal box snapping closed, could feel myself sliding the box into its slot. So how had the small bag ended up in my pocket with my phone?

Time slowed as I gaped at the shimmering velvet until Juliette reached across the table.

"Don't!" I cried, throwing up my hand to stop her from touching the small pouch.

Her eyes went wide with shock, and she recoiled as if I'd hit her. I let out a shuddering breath when she crossed her arms and tucked her hands away.

"Sorry. It's just... I don't know what it does."

"What is it?" Keeping her hands to herself, she leaned forward, curiosity overpowering her usual reticence. "I can..." She glanced at me warily for an instant, then seemed to make a snap decision about whether to trust me or not. "I can sense it. Or, rather, my magic can."

"Does it feel... evil?" I whispered hoarsely.

Surprised, she met my gaze. "No, not particularly. It feels tingly."

I frowned and glanced at the amulet. I would have gone with thick and viscous, definitely not tingly.

Catching my dubious expression, Juliette explained. "I think I mentioned that my particular magical ability allows me to reunite objects with their owners, right?"

I nodded. "You said something about the magic nagging you."

She untucked her hands and flexed them a few times. "At first, it feels a little like something is tickling me. You know, like when a bug lands on you." She glanced at me expectantly, and I nodded, knowing exactly what she meant.

"Like a phantom touch?"

She brightened. "Exactly! When that starts, I know I'm getting close to something that was valuable to someone and was misplaced. The sensation gets stronger the closer I get to the object in question."

"That sounds annoying." My own hands tingled sympathetically until I rubbed them together to dispel the sensation.

"It's the worst game of hot or cold ever." Juliette's eyes sparked with laughter as she shook her head.

"What happens when you find the object?"

The laughter in her eyes fell away as she glanced at the little pouch. Her hands fluttered, but, catching my eye, she pressed them against the vinyl to hold them in place a few inches from the amulet.

"When I find the object, the magic flares and settles just under my skin like soft pins and needles."

She flexed her fingers again, but didn't move her hands any closer. I resisted the urge to grab the pouch so I could hide it. Somewhere permanent this time. Despite having no clue where I could put it so no one would ever find it, I really didn't want to touch it again.

"You sensed it when I walked past your shop on my way back from the bank, didn't you?"

She nodded.

"And how do your hands feel right now?" I asked, knowing the answer but needing to hear it anyway, no matter how much I dreaded it.

"Like they've both fallen asleep," she whispered. "What's in the pouch, Melly? Is it what you came to ask me about? Is it what your mother left you?"

"Yes, but I changed my mind. I didn't want to endanger you or your family."

"While I appreciate the sentiment," Juliette said, smiling wryly as she flexed her fingers, "I think the decision is out of your hands."

Without saying a word, I picked up the bottom corner of the little bag and shook the amulet out onto the table. The pendant fell out first, followed by the long silver chain. An angled ray of the setting sun streamed through the window and landed on the red stone, lighting it on fire.

"Wow," Juliette breathed as I gasped.

As gaudy as the setting was, in the dancing sunlight, the stone at its center was breathtaking. The longer I looked at it, the more detail I noticed. Each layer of the stone was a different hue of red, each so intense they seemed to pulsate in an obscene imitation of a beating heart.

Mesmerized, I leaned forward to get a better look at a spot near the center that I couldn't quite make out. Was it a defect in the stone? Or an even deeper layer?

"No!" I wasn't sure if I cried out when dark blue velvet suddenly blocked the shimmering red from my sight, or if Juliette was the one who'd shouted.

Since shaking my head didn't dispel the red spots in my vision, I dug the heels of my palms into my eyes until it faded.

> *Is she okay? I hope she's okay. No idea what it
> is, but no way it's good. What if she's possessed*

*like I was? What should I do? Should I call
Cassie? I should call Cassie. Definitely. Or
Hattie? She always knows what to do. Please
be okay. Please be okay.*

Overwhelmed, I blinked at Juliette a few times before realizing that the verbal tsunami wasn't flowing from her mouth. The green door in my mind was open as wide as it could go, and light so bright it hurt poured out of it, filling the space in my head. Wincing, I threw myself at it, grabbing the edge and fighting the firehose of light and the deluge of Juliette's panicked thoughts to wrestle it closed.

*She's so red! Is she breathing? I can't believe I
let this happen. Stupid, stupid, stupid, Juliette.
What were you thinking? She's a baby witch!
She had no idea what she was doing! You
should have known better!*

Caught in the maelstrom, I vaguely noted that the voice had changed from Juliette's usual sweet, anxious tone to something much harsher and condemning.

"I didn't know! How was I supposed to know?" Juliette argued, but there was no heat to her words, just browbeaten defeat. "I've never experienced this before!"

Instead of words, I glimpsed an ancient brown book throbbing menacingly, but before I could get a good look at it, the door finally shifted under my hands.

Inch by painful inch, I pushed it closed until it slammed shut with a boom that shook my whole body. The sudden silence made the world around me spin until I dropped my head onto the table and took a shaky breath.

"Is it..." I took another breath. "Is it always like that in your head?" I asked, squinting up at Juliette.

Her eyes widened in embarrassed horror as her entire face and neck flushed a deep red. Her hands flew up to cover her face before she nodded hesitantly from behind their meager protection. "Yes," she whispered.

"I am so sorry," I replied, equally softly, aching to pull her into my arms until her mind quieted long enough to give her a moment of respite. I was no stranger to overthinking and over-analyzing, but I'd never felt anything like the anxiety that possessed her.

Suddenly parched, I lifted my pounding head long enough to drain my glass of tea and pour myself another. I wrapped my hands around the cool glass and stared at the velvet bag covering up the amulet.

"What happened?" I asked, unsure I wanted the answer.

Juliette had composed herself enough to lower her hands back to the table, though she still looked like a cornered rabbit that wanted nothing more than to sprint to safety. In her place, I would have already been halfway home.

"I'm not sure," she said, but something in her tone told me she knew more than she was letting on.

"Why don't I believe you?" I asked, cocking my head.

Without meeting my eye, she abruptly got to her feet.

"Do you have something I could use to pick it up?" she asked, looking toward the kitchen.

"Uh...would kitchen tongs work?"

Nodding, she yanked open the drawer I indicated and pulled out a set of small tongs.

"Oven mitts?"

"In the bin under the oven."

Holding the tongs with the oven mitts made maneuvering the amulet back into the little bag challenging, but when I tried to help, she glared at me. "I may not be sure what that thing is or does, but I know we shouldn't touch it with our bare hands."

My heart skipped a beat as I pictured it resting against my mother's chest. Oblivious to my distress, Juliette picked the little pouch up with the tongs. Holding it at arm's length, she walked back to the kitchen.

"Do you have any salt? And maybe a food storage container of some sort? Preferably not plastic?"

Not trusting myself to speak, I nodded and pointed at the tiny pantry above the stove and the cabinet next to the fridge.

The biggest challenge of living in a camper was the lack of storage space. Juliette made a face when she pulled out the small container of salt.

"Sorry, that's all I have," I apologized. "I can run over to the diner and get more."

She shook her head. "I think it'll be okay for now."

Finding the right lid for the small rectangular glass container she pulled out proved challenging one-handed, so I hurried over to help. While I rummaged in the back of the small cupboard, she gingerly placed the little pouch in the container and poured all the salt on top of it, quelling my protest with a stern look.

"Trust me. It's for the best," she said, taking the lid from me and snapping it into place as she looked around the diminutive kitchen. "Do you have a microwave?"

She grimaced when I shook my head. "Sorry, no. Just an oven."

"It'll have to do," she muttered, opening it and shoving the sealed container to the back. With a relieved sigh, she closed the oven door.

Even out of sight, I could still sense the amulet in the oven. From the looks of it, so could Juliette. Gritting her teeth, she clasped her hands tightly and resolutely walked away.

"Okay," she said, sitting back down. "Start at the beginning. How did that," she tipped her head toward the kitchen, "end up with you?" she asked, angling her head back in my direction.

"Give me one second, and I'll tell you everything," I replied, picking up my phone.

Might be a few minutes late, I texted Momo. **Hold the fort?**

I made sure the sound was off on my phone before placing it face down on the table. I didn't need to see Momo's reply to assume he wasn't thrilled.

Juliette waited patiently as I gathered my thoughts, and I resisted the urge to peek into her head to see what she was thinking.

"My mother passed away around six months ago." I waved off the sympathetic noises she made in response. "She'd been sick a very long time. It wasn't unexpected. And she was in a lot of pain in the end." I stared at my hands. This wasn't the first time I'd shared this part of the story, but it never got easier. "Just before she died, she pulled that necklace out from inside her shirt and begged me to have it buried with her and to promise I'd never, ever touch it."

"So, how did it get here?" Juliette asked, frowning.

"The funeral home ignored my request to bury her with it. Since it was too late to add it to her casket, I kept it with me. She'd said something about keeping it safe for someone. What choice did I have? It wasn't like I could toss it in the donation pile with her clothes and stuff."

"It's been in the camper with you this whole time?" she asked with a dubious glance around the cramped quarters.

"No. I put it in a safety deposit box at the bank." I looked away, remembering how uncomfortable I'd been with it in the camper with me. So much for that being my overactive imagination.

"Why did you take it out of the bank today?" she asked, shooting me a look that made her feelings about that decision crystal clear.

"I didn't!" I protested. "I went to the bank to look at it, but I swear I put it back in the box before I left. I have no idea how it ended up in my pocket!"

Juliette muttered something colorful under her breath. "That's a little worrisome."

To keep my brain from spiraling into panic, I focused on the clock hanging over the sink. It ticked loudly, reminding me that Momo was probably getting antsy, but Juliette stayed silent, her eyes darting back and forth as she worked through something in her head.

Suddenly, she sat up. "Tell me about your mom's illness."

The request caught me off guard, and I frowned as I answered. "There's not much to tell. The doctors never pinpointed what was wrong with her. 'General malaise,' they called it. As if that means anything."

"Weakness? Unexplained weight loss or inability to gain weight?" I nodded in response to both questions. "Chronic pain that was hard to pinpoint, but mainly affected her joints?" I nodded again. "Anything else?"

"Food sensitivity," I said. "So many food sensitivities. Like everything she ate made her sick." I paused, thinking back. "Oh, and in the end, she was often too dizzy to walk more than a few steps at a time. And she'd bleed super easily if she hurt herself."

Juliette nodded solemnly.

"What?" I asked, dread pooling in my gut.

"I'm not one hundred percent sure," she replied, glancing at the amulet, then away.

"Juliette! You have to tell me!" I cried, putting two and two together. "What does that thing have to do with my mother's illness?"

She squirmed under my gaze, her eyes darting erratically to avoid landing on me. "I really don't know. I have some suspicions, but I should really do a little research before I say anything."

"Well, I guarantee you that anything I imagine will be a thousand times worse than whatever you have to say." Already, horrors were streaming through my head. Had my mother gotten tied up in some sort of magical cult? Had she sold her soul for that amulet and the deal had gone bad?

Juliette took a deep breath. "Please understand that this is pure speculation! I don't know for sure. But there is such a thing as magic poisoning. It's super rare, but it sometimes happens to non-witches who handle ancient magical objects."

"How does that even happen?"

She shrugged. "Sometimes they inherit them, or they find them at an estate sale or an antique store. Most of the time, it's a non-issue. The magic has either faded so much it's no longer a risk, or the item was correctly imbued with power, so it doesn't leak, no matter how old it is."

"But sometimes it's an issue?" The question forced its way past the lump that had formed in my throat. "That thing might have poisoned my mother?"

"It's very possible," Juliette murmured. "I'm so sorry. There's no way either of you could have known."

"I didn't even know it existed until just before she died."

"If it makes you feel better, it wouldn't have made a difference if you did. The magic in your blood hadn't awakened yet. You would never have sensed that it was the culprit."

"But if we both have witch blood, we should be safe, right?"

She grimaced. "Again, I really don't know for sure. But I think there's something wrong with it. It doesn't feel... right. And I don't like how it tried to ensnare you earlier."

A flash of fear made my eyes widen. "Ensnare me? What does that mean?"

"When you looked into its heart, it grabbed hold of you somehow. I don't know why. But I don't like it," she said, shaking her head.

"My magic..." I said.

"What about it?" Her eyes narrowed and focused on me.

"Cassie taught me how to close it off, so I'm not constantly hearing voices. But when I stared into the amulet's stone, the door to my magic flew open without me doing anything and my magic shot out."

Her chronic anxiety made her twitchy, but she grew still in response to my words, her face darker and more intense than I'd ever seen it. It was like watching a terrifying storm roll in.

My hands shook as she got to her feet and headed for the door.

"Juliette!" I cried. "You can't leave me alone with that thing," I gestured at the oven, "and not tell me what I'm dealing with!"

"I have to go," she replied without looking back. "I need to do some research. Just don't touch it, and you should be okay."

"I *should* be okay?" I protested, but she didn't reply, letting the door slam shut behind her as she hurried down the stairs.

SEVENTEEN

"*You're not alone. What am I? Chopped liver?*" a small voice griped behind me.

My heart leaped into my throat as I jumped to my feet and spun around, instantly feeling silly. Both benches backed up to the sides of the trailer. The only thing behind me was a wall and a large window. I stepped closer to peer out the window, but the voice hadn't sounded like it came from outside, so I wasn't surprised that the yard was empty.

"*I'm in here. Hellooo?*"

I spun around in the other direction, but there was no one standing behind me. Fear sent my anger into overdrive and made my hands shake as my eyes darted around the room, peering everywhere someone could be hiding. The camper wasn't big. It didn't take me long to confirm that I was alone.

That left two options. Either I was imagining things, or... my blood turned to ice in my veins. I shivered, Juliette's casual declaration that ghosts hung out all around us echoing in my head, as I tried desperately to avoid thinking about the creepy ghost she'd mentioned.

You're fine, Melly. It's not a ghost. And even if it is one, I'm sure it means you no harm, I told myself, taking a shaky breath.

My heart was already racing, but an answering chuckle sent it into overdrive.

"Mom? Is that you?" *Please be you. Please be you.*

"I am not your mother!" If I hadn't been about to jump out of my skin with fear, I might have laughed at the indignation.

"Who's there? Come out where I can see you!" I demanded, clenching my fists to keep my hands from shaking.

"I told you; I'm in here." This time, the voice sounded more irritated than indignant. *"Wow. You are thick. No wonder I'm here."*

"Here, where? This isn't funny."

"Oh, for... Look inside already."

I was about to snap back that I *was* inside when the words clicked. Lowering myself onto the bench, I turned my gaze inward and came face to face with a small, irate person, glaring at me down their nose, fists on their hips, looking for all the world like they were ready to take down anyone who dared look at them askance.

"*Who... What...are you?*" I stammered.

"*That's better,*" the small being snapped. "*I don't like being ignored.*"

"*I'm sorry?*" I said, not entirely sure what I was apologizing for.

"*You should be,*" the being's huffy tone was accompanied by an equally petulant expression. "*Now, as I was saying, you're not alone.*"

"*I...ah...I can see that,*" I replied. "*What I'm not clear about is what you're doing inside my head? Is this another fun side effect of my head injury?*"

The little being snapped back, both eyebrows arched, and crossed its arms defensively.

"*I'll have you know that I'm a Daemon, class 3. Not some injury-inflicted delusion. Of all the rude...*" The being's sentence trailed off into a long string of muttered words that sounded suspiciously like Italian insults.

Propping my elbows on the table, I rubbed my forehead. Why hadn't I listened to the nurse and taken it easy for a few days? I'd pretended I was invincible and pushed through the pain to get the diner ready faster, then I'd jumped with both feet into the work without even taking a day to rest. And here I was, having some sort of visual and auditory hallucination of a demon in my head. A *demon*.

"Not a demon," the being huffed. *"A daemon. Totally different."*

For a hallucination, this one was incredibly detailed and seemed to know things I'd never even heard of, which brought up a ton of questions I had neither the time nor the inclination to explore.

"I am not a hallucination!" the little being said, stomping its foot. Pain shot through my head.

"Ow!" I cried.

"Could a hallucination have done that? I think not," was the only response I got.

"Okay. Fine. Not a hallucination. Which still doesn't tell me what *you are,"* I replied through gritted teeth. I'd gone to all that trouble to block other people's voices from my head, only to manifest an entity that wouldn't stop talking.

I somehow doubted that the little being's change in attitude had anything to do with it taking pity on me, but it stood straighter, tilted its chin in the air, and took a deep bow with an added hand flourish.

"Demi. Daemon, class 3, at your service. Pleased to make your acquaintance, Melody."

"Melly," I replied half-heartedly as I studied the daemon. If it hadn't been standing at attention in the center of my head, it could have entirely passed for a short, stocky human. Its straight, dark brown hair was

cut in a not-unflattering page boy style that brushed strong-looking shoulders as wide as the rest of its body. The result was a very cylindrical entity dressed in red from head to toe that vaguely resembled Linda Hunt, who my mother had adored in NCIS Los Angeles. "What *are you?*" I repeated.

The daemon puffed up, and I waved my hand apologetically. "*Yes. Yes, I know. A daemon. But what exactly is that?*"

With an exhale, Demi deflated. "*Oh. That's easy. I'm a magical construct.*"

"*A what?*"

This time, the daemon sighed. "*You were having trouble controlling your magic and sent a plea for help. I am that help.*"

"*I did? You are?*" I ran my hands through my hair and shook my head. "*I don't remember doing that.*"

The daemon shrugged. "*What can I say? I go where I'm told.*"

"*And you're just going to sit in my head... forever?*" I sincerely hoped it couldn't sense the dread and horror that inspired.

"*Well, it's no picnic for me either, you know!*" Demi snapped back. So much for keeping my thoughts to myself.

Suddenly feeling a lot more sympathy for the people horrified by my magical abilities, I shoved down any other potentially insulting feelings.

Softening, the daemon patted the air, which somehow resulted in feeling like it had patted my shoulder. *"I don't think it'll be forever. As soon as you've got a handle on things and you're no longer at risk of being controlled and exploited by an evil magical entity, I'll be on my merry way."*

I wasn't sure what had sent a cascade of cold down my back: that the daemon wasn't exaggerating or that it believed it was merry.

"I'm sorry, what?" I croaked out through suddenly parched lips.

"Don't you worry about it," Demi said, waving away my concerns. *"I'm here now. I've got everything under control."*

With that, the daemon threw itself onto the couch that had once again materialized in front of the little green door leading to my magic and lay back with a contented sigh. *"It's not so bad in here after all,"* it murmured, wiggling around to get more comfortable. *"I can totally see myself staying a while."*

Groaning, I grabbed my phone and stood up. If the fifteen unread texts were anything to go by, even a half-rate daemon protecting me wouldn't be able to save me if I didn't get back to the diner to relieve Momo from double duty.

"I heard that," Demi drawled sleepily, one arm thrown over its eyes.

"If the shoe fits…," I snapped back.

EIGHTEEN

Distracted by the daemon's running commentary on absolutely everything and anything, I'd gotten more orders wrong than right during the dinner service. Even my usually unflappable partner grumbled at me to get my head in the game before customers posted negative reviews. I couldn't wait to get home and put the whole evening behind me.

Unfortunately, not even an hour of aimless scrolling through Airstream renovation ideas online relaxed me enough to avoid a night of tortured dreams where I tried, and failed, to hide increasingly large and menacing amulets in ancient cabinets that crumbled to dust when I touched them.

At least the daemon had stopped narrating my every move, claiming that my life was too boring, even for an entity freshly freed from a century trapped in a magical void. I chose to take it as a gift rather than the intended insult.

I stumbled into the diner, bleary-eyed and exhausted, shortly before our first regular usually arrived.

"You look worse than you did last night! What is up with you?" Momo asked, narrowing his eyes at me as I snagged a piece of crispy bacon from the plate next to the cooktop.

"What's your bacon secret? I can never get mine this crispy without burning it."

"I cook it on a real griddle, not in an Easy Bake Oven." Narrowing his eyes, the big man brandished his oversized spatula. "Stop changing the subject and don't go getting any ideas about replacing that thing you call a stove so you can get rid of me."

I grinned at him around a second slice. "As if I could, partner. I'm just as stuck with you as you are with me, and you know it!"

Momo rested his hip against the cooktop and crossed his arms. He stared down his nose at me. "Out with it. What's wrong? Is it the diner? Are you having second thoughts?" If it weren't for the slight hitch of his eyebrows as he asked, I might have bought his nonchalant, just-shooting-the-breeze attitude. The bacon in my stomach congealed into a heavy lump of dread. Was he projecting his own buyer's remorse? We hadn't taken a lot of time to think things over. Maybe he was regretting our hasty decision to sink so much money into a business we had no idea how to run.

"No!" I cried, grinning almost maniacally. "I'm fine! Everything is fine! The diner is great. Honest!"

Unimpressed by my act, he pursed his lips, glanced at my feet, then stared me down until I gave up and let my smile droop.

"Okay. Not everything is fine. Obviously." I gestured at the mismatched shoes I'd somehow put on in my haste to get to work on time. "But I promise it's not the diner. I am thrilled that we bought this old place."

To my surprise, it was true.

I'd made the snap decision mostly to help Momo out, but I loved the diner. It was more home to me than the house my mother and I had shared for over a decade. Chatting with regulars and out-of-towners about their days or their travels comforted a lonely ache deep in my heart. It helped that dispensing cups of coffee and plates of meatloaf as remedies against daily stress made me feel useful again.

Momo crossed his arms and shot me a look I couldn't decipher. "If it's not the diner, is it the magic thing?"

My jaw dropped, and I blinked wordlessly at him as I processed his question.

"You..." I paused. Was everyone in this town a witch? Had I been the only one in the dark? "Are you?..." Could I even ask?

Momo shook his head. "No. But I grew up in Louisiana. Plenty of witches there. Plus, I overheard you and Cassie talking. Is that what's been eating you?"

I winced and stared at the bacon sizzling on the griddle. "The magic thing is a lot..." I let my sentence trail away as fear gripped my stomach. "How much of my conversation with Cassie did you hear?"

Momo glanced at me and frowned. "Some. Why?"

"Did you..." I didn't know how to ask what I needed to know.

A sly smirk bloomed on his usually undemonstrative face. "Are you asking if I know you can hear thoughts?" He laughed when my face turned red and my mouth fell open. "I do."

"And you don't?..." *Hate me? Want to avoid me forever?*

His expression softened. "Melly, you're a good person. You care more about people than anyone I've ever met. If anyone can be trusted with the magical ability to listen in on people's thoughts, it's you."

My mouth snapped shut as a weight lifted from my shoulders. I turned away so he wouldn't see me blink away the tears that rushed to my eyes.

"Was that it? Or is something else gonna distract you all morning?" Despite his teasing tone, I blushed.

"I'm sorry to keep leaving you in the lurch." As much as I wanted to tell him I'd do better, or at least explain what kept pulling me away, I hesitated. Between his brother and the diner, he already had more than enough on his plate without me adding knowledge about a potentially dangerous magical artifact to the mix.

"Let me guess. You want to try harder, but there's more to the story?" Momo said, tilting his head questioningly. "And you're not ready to talk about it."

"That was a little uncanny, Mo. You sure you're not a witch too?" I replied with a grin, feeling a thousand times lighter having shared even a fraction of the load weighing me down. "How about I promise to tell you everything as soon as I can?"

Momo shrugged and directed his attention back to his griddle. "As long as you're stayin' safe and pulling your weight 'round here, you can keep all the secrets in the world."

"Totally safe," I replied, resisting the urge to cross my fingers behind my back. It wasn't inherently untrue. I'd followed Juliette's advice and neutralized the amulet, plus I'd scored a magical bodyguard of sorts. Given the circumstances, I was as safe as possible.

"Oh, now I'm not just a half-rate daemon?" Demi commented peevishly. *"How convenient for you."*

Engaging didn't seem wise, so I ignored it, keeping my attention focused on my partner.

Accepting my final reassurance at face value, Momo turned back to his griddle with an indecipherable grunt.

"Coffee?" I offered, grateful that he wasn't pushing me to elaborate on why I was so out of sorts.

"Please," he replied without looking up. "Eggs with that bacon?" he asked, holding two up.

I hesitated. The bacon hadn't settled, but it wasn't enough protein to get me through the morning, especially on nearly no sleep.

"Please," I echoed, pausing to watch him expertly crack both eggs with one hand and pour them onto the cooktop without dropping a single eggshell fragment. "I still don't know how you do that."

He glanced up at me with a twinkle in his eye and a half smile playing on the corner of his mouth. "Magic." He winked.

I stilled. It was the same answer he always gave me, but it hit differently now that I knew magic wasn't make-believe.

"Really?" I asked, watching his face for any hint that he wasn't kidding.

"No!" He barked a laugh. "I told you. M'not a witch. Just got big hands and years of experience. Now, where's that coffee you promised?"

"You're a funny man, Mauricio Cruz. You're a funny man," I replied on my way out of the kitchen.

"Don't call me Mauricio," he muttered. "And you know it!" he crowed back.

The door to the diner opened, letting in a blast of frosty morning air that made me shiver as I tucked a new filter into the coffee machine.

"I'll be with you in a minute. Grab a seat anywhere you'd like," I called without turning around. If I let myself get sidetracked and the coffee wasn't ready when the early bird diners arrived, there was no telling what they'd do.

The first pot was burbling away happily by the time I was done setting up the fourth machine with decaf. Momo and I had briefly discussed investing in a single machine that could brew more coffee, but these four worked well enough to make it an unnecessary expense. I far preferred to spend the money on quality beans. Plus, my happy little row of chubby coffee carafes never failed to make me smile.

I jumped when I turned around to see where my first customers had settled themselves and found myself nose to nose with the two agents from the previous day. Agent Sterling stood on the other side of the counter with her arms crossed, feet hips' width apart, watching my every move with her steely gaze. Meanwhile, Agent Thorne was splayed across the counter, toying with packets of sugar.

He opened his mouth to speak and snapped it shut when she glared at him. I got the distinct impression that their day wasn't off to the best start. *I could peek. They'd never know. No one would. A little listen, just to see what's upsetting her enough to hold him back.* I was turning my gaze inward when I reconsidered. *It violates their privacy, Mel! You'd hate it if someone did it to you!* I flashed the two agents my best customer-service smile. They didn't need to know that their arrival had sparked the flurry of nerves tightening my chest.

"Good morning, Agent Thorne and Agent Sterling. What brings you to my diner so bright and early? Coffee'll be ready in a minute. Our chef isn't quite set up for the day, but I'm sure he could whip you both up an omelet if you're hungry."

"That sounds amazing," Agent Thorne said, beaming at me.

Agent Sterling scowled. "We're not here for breakfast. We just wanted to see if you'd remembered anything since we last spoke."

Doing my best to keep my expression neutral, I shook my head slowly. "Gosh, I wish I had, but I'm afraid that nothing came to mind. I'm so sorry. I know how frustrating this must be for the two of you. How about some coffee to go? For the road?" I gestured to the to-go cups stacked next to the first coffee machine and arched my eyebrow questioningly at them.

Agent Sterling's eyes flashed angrily, and her scowl darkened into an outright glower.

"I'm sorry. Did I say something wrong?" I asked, taking a step back. My response hadn't been helpful or forthcoming, but nothing that warranted such an intense reaction.

"Nope," she said through clenched teeth before forcing her lips into a semblance of a smile. "Nothing wrong at all."

Whoof. She is going to show our hand. She needs to chill. Pie! Pie would help. At least it would help me.

It took me a moment to realize Agent Thorne wasn't speaking out loud. When I hurried to slam the door to my magic shut, I found Demi grinning at me, holding open a tiny hatch in the center of the door.

"Helpful?" the daemon asked, grinning impishly.

"No! We can't do that! It's a violation of their privacy," I hissed at it in my head.

Demi's usual glower fell into place, eclipsing its momentary excitement. *"I thought you'd appreciate my brilliant addition."*

"Well..." For some unfathomable reason, the glare Agent Sterling was leveling at Agent Thorne somehow included me in its ire. She was impossible to read. Even a hint could help me get my bearings. *"Fine. Yes. It's helpful."*

I was rewarded with a smug smirk.

> *Oh, for crying out loud, is he thinking about*
> *pie again?*

Agent Throne yelped and rubbed his arm where his partner had jabbed him with her elbow. "What was that for? I didn't even do anything!"

"You were thinking about pie!" she snapped.

To my surprise, he dropped his eyes like a little boy caught misbehaving. "Yeah, I was," he admitted sheepishly.

"Focus," she snapped, rolling her eyes. "We have better things to do than think about pie."

"But pie!"

I was trying to get a read on Agent Sterling, so I couldn't tell if he'd said that out loud or in his head. Still, I swallowed the laugh that bubbled up in response to his impassioned protest. The man really had a one-track mind.

"How about I box you up a slice to go with your coffee?" My grin grew when he nodded enthusiastically, studiously ignoring his partner's glare.

We need this woman to spill whatever she wasn't telling us yesterday, but this yahoo only thinks about his stomach.

I didn't need to hear more to know that, despite her internal grumbling, she didn't truly mind being partnered with him.

"Right, well, we probably should get going," she said, interrupting my train of thought. Instead of turning away from the counter, she leaned closer and narrowed her gaze. "Ms.... ah... Melly, I cannot stress enough how important it is for us to find this amulet. I don't mean to sound overly dramatic, but lives are at stake. If you know anything, anything at all, it truly would be better for everyone involved if you told us what you know." She paused, raising her eyebrow to make sure I caught her meaning. "For *everyone* involved," she repeated.

My blood froze as she held my gaze a moment longer than necessary, and I nodded silently in response.

"Wonderful. I'm glad we understand each other." She dropped a white card with just her name and a phone number and stabbed it with her index finger. "We'll be expecting your call. Now, I'm going to powder my nose. If you happen to have two coffees and a slice of pie," she said as she rolled her eyes, "ready by the time I get back, I'm sure my partner here would be eternally grateful."

The icy chill that had settled over me under Agent Sterling's piercing glare thawed as Agent Thorne perked up in response to her comment.

Aw, maybe she doesn't hate me quite as much as she lets on!

"I'm sure she doesn't," I replied, turning away to get their coffees.

"Excuse me?" he asked, confused.

"Sorry, just thinking aloud," I replied, wishing the ground would swallow me whole.

NINETEEN

"**W**as that who I think it was?" Juliette asked, after holding the door for Agent Thorne, whose hands were too full of coffee and pie to open it himself. Agent Sterling followed in his wake, too busy typing furiously on her phone to acknowledge the shy bookshop owner pressing herself against the door to get out of her way. "What did they want?"

"The amulet." The best I could muster after the uncomfortable encounter was a wry grimace.

Juliette's eyes flew open in alarm. "You didn't give it to them, right?"

I shook my head. "No. Nor did I tell them anything new." On the other side of the large diner window, Agent Thorne stacked the two cups of coffee and attempted to balance the pie box on them to free up a hand to open the passenger door of their rental. To be nice, I'd given him three kinds, so the box wasn't exactly small. I was torn between being mesmerized by the impending disaster and concerned that none of his cherished pie slices would survive his acrobatics.

Catching my amused grin, Juliette followed my line of sight and gasped. The stacked treats teetered in the agent's hand, and we both held our breath as his arm wobbled alarmingly.

"Oh, for crying out loud!" Agent Sterling cried loud enough for us to hear clearly through the thick plate glass. She dropped her voice as she slipped her phone into her pocket to grab the box and one of the two cups of coffee, but it was easy to imagine what she was saying to him as she gesticulated and shook her head.

Without turning to look at Juliette, I gave voice to the anxious turmoil churning in my gut since she'd asked about my mother's illness.

"They said lives could be at stake. Do you think they were trying to scare me into telling them what I know?" I looked over at her, but she was still watching the two agents squabble. Agent Sterling was jabbing her finger at her phone screen while Agent Thorne shrugged dismissively. "Yesterday, you implied that thing killed my mother. Did you find out more?"

I left my real question unspoken, hoping she wouldn't make me say it, but her only reply was a side glance filled with such sorrow, I almost burst into tears. Shoving aside the grief threatening to overwhelm me, I focused on the issue at hand. There would be more than enough time to wallow in the what-ifs of my mother's final years after any potential danger was eradicated.

"I don't have any concrete reasons to distrust them," I said, picking up where I'd left off. "And I don't get any concerning vibes from them. Anyone who likes pie as much as that guy can't possibly be bad, right?"

Juliette shrugged. "Eh. In novels, the bad guys always seem like the good guys until they turn on the main character."

I made a face. "I guess I don't have any real reason to trust them, do I?"

She shook her head. "Not until we know more about the amulet, at least."

"And since I'm making zero headway in that direction…" I let my voice trail away with a defeated shrug. A swell of tears rose into my throat, but I swallowed them down and focused on the one thing I could manage. "Coffee?"

I made my way behind the counter and fussed with the machines until I was sure I had my impending meltdown under control.

"What brought you out here so early, anyway? You're not usually one of our early birds. I'd think living over a bakery with an Instagram-famous barista would keep you from having to venture into the cold to get yourself coffee. Have you found out something about the amulet?"

"You'd be right about the coffee. I'm perfectly caffeinated, but I wanted to catch you before the morning rush." As she spoke, the diner door opened to let in half a dozen customers. Behind them, I could see at least three more getting out of their cars.

"Better talk fast. The hordes are descending, and they look hungry." Raising my voice, I called out to the new arrivals, "Grab a seat wherever you'd like. Everyone for coffee?"

I spun around to plunk ten mugs, five little pitchers of cream, and a handful of sugar packets on a tray as a chorus of yesses echoed around the diner.

"I found a spell that might get us started on our quest," Juliette whisper-hissed at my back.

Glancing over my shoulder at her, I arched an eyebrow. "Our quest?"

Juliette's ears turned a darker shade of pink. Flicking her fingers nervously, she shrugged her left shoulder. "It sounded more fun than 'research on a potentially deadly magical device,'" she muttered.

Snorting a laugh, I nodded. "You're not wrong about that. Did you say a spell?" I lowered the heavy tray to the counter so I could adjust the balance and grabbed one of the full pots of coffee. "How does that work? What does it do?" Visions of pimply teens in flowing black capes waving shimmering wands in the air popped into my head. Somehow, I didn't think that was what she meant.

"Don't worry about that now. I'll give you the details later. When's a good time for me to come back?"

Glancing around the diner, I frowned. I didn't know what casting a spell entailed, but I doubted the small space packed with booths and counter stools would lend itself well to the task.

"How about I come to you? I can be there around three. Does that work for you?"

She clapped her hands, her face lighting up. "That's perfect. The toddler story hour group will have gone home for their naps, and the after-school crowd won't arrive until after four."

"After-school crowd?" I asked, surprised. I didn't usually equate bookshops with after-school hanging out.

She laughed. "You'd be surprised how appealing YA shifter romances are to teens."

"Do I even want to know what that is?" I asked, hoisting the tray to my shoulder in a practiced move that barely hurt after doing it repeatedly day after day for months, even after having slammed it into a jukebox.

"Probably not," Juliette answered with a chuckle on her way out. "See you later! Don't forget to bring the you-know-what!"

Momo and I were settling back into a semblance of the routine we'd perfected under Aggie's watchful eye. Being in charge of the front-of-house was changing my perspective on the useless busy work I'd assumed our tiny boss dreamed up to keep me busy during lulls. She'd always demanded that the sugar packet stash on each table be replenished between each service, along with the ketchup, mustard, and salt. I also had to check the state of the bathroom at least six times a day and check the floor under each table as soon as it was cleared.

A few days of running around delivering more sugar, salt, or ketchup to tables while also dropping off meals, topping off drinks, and popping into the bathroom every time the toilet paper ran out was making me see the light. And wondering how soon I could hire help.

"My feet are killing me. Was it always this hard? Or are people suddenly extra ornery?" I grumbled to Momo after the last of the breakfast diners had waved goodbye on their way out.

Momo popped his head up to look at me through the kitchen window and shrugged. "Seems the same back here. Maybe you're not getting enough sleep."

"I'll get on that as soon as I start drinking a million ounces of water every day, getting more exercise, and eating more protein." I rested my left ankle on my right knee and rubbed my calf.

"All phenomenal ideas," Momo replied, totally ignoring my snarky tone. "Do you even have a bed in that tin can of yours?" he teased.

"Hardy har," I replied.

I didn't regret buying the diner with Momo. But between disturbing dreams of evil amulets coming to life, were actual nightmares about the diner failing miserably. Invoices were arriving for food and restaurant supplies, not to mention the small upgrades that had seemed smart to make while we repaired the damage from the accident. Meanwhile, it seemed like we were getting fewer customers, though that could have just been my panic feeding me incorrect information. Still, I didn't remember any empty tables at breakfast when Aggie had been in charge.

"Hey, Momo?" I called.

"Yeah?" he replied without looking through the window.

"Are we getting fewer customers, or am I imagining things?"

Instead of appearing at the window, he came through the swinging doors into the front of the diner, drying his hands on his apron. The furrows between his eyes looked deeper than they had the week before. Or maybe I was imagining that, too.

"Wasn't gonna say anything unless you brought it up, but yeah. I think so. Not going through the bacon as fast as usual." His expression didn't change as he glanced around the empty diner, so I had no idea what he was thinking.

"Nope," Demi declared, leaning against the door to my magic with its arms crossed defensively.

"Nope, what?" I replied. *"You have no idea what I was going to do?"*

Demi replied with a look that said we both knew exactly what I was going to do, and we both knew we knew.

"Fine. I was going to peek. So what? You almost made me spy on the other two earlier."

"Government agent thoughts, fine," Demi said with a decisive nod. *"Friends and business partners, totally different story. If you want to know what he's thinking, ask. Or wait until he volunteers the information. Your choice, but you're not getting it this way."* For extra emphasis, it rested its head against the small opening in the middle of the door.

Reluctantly, I mentally backed away from the small door in my head. One tiny peek would allow me to pivot and do what Momo wanted. He was largely the reason I'd bought the diner. What if he'd been projecting his remorse onto me earlier?

"Just one small peek?" I implored the daemon. *"Please? One second. Nothing more. Just enough to know how to keep him happy. That's an honorable reason, isn't it? I just want to help him! It would be for his own good!"* Demi glowered at me, pointedly leaning its small frame against the green door. In its black combat gear, it was far more intimidating than it had any right to be. I turned away reluctantly.

How often had I wished I knew what my mother wanted so I could just do it and spare myself her disappointed looks? It seemed cruel to have developed this ability when it was too late to make her truly happy.

As for peeking into Momo's head to guide me today, my magic's new guardian's posture said it all. If I wanted to see what Momo was thinking, I'd have to get past it first, and it didn't plan on making it easy.

"Fine. I'll do it your way," I grumbled internally. "You'd tell me, right?" This, I said out loud.

"Tell you what?" Momo asked, frowning down at me.

"If you thought we'd made a mistake? I could take it." I grimaced and reconsidered. "Maybe."

He glanced around the restaurant and shrugged. "Regretting the past is a waste of time better spent course correcting to make the future what you want it to be." With a sharp nod, he turned and headed back into the kitchen.

My jaw dropped. Momo was a man of few words, and they were rarely this profound. I pondered what he'd said as I checked the condiments in each booth and made sure no one had left anything under the tables. He wasn't wrong. It wasn't as though we could call Heather up and tell her we'd made a mistake. She'd laugh herself silly before hanging up on us.

The diner was ours, for better or worse. If we didn't want to end up bankrupt and desperate, it was up to us to figure out why we were losing customers and what we could do to fix it.

Magic?

Before the thought had fully formed, I'd already discarded it. Cassie, Juliette, and Hattie all had thriving stores, but as far as I could tell, it was because they worked their tails off, not because they were witches.

Though maybe...

I tucked the tiny, hopeful thought into a corner of my head where it wouldn't wither under the cynicism that had kept me safe for years and greeted the people walking in.

"Hello! Are we here for a late breakfast or early lunch? Either way, grab yourselves a seat and I'll be right over with water and menus."

TWENTY

The bookshop's soothing scent wrapped itself around me as I walked in. The door closed behind me with a soft jangle of bells.

"Right on time!" Juliette said, appearing from what I assumed was an office in the back. The baby raccoon she was rumored to have adopted after finding him under a dumpster scampered alongside her.

He held up his little arms and chirruped something that made her lean over to hoist him onto her hip like a tiny, fluffy, particularly bendy child.

"That's right, you two haven't met!" she said. "Harvey, please meet my new friend Melly." Her cheeks flushed slightly as she spoke, and she kept her eyes firmly fixed on the raccoon's small gray and black face. "Melly, this is Harvey. He's a good boy who sometimes gets overly enthusiastic about things." Her stern look and arched eyebrow were tempered by the smile tugging at the corner of her lips. Harvey ducked his head sheepishly and placed his tiny hands over his eyes.

"Nice to meet you, Harvey. I'm sure that whatever you did isn't half as bad as Juliette is implying."

Juliette laughed. "Don't believe a word he says. I should rename him Harvey Destroyer of All." She smiled at the fluff ball resting in the crook of her arm. A sharp pinch of longing stole my breath when he stretched his head to touch his nose to hers.

Harvey twisted the upper half of his torso, dug his claws into her sleeve to climb onto her shoulder, where he wobbled alarmingly before darting across her back to launch himself onto the store counter. He landed with a skid that sent a stack of papers flying in every direction.

Juliette laughed, rubbing her shoulder with a wince. "And that's Harvey, a bundle of sweetness mixed with a whole lot of mischief."

"Seems... fun?"

"Something like that," she replied with another laugh. "I have us all set up in the back. Tybalt should be here any minute. He promised to watch the store while we were doing the spell, but he has to go pick Emma up from school at 3:45, so we don't have a ton of time. Come on, you. I'm not trusting you alone in here," she said to the raccoon, scooping him up from a precarious position on the cash register before leading the way.

I followed her down a towering row of shelves packed with colorful books. Enticing titles caught my eye as I passed, and I silently promised myself a long afternoon of browsing just as soon as we sorted out the amulet thing and I got a handle on the whole diner thing. So, basically, in the very distant future.

Catching the tired groan I thought I'd muffled, Juliette peered over her shoulder at me. "Everything okay?" she asked.

My smile must not have been as convincing as I'd hoped, because it didn't lighten her worried gaze. She lowered Harvey into a playpen overflowing with toys before resting her hand on my arm. "We don't have to do this if you're uncomfortable. I know all this magic stuff is a lot to swallow at first."

Chuckling, I waved my hand dismissively. "I'm fine. Really." She arched her eyebrow at me, and I suddenly felt a little like a chastised raccoon. I sighed, glancing away from the intensity of her worried gaze. "It's all just a lot, you know? Too many changes in too short a time frame."

Something shifted in her expression, but she let my vague answer ride with a small squeeze of my arm.

"I know we're not really friends yet," she said, blushing again at the word friend. "But I'd like us to be. I'm here if you ever need someone to talk to." Her entire face was pink, and she was staring fixedly at the floor by the time she finished her sentence. "Sorry." She grimaced. "I get a little overwhelmed by interpersonal relationship things. But I mean it."

"Thank you," I replied gently. "I appreciate it." Not that I entirely believed her. She was already part of a large group. Why would she need to befriend me?

Maybe she means it, a different, more hopeful little voice suggested deep in my head.

I didn't bother answering it.

"So, what's the plan here?" I asked instead.

Juliette's shoulders relaxed, and she grinned at me as if equally relieved that I was changing the subject. "The plan is that we are going to peek into the past."

My eyebrows jumped halfway up my forehead. "We're what?"

"I have a spell that lets me glimpse important moments in an object's history. I'm hoping it'll shed some helpful light to point us in the right direction."

"Ohhhh-kay," I said uncertainly.

"Trust me, there's nothing to worry about." Her smile didn't quell the anxious flutter in my chest.

"If you say so."

"I do!" Her confidence was somewhat reassuring, at least. "Did you bring the things I suggested?"

Nodding, I reached around to bring my cross-body bag forward. "I have the amulet and a bracelet that belonged to my mother. I don't have many of her things, so I hope it's enough."

"Was it something meaningful to her?" Juliette asked as I pulled the little pouch containing the braided strand of colorful glass beads from the inside pocket of the bag.

"Yes. We got it together when I left for college. I wore a matching one. We joked that we'd be able to sense each other's emotions through it. She never took it off, not even when I came home to take care of her or after I lost mine." I tipped the bag into my hand, grabbing the bracelet before it slipped off my palm.

"Oh! It's beautiful!" Juliette exclaimed, leaning closer to get a better look at the multicolored Venetian beads.

Juliette gestured for me to put the bracelet into the small wooden bowl in the center of the table laden with a strange assortment of items. Then I pulled the amulet's storage container out of my bag.

Despite being doused in salt, which Juliette had explained would help neutralize, or at least temper, the pendant's magic, I could still sense the amulet inside its blue velvet bag. Other than being faintly aware of its presence, it hadn't bothered me much from deep inside my bag. Though I had reached for it a few times while walking to the bookshop.

"Not with your hand!" Juliette cried as I snapped open the lid and reached into the container to pull out the little velvet bag.

"Oh. Right." I snatched my hand back and took the wooden tongs she handed me.

"I don't think it'll harm you if you handle it, but we should probably err on the side of caution. Put it there," she said, gesturing to a small circle of what looked like salt at the other end of the table.

Acquiescing with a tip of my head, I gingerly pinched a corner of the pouch with the tongs and upended it where she gestured. The amulet's inner light pulsed once brightly before fading to an ominously dull glow. I almost leaned forward to get a better look before remembering what had happened the last time I'd let it get its hooks into my brain.

My hands shook as I wiped them on my pants to dispel the greasy feel of the amulet's proximity. To keep myself from giving in to the urge to stare into the amulet, I glanced at the other items on the table. I could identify the individual things, but I didn't know how they related to each other. What did a tall white pillar candle like the one I used when the camper's solar panel failed to provide enough light for me to see by at night have to do with a crow feather? The iridescent feather shimmering in the dancing candlelight looked like it had just been plucked from my new friend's back.

"What is all this for?" I asked.

"Gimme a second," Juliette said, holding up a finger as she ran her eyes down the page of a well-worn antique journal. From where I stood, it looked like many people had added to it over the years.

"What's that book?" I couldn't help asking, my curiosity firing on all cylinders.

"Almost there," Juliette muttered without looking up.

"Hello? Where are you all?" a female voice I vaguely recognized called from inside the shop.

"Back here!" Juliette replied, still without taking her eyes off the page.

I don't know who I expected to see, but it wasn't Amy. I hadn't realized she was part of Cassie and Juliette's inner circle beyond being Crystal's girlfriend. But as she came into the office and threw her arm over Juliette's shoulder for a quick side hug, it occurred to me I'd never seen the group of friends outside of the diner.

"Hi, Melly! It's fun to see you out of the diner for a change." Amy grinned at me from the other side of the table. "Are we ready to talk to some ghosts?"

"Ghosts?" My eyes flew open in alarm. "Juliette didn't mention ghosts."

I'd tried very hard to forget about the one she'd seen hovering around me. Between the diner, the mind-reading chaos, and the general witch thing, my freak-out bank was maxed out. Presumably, my ghost was already dead and could wait until I sorted everything out to be dealt with. Hopefully, after I read a book or two.

"This spell doesn't always involve ghosts," Juliette said reassuringly, rolling her eyes at Amy. "We don't even know if the person connected to it is dead or not."

"My mother was connected to it, and she's dead." The words, straining to get past the swell of grief that filled my throat, came out in a hoarse whisper.

Juliette instantly paled and covered her mouth with a shaky hand. "I'm so sorry!" she cried. "That was horribly insensitive. I don't know what I was thinking."

"It's okay, Jules. It was an honest mistake," Amy murmured, grabbing hold of Juliette's elbow and giving it a firm squeeze. "You're okay. Take a breath."

Confused, I glanced back and forth between them. "Of course it's okay. I'm not upset. I just got a little overwhelmed. That's all. And I'd rather not see my mother today, if that's all right. I didn't do my hair the way she liked."

My joke had its intended effect. Juliette drew in a deep breath and let out a watery chuckle. "Sorry... I..." She shrugged.

"Anxiety attacks?" I suggested. I'd never had one myself, but Juliette's fluttering hands had triggered the memory of an old college friend who'd been prone to them.

"Yeah." She smiled self-deprecatingly. "Anyway, as I was saying, this spell doesn't always conjure ghosts. Though Amy isn't wrong, it has been known to happen."

Amy visibly shuddered.

"Don't worry, I warded the room and added new salt to the perimeter. That won't happen again," Juliette said with a grin directed at her friend.

"You'd better have," Amy replied in a stern tone that I would have taken seriously if her eyes hadn't been full of teasing laughter.

The sadness in my throat swelled again in response to their easy camaraderie. My college friendships had fallen away after I'd left to take care of my mother. Some of my closer classmates had tried to stay connected, but our efforts had fizzled as their futures had grown brighter and bigger while mine grew darker and smaller. We'd run out of things to talk about, and there were only so many times someone could have *How's your mom doing? Not much better, thanks for asking* text exchanges before admitting it was futile to keep chatting.

Catching something in my expression, Juliette's smile faded. "I'm sorry. I should have told you that Amy was coming over. She's done so many of these with me, I didn't think..."

Banishing whatever she'd seen lurking on my face, I flashed her the most reassuring and encouraging smile I could. "Of course. It's no problem at all. The more the merrier, right? Plus, it's not like I'm going to be of any use. I have no idea what's going on!"

"Oh! Let's change that!" Amy cried, clasping her hands excitedly. "Have you walked her through what's on the table yet?" she asked Juliette.

"No. I was..." She waggled the book that she'd closed around a finger to mark her place.

"Is the spell ready?" Amy asked, glancing at the book.

"I think so," Juliette said, opening the book and frowning down at the page as she reread it one more time.

"Good. Then let's get this party started!" Amy's delight was palpable. "I love this part. Let's start with the basics. Melly, what do you know about magic?"

"Nothing," I said with a half shrug. "Or, rather, only what Christina and Cassie taught me this week, which isn't much, and what I learned from *Buffy* and *Charmed*, which I assume is all bunk."

"Eh?" Amy smiled wryly. "Not all of it. To be honest, I've only been *in the know* for a short while," she said, winking suggestively. "But I've picked up a few things. Ready for a crash course?"

I nodded. "As I'll ever be."

"Awesome!" Amy grinned reassuringly. "There are two ways witches can use magic. One is casting spells, which I'll get to in a minute. The other involves tapping into the greater flow of magic." When I frowned, she elaborated. "Magic flows all around us all the time. Some people call it the chi, or the universe. I like to think of it as the energy that connects all life. On some level, many people can sense it. Even if it's just the hair on their arms tingling every so often or a particular ability to manifest things. And, of course, witches can actively tap into the flow and manipulate it."

She paused to see if I was keeping up. Amazingly, so far, I was having no trouble following her line of thinking. "Are you saying that every time I've manifested a good parking spot, I was unknowingly performing magic?"

Hesitating, Amy glanced at Juliette. "Was she? Do you think everyone good at manifesting things has dormant witch blood? Or unawakened witch blood?"

Glancing in the air, Juliette thought about it for an instant, then shrugged. "Maybe?"

"Just how many people have witch blood they know nothing about?" I asked, glancing back and forth between them.

This time, they shrugged in tandem. Juliette explained, "There's no way to know. During the witch trials, countless witch families turned their backs on their heritage out of fear. They stopped accessing their magic, stopped practicing, or even talking about their abilities. It only takes two generations for grandma's outlandish habits to become a family joke. Two more generations and no one even remembers that woman, let alone that she could heat the bath water without using a fire."

"If a witch doesn't access her magic as a child, she loses the ability to do so when puberty hits," Amy added.

"So... why am I different?" I asked, frowning.

"Shock," they said at the same time.

Amy's eyes tightened slightly. "The only way witch blood can be awakened after puberty is if the witch in question experiences a massive shock. Physical or emotional." She tipped her head toward the bakery connected to Juliette's bookshop. "Cassie's husband dumped her out of the blue and kicked her and her daughter out. The trauma woke up her witch blood. It's safe to assume that being hit by a car driving through a diner did the same to you."

"What about you?" I asked Amy. "You said you've only been in the know for a little while. What triggered it for you?"

She shrugged and opened her hands in a *beats me* gesture. "Some of us never know what does it." The way her eyes darted to the left and the crease between her eyes deepened gave me the distinct impression she was hiding something. If the worried look Juliette threw her was any indication, I wasn't the first to think so.

Amy clapped her hands once and rubbed them together, like a child salivating over a dessert buffet. "Other than being able to tap into the greater flow to use the magic, witches also have a close relationship to the natural elements."

"Christina mentioned something about that, but I don't think I really get it," I said, frowning. It sounded a little too science fiction to be real to me.

Amy glanced down at her hands as she worked out how to explain. "I think it's a bit like the flow of magic. The elements are all around us all the time. There's water and earth in the air, and even the occasional lightning bolt. Tapping into that is like an unavoidable side effect of tapping into the magic. Or maybe the magic is just the elements combining on a cellular level..." Amy's voice trailed away as she lost herself in her thoughts.

"Huh. Interesting," Juliette said, glancing up from her book. "I've never thought of it that way."

Shaking her head, Amy snapped back to the present. "That is some deep thinking that will have to wait for another day."

I couldn't help grinning at the two of them.

"Anyway," Amy said with a sheepish smile. "Sometimes witches have no trouble siphoning out the magic they need from the greater flow. For others, it's like trying to fill a shot glass with water from a firehose at full blast. If you try, the water shoots out in unexpected directions, and the glass remains empty. We use spells to point the magic in the right direction, and an assortment of tools to limit how much magic is directed at the target."

"That makes sense," I said, nodding. "What kinds of tools?"

"Well, for one, the five elements," she said, pointing to the candle.

"Five?" I interrupted. "Are we counting love?"

Amy grinned. "No, but good reference. In our case, the fifth element is spirit. But I'll get to that. Fire." She pointed at the candle again. "Wind." She indicated the feather. "Water and earth." She gestured at a glass of water and a small bowl of what I'd first thought were coffee grounds. "Spirit, or our ability to tap into the magical flow, is represented by the altar itself." She waved her hand to take in the whole table.

Amy tipped her head at Juliette, who picked up the narrative. "We also invoke the four corners to keep us centered and safe." I'd barely opened my mouth to ask before she answered, "The corners represent cardinal directions. You'll see what I mean in a second."

"And, for extra precaution, because we now know what happens if you aren't extra cautious..." Amy glanced sideways at Juliette. "We cast a protective circle of power to keep our magic contained. For the same reason, we work from within a circle of salt to keep evil out while we are connected to the greater flow."

"Evil?" I gulped and wiped my increasingly sweaty palms on my jeans. How had we gone from *Stop by to cast a little spell* to *We need to protect ourselves from evil?* "I assumed you were all good witches." The words sounded even more naïve spoken out loud than in my head.

"We are." Juliette's warm smile held no trace of malice or duplicity, and visions of magical knives and flowing blood faded away. "Technically, good and evil are human constructs. Magic is neither, but it contains equal amounts of light and dark, which keeps it neutral. We choose to work within the light. Sometimes dark magic tries to hitch a ride."

I nodded and looked down at the amulet. "And some witches intentionally harness the dark parts?"

Juliette's smile drooped. "Dark magic is far stronger than good magic. That makes it irresistibly tempting to those who think they can control and harness its power. The rule of thirds makes the cost of doing that usually far too high."

She perked up when Amy squeezed her arm. Patting her friend's hand, she smiled grimly. "But that is a story for another day. Today, we are here to glean whatever we can from this amulet. Are we ready?"

"Wait. What's the rule of thirds?" I asked, my stomach doing a loop-de-loop that left me faintly nauseated. Cold sweat cascaded down my back as I grasped just how little I understood about magic. My gut wanted to be anywhere but in Juliette's bookshop, surrounded by what looked like the entire Witches-R-Us catalog, on the verge of, what? Summoning my mother? Taking a little spiritual walk into her past? Inviting a demon into the world?

"It's going to be okay," Amy said, grabbing my arms and turning me to face her. "You may not know what's going on, but we do. This is not our first time doing this. You can trust us, I promise."

I gulped again. "Okay. But the rule of thirds? That seems important."

Amy squeezed my arms and released them with a grin. "Simply put, intention matters in magic. Every magical act comes back to you threefold."

"Ah," I said. "That would certainly be a powerful motivator to stay in the light."

"Are we ready?" Juliette repeated. "Don't worry," she said to me. "As Amy said, we're both going to be here the whole time, and nothing we see can hurt us."

TWENTY-ONE

*S*peak for yourself; you're not potentially about to see the mother you're still very much grieving.

Amy and I watched silently as Juliette painstakingly poured salt out into a circle surrounding the table, chanting the spell they'd explained would add an extra layer of protection.

> *"I call the North, the East, the South, and the*
> *West.*
> *By the elements of Air, Fire, Water, Earth,*
> *and Spirit,*
> *I cleanse this space of the Negative, the*
> *Harmful, the Unwelcome,*
> *And invite in only Love, Light, and*
> *Harmony.*
> *By the power of the Maiden, Mother, and*

Crone,

So mote it be."

"So mote it be," Amy echoed as Juliette connected the two ends of the circle.

Juliette straightened with a little grunt and put the nearly empty salt container on the table, then wiped her hands on her dress. "Everyone okay?" she asked, casting an assessing eye over me.

The spell had only unsettled me more, but I tried not to let that show in my answering smile. Something in the way Amy's grip tightened on my arm gave me the impression she hadn't believed me.

"Why?" I asked, running my eyes over the things on the table and the salt on the ground.

"Like we said, the salt creates a barrier that the spirits can't cross," Juliette said, shooting me a worried look.

I dismissed her answer with a wave. "No. I get that. Why are you doing this for me?"

Amy and Juliette glanced at each other, communicating silently in that way only good friends can. Juliette's shoulder hitched slightly up, and Amy took a deep breath.

"It's not entirely for you," Amy said, wincing and glancing away.

"What do you mean? It's my amulet... or.... whatever, the amulet is in my possession." I frowned at both of them.

"It's her magic," Amy explained. "Once it latches on to an object that needs to be reunited with its owner, it doesn't let go until the job is done."

I turned my attention to Juliette. "You said the magic nags you. Why am I getting the sense it's more than that?"

She grimaced slightly. "It nags at first. Then it gets more and more insistent until I can no longer ignore it."

"It hurts you?" I asked, my eyebrows jumping up.

"Eh. Hurt is a strong word. It's like the worst case of pins and needles you've ever felt."

"Juliette! That sounds terrible!" I cried, throwing up my hands, not entirely sure why I was suddenly yelling.

"This is why I didn't want to tell you. I don't want you to feel obligated," she said softly.

But not so quietly that I didn't hear the subtext loud and clear. "But you'll do the spell whether I stay or go?" I kept my eyes trained on her face, watching a series of micro-expressions ranging from embarrassment to determination dance across her features.

"I don't have a choice," she said, nodding firmly.

Grim resolve settled over me like a heavy wool cloak when she flexed her fingers absentmindedly, as if the magic was already paining her. I pulled my shoulders back and nodded.

"Then I'm staying. It's my fault the amulet is here. It wouldn't be fair to let you deal with it on your own."

"Fair has nothing to do with it," Juliette protested. "It might be your amulet, but it's my magic torturing me!"

"It's not, though, right?" I asked.

She shook her head, confused about the change in direction. "What's not what?"

"Mine." I glanced at Juliette and Amy. The two women looked back at me with identical baffled expressions. "If Juliette's magic... activated, or whatever, that means the amulet doesn't belong to me. Otherwise, her magic wouldn't be torturing her until she returns it to its owner."

Understanding brightened their faces, only to be immediately replaced by frowns.

"I mean..." Amy glanced at the amulet, then back at Juliette. "I guess? This is a bit of a new one for us."

"My magic usually picks up on things at estate sales," Juliette explained. "But it does imply that the amulet doesn't belong to you."

"All the more reason to figure out who it belongs to, then, right?" I asked, gesturing at the occult paraphernalia on the table, tilting my head and arching an eyebrow invitingly.

"Indeed," Juliette said, nodding her head and stepping closer to the small, ancient leather book perched and open on the edge of the table. "I tweaked the spell so it would fit," she said to Amy, who nodded in response. "Melly, would you please stand at the head of the table? Amy, you're on that side," she said, pointing to the other side of the table. "I'll be here."

My spot placed me in front of the pillar candle. Juliette leaned over to light it with a long match that she pulled from an ornate metal box. When the wick caught fire, she extinguished the match by waving it in the air and burying the smoking tip in a bowl of black powder.

I took the hand she held out as Amy grabbed my other one. Once they'd clasped hands, our arms formed an awkward triangle straddling the rectangular table that neatly encircled the pentagram.

"I'm going to recite the spell twice on my own, then you're going to say it a third time with me. Okay?"

When we both nodded, she took a deep breath and looked up, fixing her gaze somewhere near the ceiling.

> *"In today's embrace, mysteries dwell,*
> *Whispered truths, secrets to tell,*
> *Ancient wisdom's protective spell,*
> *Reveal the answers that we ask,*
> *From darkness at long last,*
> *Show us the shadows of the past.*
> *By ancient powers, this spell be well."*

Nothing happened the first or second time Juliette chanted the spell, but as the three of us launched into the third round, the hair on my arms and the back of my neck prickled. The last words swelled to fill the back office, and when they faded away, the air in the center of our triangle of arms shimmered like a mirage.

"Is that..." I whispered.

Juliette interrupted me without looking away from the image taking shape in the air. "Shhh. Watch."

It was like trying to watch a TV show in a reflecting pool. The image wavered, fading in and out, focusing on one aspect, then another. But it was clear we were watching an injured man making his way up a nearly deserted downtown main street in fits and starts. He was curled in on himself, dragging a bloody left foot and leaving bright red handprints whenever he leaned on the walls for support.

I was so focused on trying to get a glimpse of his face that I didn't notice when the backdrop of shops closed up tight for the night gave way to a brightly lit corner diner window. At first glance, the place looked empty. The red vinyl benches reflected in the freshly cleaned Formica table tops gleamed under the overhead lights, and the counter and its matching red round stools stretched the entire length of the diner. In comparison, our vintage diner looked almost shabby.

My heart slowed when I saw her at the far end of the counter, scrubbing away at a stubborn stain. She looked like she was in her late 30s or early 40s, which would have put me in my late teens or early 20s. The bracelet that caught the light and sent a riot of colors dancing on the far wall of the diner when she raised her hand to shoo off the man now leaning against the diner's glass door instantly revealed her age. That same bracelet was sitting in the bowl in front of me. This had to have taken place at some point during the six months I was away at school, presumably on the early side of my short college tenure, since she wouldn't have been wearing short sleeves in the winter. She used to complain bitterly about how all the large windows and the perpetually open door made that diner so cold. She'd taken the job after I left, only accepting the position that required her to close every night once I was no longer home for her to worry about. Her failing health had forced her to quit shortly after, so I'd never seen the place.

The man suddenly slipped in the puddle of blood forming under his feet. We all jumped along with my mother when he landed hard against the door.

Juliette gasped when his face became visible for the first time, but I couldn't take my eyes off the wavering vision long enough to see what had surprised her.

My mother's eyes widened as color leached from her face. She opened her mouth to say something, but if she got any words out, we couldn't hear them. It looked like she was telling him to stay out, or she'd call the police. At least, that's what I would have been saying, and it fit with the panicked glance she shot at the phone hanging on the wall three feet behind her.

It was unclear whether the man heard and ignored her, or if her words didn't even register. He pushed the door open and dragged himself into the diner. With strength I didn't expect him to have, he closed the door behind him and engaged the deadbolt.

My mother stumbled back and fumbled for the phone without turning away from the man. She gestured menacingly with the receiver, likely giving him one last chance to leave before calling the police.

Just call them, Mom! What is wrong with you?

Yelling at her in my head had about as much effect as shouting advice at actors on TV.

The man clutched the counter with one hand to steady himself and held the other one up imploringly as he lowered himself onto the nearest stool. I held my breath as his head fell forward.

Was he dead? Had a bloody man in obvious distress stumbled into the diner where my mother worked and died on the counter? No. It wasn't possible. There was no way she wouldn't have told me. We had talked nearly every day when I was away at school.

My mother hung up the phone without dialing. Then, reaching for the closest thing to a weapon that she could find, inched her way closer to the man, brandishing an empty glass coffee carafe. Honestly, as weapons went, it was a solid choice. It was easy to hold and could cause a lot of damage if she bashed him over the head with it. Even more if it shattered on impact.

She was only a couple of feet away from him when he suddenly jerked awake and sat up. My heart jumped about as high as my mother's entire body. Clutching her chest, she took a huge step back. We couldn't hear the brief exchange that ensued, but we got the gist of what transpired. The man reached into his jacket and pulled out a thick manila envelope that he pushed across the counter to my mother. The vision seemed to stall for a second, focusing on the bloody smear he left on the envelope when he withdrew his hand. When the vision sped up again, my mother and the man both looked a little fuzzier than they had a moment earlier.

His mouth was moving as he slid off the stool and stumbled back to the door, ignoring my mother's frantic *do not leave that here* gesture. A second later, the door was open, and the man had vanished down the street, leaving my mother alone in the diner, eyeing the stained envelope with a wary frown.

The vision faded to a shimmering black, and my heart wedged itself in my throat. If Juliette hadn't tightened her grip on my hand, I would have lifted it to reach for my vanishing mother.

"It's not over," she murmured as the vision brightened again, this time to reveal the kitchen in the apartment Mom and I had shared until she'd died.

My mother kicked off her shoes and dropped the oversized tote she used as a purse despite her doctor's admonitions that it was the sole reason her shoulder constantly hurt. Glancing around furtively as though someone might have followed her in, she pulled the bloody manila envelope out of her bag, and, after a moment's hesitation, pried open the top flap. She hesitated only an instant before tipping the contents onto the table.

Even though I was fairly sure I knew what the envelope contained, I gasped along with Juliette and Amy when wads of cash tumbled out, followed by the amulet. My mother stared at it, mesmerized by how the deep red of the stone shone under the bright kitchen light. So bright it almost looked like it was glowing from within.

No! No! No! Don't touch it! Please don't touch it! My heart screamed at her as she stroked it with a tentative finger. The instant she came into contact with the stone, the color flared so intensely, all three of us flinched away. When I opened my eyes again, my mother was slipping the amulet's chain over her head and tucking the pendant into her shirt. The last thing I saw before the vision faded to black and vanished was her placing a protective hand over it as something red flared deep in her eyes.

"No! Come back! Bring it back! I need to see what happens next!" I cried to Juliette, yanking my hands free.

She shook her head apologetically. "I'm sorry. I can't. That's not how the spell works. We've tried repeating it before. All we get is the same vision."

"But..." I stared at the spot where my mother had just been standing, willing her to come back, even if only for an instant. Even in the handful of seconds that had elapsed, I'd already forgotten some of the details of her face. When she'd died, I'd been horrified to realize that it had almost instantly faded from my memory. I could hear her laughter and her voice, but I could never seem to see more than fuzzy features when I tried to conjure her in my mind.

To my utter embarrassment, a sob so strong it shook my shoulders burst from my mouth. I took the tissues Amy held out without making eye contact. I didn't realize my face was sopping wet until the tissue came away drenched after I used it to dab my eyes.

"Sorry. I didn't think I was going to get so emotional," I said, taking the box of tissues from Amy.

"Grief is grief, right?" she said knowingly. "You never know when it's going to take you. Your mother was beautiful."

I nodded, sending a fresh wave of tears cascading down my face. I smiled through them. "She really was. She lit up a room." For an instant, remembering her like that brought a smile to my face despite the continuous waterfall of tears. It faded as I pictured her at the end. "Until she didn't. There was so little of her left when she finally passed away. I'd forgotten how vibrant and alive she'd been before she got sick."

"The amulet drained her of that life force," Juliette said grimly, eyeing the little pouch with distrust. "We have to put it somewhere safe before it latches on to someone else."

The words had barely left her mouth when the bell over the shop door jangled and a happy child's voice sang out. "Hi, Mama! We're back! We brought you a treat! Where are you?"

Juliette straightened and shot Amy a weighted glance before heading into the bookshop to greet her daughter.

With her lips pulled back in a grim line, Amy gestured to me to grab the little velour bag. Pinching its chain with the tongs I'd used earlier, she picked the amulet up and cautiously lowered it into the bag, keeping it away from the drawstrings I held in my shaky fingers.

We both let out tremulous breaths when the lid to the container snapped closed over the amulet and fresh salt.

"Are you okay?" Amy asked, blowing out the candle and pulling an empty cardboard box out from under the table.

"Yes. It didn't touch me," I replied, handing her the bowl of black sand she gestured to.

"I meant with the vision." She glanced at me, worry pulling at the corners of her eyes.

"Oh. Yeah. I think so," I said, focusing on the remaining occult items scattered around the table.

"Seeing my mom like that would have shaken me. If you change your mind, call one of us. All right?"

I nodded, confident that I wouldn't be disturbing either of them. Seeing my mother so vibrant and healthy had blown open the door to the memories related to her illness and released a geyser of emotions I was nowhere near ready to process. I'd slammed the door shut so fast, I could still hear a faint ringing in my head.

TWENTY-TWO

"**G**ood morning!" Amy called out as she entered the diner the next morning.

A dozen heads swung in her direction, causing Juliette's face to burst into flames behind her. At least, that's how I imagine turning quite that shade of red felt.

"Sorry!" Amy whisper-shouted. "Way too loud."

Juliette rolled her eyes at her friend and led the way to two open seats at the counter, where I was topping off coffee cups for three of our regulars.

"Can I get you two some coffee? Maybe some breakfast?" I asked, holding up the coffee carafe in my hand.

"No, thank you. I've already eaten," Juliette replied, as she lowered herself onto a stool with a grateful groan. Glancing at the mug I'd poured for Amy in response to her enthusiastic nod, she relented. "Okay, that smells amazing. Can I have a cup, too, please?"

"Momo," Amy called toward the pass-through window, "are you cooking hash browns or home fries today?"

His face popped into view, wearing his usual neutral expression. For someone who didn't know where to look, the pleased glint in his eyes would have been easy to miss. "For you, I can make either." His wink must have gotten the desired response, because her bubbly laugh almost brought a smile to his lips.

"Can I have a heaping portion of your world-famous home fries then, pretty please? Maybe with a side of hollandaise?" She batted her eyes coquettishly at him as she made the request.

Momo rolled his eyes. "Next, you're going to want bacon and two poached eggs with that," he replied, not sounding put out in the least.

"Yes, please!" she cried. "That sounds amazing."

"That's what you have every time we're here in the morning," Juliette remarked, picking up her steaming mug and taking an appreciative sniff.

"And every time, it's amazing," Amy replied with a laugh, nudging her friend with her elbow just hard enough for the very full mug to slosh coffee all over the counter. "Oh, no! I'm so sorry. Are you okay?"

"I'm fine." Juliette smiled reassuringly at her friend. She took the napkin I held out as I quickly wiped down the counter with a rag.

"But I got coffee on your dress!" Amy said.

In an out-of-character move, Juliette winked at me before looking down.

My hand hovered over the box of salt I kept on the counter for moments like these as the stain visibly started to shrink. "Whaaaat?" A small bubble of water formed just above the coffee splotch and hung there, growing as the stain slowly disappeared.

Amy glanced around the diner to make sure no one else had noticed the magic show unfolding right under their noses. She turned back to us with a little shrug. "It's true what they say. People only see what they expect to see. Never fails."

My mouth fell open as the small drop of water flew up and settled on a discarded napkin. Grinning proudly, Juliette swiped at the few brown flecks remaining where a sizeable brown stain had just been. "All better!"

"You just..." I blinked a few times at her pristine dress. "You just magicked that stain right off your dress. How?"

Her smile grew as she leaned forward and gestured for me to do the same. My heart swelled as Amy scooched in and brought her head close to ours. As pathetic as it sounded, it had been so long since I'd hung out with peers that I'd forgotten the joy of being included in a shared moment.

In a low voice intended for just our ears, Juliette explained, "Remember yesterday when I told you that all witches have some affinity for one or more of the five elements?" She grinned when I nodded. "Well, I can exert a tiny amount of control over water. Enough to suck the water out of the stain and leave the coffee dust behind."

"Wow," I said. "That's...cool."

"Fire," Amy said when I glanced at her.

"And me?" I didn't think I'd even been more attracted to one element over another. I enjoyed swimming as much as the next person and appreciated a good bonfire, but I certainly didn't have a green thumb worth writing home about, or... My train of thought ground to a halt, suddenly remembering the heady sensation of swinging higher and higher on the school playground, the wind whipping at my hair and caressing my face as the teacher howled at me to get down before I hurt myself or someone else.

"It can take a little time for that affinity to make itself known when magic emerges late," Juliette explained with an apologetic smile.

"Yeah, I was imbuing my jewelry with magic long before I first connected with fire," Amy said. Her eyes widened, and she chuckled. "That was a weird day in my studio. And I'll forever have that mark on the ceiling to remember it by."

Juliette laughed, then, catching my baffled expression, explained. "She was working on a fiddly piece of glass. I was pestering her with questions, and she was calmly explaining how the intensity of the heat was crucial to the outcome when the tiny flame on her blowtorch exploded into a massive column that shot right up to the ceiling. It seems I was irritating her a little more than she was letting on."

The two women laughed, leaning against each other for support as the giggles took over.

"Your poor shop assistant!" Juliette gasped.

"Chloe! No! Amanda! Poor girl never came back." Amy laughed even harder at the memory.

I chuckled half-heartedly, not seeing the humor in a moment that had probably freaked out the assistant.

"She's okay," Amy reassured me, wiping an errant tear from under her eye. "Teen witch. I think it was the hysterical laughter that scared her off."

"Or getting doused in the water I threw at the flame just as she walked in to check on us." Their laughter, which had somewhat died down, flared again.

"I guess you had to be there," I muttered, pretending that a customer at the other end of the counter needed my attention. It probably would have been hilarious if I'd been there, but I hadn't been, and although they probably weren't intentionally shoving me out of the moment, watching them relive the memory from the outside stung just as much.

"You're jealous because they were friends before they knew you?" Demi asked, snorting condescendingly at me.

"I said I knew it was irrational," I argued. *"Great, now I'm arguing with a figment of my imagination."*

"I am a figment of your magic, not your imagination!" Demi protested, sticking its tongue out at me. *"Can a figment do this?"* the daemon said, jabbing a finger into the wall next to the little green door.

A flash of pain exploded behind my left eye, startling a yelp out of me that made everyone at the counter look over at me.

"You okay, Mel?" Joe, one of our more taciturn regulars, had lowered his newspaper to peer at me with concerned eyes from under his bushy eyebrows.

"All good, just stubbed my toe. You know how it is." I smiled reassuringly, resisting the urge to rub my forehead.

The glare I leveled on Demi had no effect on the smug look on its face. *"Fine. You're not a figment of my imagination. But you know what? I do not have the time or the energy to deal with you, so I'm going to need you to keep your snarky commentary to yourself."*

"Whatever," the stocky little daemon rolled its eyes at me as it dropped onto the floor, cross-legged, and scowled. I could no more explain how I sensed its back slide down

the wall next to the little green door than I could explain how I knew it felt just as rejected by me as I did by Juliette and Amy.

Grief has finally sent you around the bend, Melody. That is the only plausible explanation for any of this. Even without looking, I knew the daemon was smirking at me.

While a bit more of my sanity slipped through my tenuous grasp, Momo slipped Amy's heaping plate of food under the heat lamps, and I snagged a set of cutlery on my way to grab it for her.

The two women had settled down and looked mildly sheepish about their outburst.

"Sorry about that," Juliette said as I placed the plate in front of Amy.

"Careful. Plate's hot," I said, knowing full well she'd instantly touch it to see how hot. To my credit, I didn't laugh when she snatched her hand back with a small hiss of pain. "Nothing to be sorry about," I said to Juliette.

"We didn't mean to make you feel left out."

Stunned by her astute assessment, I gaped at her. Her ears and cheeks flushed as she half-shrugged and glanced away. "I don't read minds or hear thoughts," she reassured me, glancing back. "But I've been where you are, and I recognized the signs."

"She analyzes micro-expressions and overthinks things," Amy explained after gulping down a steaming forkful of home fries. I winced sympathetically. That had to have hurt. Undaunted, she stabbed another potato and popped it into her mouth.

"Anxiety. The gift that keeps on giving," Juliette deadpanned, holding her coffee up as if giving a toast. "Anyway, I'm sorry we were rude. Can we make it up to you with pastries this afternoon?"

Amy snorted a laugh. "Nothing says forgive us like pastries stolen from your cousin's bakery."

"Hey! I was going to pay for them!" Juliette protested, winking at me as she did.

I laughed. "Stolen pastries sound amazing. I was going to come see you this afternoon, anyway."

Juliette sat up and focused her attention on me. "Oh, yeah?"

"Yeah. I went over that vision again and again last night, and I just don't see how it helps us. We already knew my mother had the amulet, and it's not like we got anything from the guy that could help us identify him." I lowered my voice. "If he even survived. He looked like he'd lost a lot of blood."

The two women grimaced and nodded in agreement.

"I don't think he survived," Juliette said, shooting me a worried glance.

"How do you know?" I asked, leaning closer.

"He's the ghost."

"What ghost?" Amy asked when I didn't reply.

"The other day, when Melly stopped by the bookshop, he was hanging around her. I guess now we know why," Juliette explained.

"Is he gone?" I resisted the urge to turn around to look for myself.

"I haven't seen him since that one time." Juliette shrugged apologetically. "It doesn't mean he's gone forever, but I get the sense that we won't see him again unless we completely fail to figure out the amulet's secrets. To that end, did anyone notice anything that could help us identify him?"

"I didn't pick up any identifying markers on his clothing, and there was nothing remarkable about his face." Amy shook her head. "I could draw it and run it through a facial recognition program, but I doubt that would get us anywhere. Especially if he's no longer alive. He looked like half the middle-aged white guys out there."

"You have access to facial recognition software?" Juliette asked Amy, looking as curious as me.

Glancing away, Amy waved dismissively. "That's not the point. The point is that it wouldn't help."

"There was something on his jacket. I saw it when he pulled the envelope out," I admitted. "It looked like a company logo. I thought it might have been two crossed tools of some sort, but I didn't see it clearly enough to find anything helpful online." I'd spent well over an hour typing every permutation into the search bar and had been rewarded with dozens of options that didn't look right.

"Huh," Amy said, her forehead furrowed, and eyes glazed over as though she was replaying the vision in her head. "Maybe..." her voice trailed away.

When she didn't continue, Juliette cut in. "There is another spell that might help us."

I perked up. "That's great! Let's do it!" Juliette winced in response to my enthusiasm. "What? Does it require something hard to get? Or something gross?"

She laughed at my preemptively disgusted expression. "Nothing like that."

"Then what's the issue?" I pressed. Between the agents nosing around and my need to figure out what to do with the amulet before it did whatever they thought it was going to do, not to mention that Juliette was flexing her fingers increasingly frequently, it didn't seem like we had much choice in the matter.

"It's a spell for speaking to the dead. We could try to connect with the guy who gave her the amulet, but the ghosts of people who died violent deaths sometimes get stuck in a trauma loop. It makes communicating with them challenging. When I saw his ghost hovering around you the other day, something felt off about him. I think that might have been why." Juliette grimaced and glanced away. "I think that your mother is our best bet."

The sympathy in her eyes hurt almost as much as the thought of seeing and potentially talking to my mother again. As grief welled in my throat, threatening to overwhelm me, Juliette reached over to place her hand over mine. She squeezed it gently and lowered her voice.

"I'm worried it'll be too hard on you. It's why I didn't suggest it yesterday."

Tears pricked my eyes. She wasn't the only one.

TWENTY-THREE

Juliette's office was configured differently from the previous day. More like it typically was, I suspected. The table we'd used was pushed against the wall. Instead of an assortment of occult things, a closed laptop and a notebook sat on it, along with a massive mug filled with pens and a towering stack of papers. My heart sank as I pictured the equally daunting stack awaiting me on my desk back at the diner.

More disconcerting, energy crackled through the air, making all the hair on my body stand at attention.

"Hi," I said, rubbing my arms.

"Hi!" Juliette and Amy greeted me in tandem from an overstuffed green corduroy loveseat at the far end of the narrow room. I couldn't tell if the small couch's resemblance to the famous teddy bear with the same name was accidental. Given Juliette's passion for all things books, I was leaning toward intentional.

A smaller assortment of occult stuff than had been on the bigger table crowded a small, round coffee table. Even if a bigger table had fit in the tiny nook, this one suited the diminutive seating area.

A third woman I'd never met sat in a coordinating armchair. Astoundingly, the green in her multicolored boho skirt perfectly matched the green of the upholstery. The golden kerchief accented with tiny gold coins that held back her dark curls was the type of gorgeous accessory I'd never found the courage to attempt wearing. She wore it effortlessly. Same with the dozens of bangles that jangled when she raised her hand to wave hello.

"Hi! I'm Zabrina. Friend of Juliette's."

"And me!" Amy protested.

A warm smile lit up Zabrina's eyes as she tipped her head graciously at Amy. "And Amy's. It's lovely to meet you. I hear that my arrival is auspicious."

"Uh, hi. I'm Melly," I said, holding out my hand.

Juliette responded to my questioning glance with an excited grin. "Zabrina is a fortune teller!" she exclaimed, bouncing up and down in place before bursting into laughter at the exasperated eye roll the woman shot her.

"Tell her the whole truth, please," Zabrina admonished with zero heat in her voice.

"Fine," Juliette said. "Melly, I'd love for you to meet my friend Zabrina. She is a fortune teller, which is how

I first met her, but is also the person who taught me everything I know about connecting and communicating with ghosts."

I narrowed my eyes at Juliette. Nothing I knew about her resonated with her being friends with a fortune teller. "You?..."

I didn't even have to finish the sentence before Zabrina burst into a melodious peal of laughter. Juliette scowled at both of us.

Zabrina leaned toward me to whisper conspiratorially, "She wasn't a fan at first. Thought I was full of..."

"I did not!" Juliette protested, *thwapping* her friend with a cauldron-shaped throw pillow.

"Did, too!" the graceful woman replied, fending off the attack with another peal of laughter.

Juliette straightened up and lifted her chin. "I might have maybe thought you were..." She rolled her right hand for emphasis. "Embellishing a bit."

"Ha!" Zabrina cried. "That's a good one." She winked at me. "I told her she'd have a family soon, but that it wouldn't look how she expected."

Dropping her chin and her shoulders, Juliette relented. "I thought she'd taken one look at me and made assumptions about what I wanted in life. But she turned out to be right." Her eyes softened as they landed on Zabrina, and a beatific smile bloomed on her lips.

"I'm always right," Zabrina said to me, without a hint of arrogance.

She stilled, the laughter fading from her eyes as something about me caught her attention. I squirmed as she tipped her head to the side and studied me. Other than the loveseat and armchair, there was nowhere else to sit at that end of the room, and I'd never felt more exposed than I did then, helplessly caught in the fortune teller's gaze like a fly caught in a spider's web.

"I'm sorry! How rude of us!" Amy cried, sensing my discomfort and jumping to the wrong conclusion. She jumped up and waved at the spot she'd vacated. "Sit! Sit! I'll grab myself a chair."

"No, no!" I protested. "I can grab one."

"Don't be silly. You're the guest of honor here. You need to be comfortable." She nudged me toward the loveseat as she pushed past me to grab the desk chair from the other side of the room.

Zabrina's eyes tracked me without wavering as I lowered myself into Amy's spot.

"Don't mind her," Juliette whispered, leaning toward me. "She does this. She'll snap out of it in a minute."

In less time than that, Zabrina snapped upright and blinked her eyes a few times, shaking her head to clear it. "Was I out long?" she asked Juliette, arching an eyebrow questioningly.

Juliette shook her head. "Only a few minutes. Did you learn anything interesting?"

"Nothing we need to concern ourselves with at this moment," Zabrina replied, turning her warm smile on me. "Your mother? That's who we're here to talk to, right? She's anxious to connect with you."

I braced myself as I glanced around the room. Toward the end, my mother's skeletal thinness had terrified me every time I had to tend to her. The softest touch either ripped or bruised her papery skin. And on more than one occasion, I'd been unable to banish the thought that she was nothing more than a barely alive, mummified corpse. It had taken me weeks of actively forcing myself to remember her at her brightest and liveliest to banish the haunting images of her last days.

"She's here?" My hoarse whisper earned me sympathetic glances from all three women.

Zabrina leaned over to grasp my shaking hand in her own warm and steady one. "She is. She means you no harm. All I sense from her is deep, deep love and affection and a strong desire to make sure you're okay."

My eyes filled with tears that instantly overflowed onto my hot cheeks. "Will she... what does..." Unable to find the right words, I fell silent, willing Zabrina to understand me, anyway.

The fortune teller was beautiful, but when she smiled, she became almost otherworldly. My hands settled, and some of the tension that had been building since I'd first walked in melted from my shoulders.

"Ghosts often appear to us in the form that is most comfortable for them. Some look the way they did when their confidence and accomplishments peaked, others the way they did when they were most loved and welcomed."

"But not..." I whispered.

"Unless the person's death was so traumatic that it blocked everything else they know about themselves, no, they don't appear the way they did when they crossed over." I didn't need to ask to know that she'd already seen that my mother's death had been the opposite of that.

When it had become clear that my mother's time was ending, the hospital had let me take her home. For five days, I'd sat by her side and read to her even as she slept while hospice nurses popped in and out to check on her. When one of them had taken me aside to let me know it was a matter of hours rather than days, I'd played my mother's favorite music softly in the background, dimmed the lights, and crawled into bed with her. Holding her hand gently in mine, I'd rested my head against hers and murmured in her ear all the ways I loved her, how much she meant to me, and everything I'd learned from her that would keep me going long after she was gone. And then, when she fought the inevitable, refusing to surrender, I'd given her permission to leave me, promising that we'd be together again after I'd lived enough for both of us and done all the things her illness had stolen from her.

It had somehow taken forever, and no time at all.

If I had to guess, she'd appear looking the way she had in high school, or maybe her young 20s, flitting her way between music festivals and protests at the height of the social revolution of the 60s. I'd never tired of seeing her light up when she told me about those days.

"Whenever you're ready," Zabrina murmured, patting my hand one last time before sitting up.

I took a shaky breath and straightened my back. Nodding with confidence I did not feel, I said, "I think I'm as ready as I'll ever be."

"Wonderful," Zabrina said. "Juliette, do you want to take the lead?"

Juliette's answering laugh broke the tension in the room. "Wouldn't that be like going to a Michelin-rated restaurant and asking to cook my own meal?"

Zabrina's eyes twinkled with mischief as she countered, "I'm not sure I'd compare myself to a stuffy restaurant graded by an outdated French organization invented just to get people to travel more, but I think I get your meaning."

Laughing along with the three of them made the last of my apprehension fall away. Knowing that I was going to see my mother the way I'd longed to see her for years had turned low-grade terror to near-giddy excitement.

I could not wait for her familiar voice to wrap itself around me.

"How does this work?" I asked, glancing down at the paraphernalia on the table.

"A lot like yesterday," Juliette said. "First, we'll do the protection spell. Just in case. Then we cast a spell to call forth your mother." She rolled her eyes affectionately at Zabrina, who'd made the tiniest scoffing sound.

"What?" I asked, glancing back and forth between them.

"Nothing," Juliette said.

"You know I'm right!" Zabrina answered.

"Right about what?" I asked, glancing at Amy, who'd folded herself into a pretzel on Juliette's desk chair.

"Don't mind them. Ongoing argument. Zee doesn't think Jules needs the spell to call forth the ghosts. Jules maintains that she does."

"Don't call me Zee. And she doesn't," Zabrina said, her voice just as calm and melodious as it had been when she'd introduced herself. I had the feeling that it would take a lot to ruffle the fortune teller's feathers.

"If I don't use the spell, no one else can see the ghosts!" Juliette protested. "How could they?"

Zabrina took a deep breath. "Juliette, I promise that your power is strong enough to connect everyone. How about we try it? If it doesn't work, we can always use the spell."

The corners of Juliette's mouth turned down slightly, and she buried her hands in the folds of her skirt. "I guess we can try," she said in a timid voice I'd never heard her use.

Zabrina caught Amy's eye and tilted her head in her direction.

Understanding the assignment, Amy jumped in. "It's going to work. I'm sure of it."

The baleful stare she got in response from Juliette would have withered most people.

"Fine," Juliette said, a bit more convincingly. "But can we at least do the protection spell first?"

Grinning, Zabrina nodded. "I wouldn't have it any other way."

Juliette jumped out of her seat and grabbed a box of salt that had been stashed under the table, likely because there wasn't a spare square inch of space on the table itself.

"I can't go around the loveseat. We're going to have to stand in the middle of the room to do this," she said, nodding to the empty space between the desk and sitting area.

"Sounds good," Amy said, jumping to her feet.

"You all stand there, I'll pour the salt circle around us and recite the spell, then I'll call Melly's mom. Okay?" It seemed to me that Juliette was only telling us what she was going to do to reassure herself, but we all nodded in agreement anyway.

We gathered in the center of the space she'd indicated and watched as she poured the circle.

> *"I call the North, the East, the South, and the West.*
> *By the elements of Air, Fire, Water, Earth, and Spirit,*
> *I cleanse this space of the Negative, the Harmful, the Unwelcome,*
> *And invite in only Love, Light, and Harmony.*
> *By the power of the Maiden, Mother, and Crone,*
> *So mote it be."*

"So mote it be," we echoed.

"As long as the circle isn't broken, no ghosts can touch us or harm us?" I asked, not sure if that was reassuring or disappointing.

"It's not your mother. It's your mother's spirit. Not like a ghost can hug you, you know."

I ignored Demi's snarky comment and kept my focus outside my head.

"That's right. I broke the salt seal around the room so your mother can get in, but she won't be able to cross the circle," Juliette said to me. "Everyone ready?"

In for a penny, in for a pound, as my mother would have said, even though she'd never so much as set foot outside the United States, let alone in England where the idiom would have made sense.

"I'm doing it," Juliette said.

"You've got this," Zabrina replied. "We're not going anywhere."

Juliette clenched her entire body and screwed up her face, radiating intensity, but nothing happened. The room remained blissfully empty of ghosts. Amy shrugged slightly when I caught her eye. Zabrina ignored our exchange and kept her entire focus trained on Juliette.

After a few painful minutes, Juliette released the tension she was holding and let out a frustrated sigh. "Nothing. I've got nothing."

"It's okay. I'm proud of you for trying. It'll happen one day. I know it," Zabrina said, her voice so soothing that even I was comforted. "Want to try holding everyone's hands? That could boost your power."

Juliette shook her head. "No, let's just do the spell and get this over with."

"Fine by me," Zabrina said, plunging a hand into a hidden pocket of her flowing skirt.

Juliette's eyes narrowed as she pulled out a handful of deep blue stones. "You didn't think I could do it!"

"*You* didn't think you could do it," Zabrina replied softly. "And so, you were right. I just like to be prepared for every eventuality."

With a gentle smile, she handed each of us a shiny stone. "Lapis Lazuli. To boost your spiritual communication. Hold hands around it."

Palming the stone, I took Juliette's hand in mine and reached for Amy's with my free one.

Gripping my hand tightly around my stone, Juliette took a shuddering breath. "Just like yesterday, I'll recite it twice, then we all say it together the third time, okay?"

As soon as we all nodded, she launched into the spell.

> *"In liminal space, mysteries dwell,*
> *Whispers hushed and lanterns gleam,*
> *Summon those from dreams unseen.*
> *Beyond the veil, let truths be gleaned,*
> *Spirits tell, what mysteries mean.*
> *By ancient powers, this spell be well."*

"Melody! What on earth have you done with your hair?" My mother's appalled voice echoed around the small room the instant we'd said the last word. "Stand up straight. You'll give yourself a hunchback," she added, almost like an absentminded afterthought.

To my surprise, she didn't look like the flowers-in-her-hair hippie version of herself from faded photographs. She looked exactly the way she did when I was a teen. Her auburn waves, bleached blond and coiled into tight curls from repeated perms, framed her slightly plump face from which peered eyes that had never let me get away with anything. I reacted accordingly: pulling my shoulders back and down into their correct position, feeling like I was 14 all over again.

"Hi, Donna. Is it okay if I call you that?" Zabrina asked softly, graciously pulling my mother's attention away from my appearance.

"Well, that is my name," my mother replied. "I'm not sure what else you could call me."

She snapped her mouth shut and frowned down at us, distracted from one of her favorite jokes by the realization that she wasn't standing on the ground. "Why are you all down there? Wait. That's wrong. Why am I up here?" The words were barely out of her mouth before she was bobbing up near the ceiling. "That's fun. Wonder if I could be over there." She blinked out of sight and reappeared on Juliette's desk. Or rather, in Juliette's desk, split in half by the desktop.

Wincing, I glanced away. Being criticized by her ghost was bad enough. I didn't need to see her cut in half.

"Oh! That's fun! Melody! Come over here! Try this! It's so fun!" Surprised laughter filled the room as the effort of pulling herself out of the table sent her flipping through the air head over heels.

Her laughter and childlike delight triggered a flood of memories that clogged my throat with grief. I'd forgotten how much she loved to have fun or even how fun she could be. I couldn't remember the last time she'd been able to muster more than a sad, half-hearted chuckle in response to any of my attempts at lightening the mood.

Before the amulet had sucked her dry of her life force, she'd been the queen of actually funny practical jokes and the first to jump into any adventure that presented itself.

We'd ridden every roller coaster and every carousel we ever came across. She was a menace when it came to arcade games and had challenged little kids to dance-offs on those electronic dance machines more than once. If we ever stumbled upon a store that sold outrageous clothing, you could be sure she'd be dragging me into their changing room five minutes later with an armful of the most absurd things they sold. She skipped instead of walking and sang in the rain as if no one could hear her off-key rendition of classic rock ballads or notice that she never got the words right.

She'd been the life of the party, and I had resented her carefree approach to life, assuming it meant she took nothing seriously. It had taken me years to realize that she tackled everything with a can-do, daredevil attitude to keep from following in her mother's footsteps by talking herself out of experiencing everything life offered.

"Wheeeee!" she cried, doing figure-eights above us, pretending to dive-bomb us, then soaring back up to the ceiling at the last second. "Come on, Melly! Don't be a stick-in-the-mud!"

The words stabbed me in the gut, making me regret all the times I hadn't given in to her pleas to come play with her.

"I'm sorry, Mom. I wish I could. That looks like a lot of fun," I replied, doing my best to keep my voice light and cheery.

Because she was the woman who knew me best in the world, she heard everything I didn't say and instantly floated down. She landed softly at the edge of the salt circle, her glee replaced by the concerned frown she'd worn so often when talking to me. "Are you okay, baby?" she asked, lifting her hand to caress my face. She frowned when she encountered the protective field created by the salt.

The mild surprise that registered in her eyes when I didn't protest the infantilizing nickname grew when I lifted my hand to hers instead of jerking away from her touch. Except that there was no touch. I could see her, and hear her, but only the barest brush of air caressed our hands where they met. My heart collapsed in on itself.

"Mama," I said, pushing the word past the lump of grief lodged in my throat. "I miss you so much, Mama. I don't know how to do this without you."

The truth didn't hit me until I said it out loud, but the limbo I'd been trapped in since her death boiled down to not knowing how to keep going without her cheering me on or guiding me or even nagging me as I stumbled through life.

"Oh, my darling, darling baby," she murmured, bringing her other hand up.

With a sob, I stumbled toward her embrace, pulling my hands from Amy's and Juliette's, ignoring the cries of protest erupting around me. My mother's ghost flickered, growing more translucent for an instant before solidifying again.

Juliette's grunt of pain and Zabrina's murmured reassurance to her barely registered as my foot scuffed the salt circle, and twin arctic circles bloomed on my cheeks when my mother attempted to cradle my face in her hands. I didn't care. I'd wept for this every night for months.

My tears overflowed when a kiss like the gentle flutter of butterfly wings landed on my forehead. Floating closer, she rested her head against mine.

"You can do anything," she murmured. "I know you can. You are the brightest, strongest, most capable person I have ever met. The reason my life was so amazing. Melody, *you* are my everything."

A sob shook my body, and I leaned in closer, desperate to feel her embrace, but the only thing that wrapped itself around me was more cold.

She smiled lovingly down at me. "I will be eternally grateful for how well you cared for me. But now it's time for you to take care of *yourself*. You have so many years to make up for. So much to experience. You haven't even fallen in love yet! Or lived, really. Which is my fault, I know. But now you're free to do everything we always said we'd do."

"But I don't want to do them without you," I wailed. "It's not fair."

"Oh, but it is." She laughed softly. "I'll be with you every step of the way. And I fully expect a detailed report on what had better be a full, happy life when you finally join me here. You hear me?"

"Yes, Mama," I said, laughing wetly. "How long does the report have to be?" The age-old homework question had always driven her into a rant.

Her answering laugh wound its way into my heart, healing some of the constant ache that had settled there when she took her final breath. "You make it as long as you want, my love. I promise it'll be perfect no matter what."

"What? No rant?" I asked, finally daring to look up into her eyes.

She grinned at me. "The time for ranting is over. Now it's time to fly!"

With that, she pushed herself off me and propelled her way to the ceiling again, where she lay on her back, with her arms out to her side in a *T* and her feet crossed at the ankles, floating back and forth as though relaxing in the ocean. The faint strains of her tuneless humming floated down to us.

"Do we know what we want to ask her?" Juliette said softly after I'd fully composed myself.

"I think so," I replied. "Whether she gives us a straight answer is another thing."

TWENTY-FOUR

"**M**ama, can you come down here, please? I can't talk to you when you're all the way over there," I called up to her. She ignored me in favor of doing another forward roll.

"Did you see that, Mel? I did three in a row!" She clapped her hands, giggling like a little girl.

"I did. That was cool! How many would it take you to get down here?"

Amy twitched next to me, and when I glanced over, I saw why. She was biting her bottom lip hard to keep herself from laughing out loud. The glare I leveled on her only made her laugh harder.

"Six!" my mother said from much closer than I expected.

"Six?" I asked, turning my head and jumping when I found myself nose to nose with her.

"Six flips to get down here." She grinned. "Is this close enough? I can get closer." She floated a few inches closer, and the temperature of the entire left side of my body dropped noticeably.

Shivering, I glanced over at Zabrina. Even at her sickest, my mother hadn't lost her sense of humor, but this behavior was strange, even for her. The icy hand that ran down my back when Zabrina mouthed, "We're running out of time," had nothing to do with ghostly proximity.

Tears pricked my eyes. I wasn't ready to let her go again. As if they could read my mind, Juliette and Amy smiled encouragingly.

"It's going to be okay. We've got you," Juliette murmured.

Her words thawed some of the chill that had settled in my core. Our friendship, if I could call it that, was so new we hadn't even taken it out for a test drive, but knowing they'd be there when my mother was gone again was comforting.

"That's perfect. Thank you, Mom." I said, turning to look at her. She'd floated back a few feet and was scrutinizing my face with a look that had always made me feel like she was seeing to the bottom of my soul.

"You've changed," she said, more curiously than accusingly.

"I have?"

She nodded slowly, a small smile brightening her serious expression. "There's something more…" she hesitated. "Confident. That's it. More self-assured. It's a good look on you."

The laugh I barked surprised both of us. Of all the words I'd have used to describe myself these days, self-assured wasn't at the top of the list. Or even on the list.

"I mean it!" she protested. "You might not feel it yet, but it's there. You seem more settled, like you've found an important part of yourself. I'm happy. I was worried about you." A frown split the tender expression on her face. "Why was I worried, Melly? What happened?" She looked around, more and more panicked as her eyes darted back and forth, bouncing over the three other women and the unfamiliar room. "Melly? Where are we? Why aren't we at home?"

"We're losing her," Zabrina murmured. "This is normal, but it means we're almost out of time."

"Mama. Mama!" I called, wishing I didn't have to say goodbye again so soon. Zabrina had been clear; this was our one shot. Her ghost was too new. It took decades for ghosts to store up enough energy to communicate regularly with the living. She'd warned me that this would drain her for months, if not years. "Mama, eyes on me."

Our secret code for commanding each other's attention, no matter what the other was doing, did the trick. Eyes wide with panic, she looked down at me.

"What's happening, Melly-boo? Why can't I remember?" Her despair ripped my grief wide open, and it took me precious seconds we didn't have to catch my breath.

Juliette and Zabrina smiled reassuringly when I shot them a panicked glance.

"It's normal for her to be a little jumbled," Zabrina murmured. "Being here drains her energy."

I nodded and squared my shoulders against the sobs threatening to overwhelm me.

"You're okay, Mama. I promise. You're fine. I'm fine, too. Everything is okay. We are both safe, and everything is as it should be." It nearly broke my heart in half to say it, but it had been what she'd say to me when I was scared late at night or when I was worried about pretty much anything. She was here because of me, and I was going to do everything possible to spare her as much pain and confusion as possible.

Her answering smile was tremulous at best, and the trust in her eyes almost did me in. The hand she lifted to caress my cheek was more translucent than it had been a few minutes earlier. She was vanishing right in front of me. I forced all the grief and longing into a corner of my head and walled it off. I'd cry later. If I didn't ask her what I needed to know, we risked being reunited much sooner than expected. No use wasting unnecessary tears.

"Mama, I need to know the truth," I said, pinning her with my stare, willing her to understand I wasn't kidding.

"Of course. Whatever you need," she answered in a dreamy voice that sped up my heart.

"The truth about the pendant. And the money."

Alarm sharpened her focus. "What money? You know we have no money. No fault of mine. I worked my tail off taking care of you."

Undaunted, I pushed on. "The money in your closet."

Her nostrils flared, and her eyes widened as she fisted her hands on her hips. "Melody Ashlyn Miller, how dare you go snooping in my closet? I raised you better than that. What's our only rule?"

"I know the rule, Mama. And I'm sorry, but I had no choice. And now I need the truth. Please, Mama. Just this once, can you do what I'm asking without arguing?"

She snapped upright and floated a few feet back, arms crossed, and mouth puckered into a tight ring of disapproval. "Just this once? What exactly is that supposed to mean, young lady? Is that how you speak to your mother? How dare you call me a liar? I have never once..."

"Mama! Please!" I think it was the way my voice cracked more than the plea that snapped her out of her defensive stance.

Her expression melted, and she floated a little closer. "What is it, baby? Tell Mama. You know you can tell me anything."

I resisted the urge to roll my eyes at the hypocrisy and took a deep breath instead. Keeping my voice calm and cajoling, I tried again, keeping my eyes trained on the ground. "Mama, I know I wasn't supposed to go into your closet, and I'm so sorry I did. But what's done is done. And now I need your help. Can you help me?" Bracing for another outburst, I side-eyed her surreptitiously.

"Well, that was naughty, but since you apologized, I think I can let it go. What do you need?"

"Like I said, I need to know about the pendant. And the money. Mostly the pendant. But knowing why you had a quarter of a million dollars in cash just sitting in your closet would also be nice." By the time I was done, I was yelling. All three women had their eyes glued on me, their mouths hanging open in various degrees of shock or surprise. I hadn't told them about the money. I hadn't told anyone. And now three more people knew. I stabbed the mounting panic with a pin and turned back to my mother, who, contrary to the women at the table, had caved in on herself.

"I'm sorry, Mama. I didn't want to upset you. But I need to know. These two government agents…"

Her head snapped up, alarm leaching what color she had left on her face. "Government agents? What agency?"

I frowned. "I don't know. Something weird I'd never heard of. Why?"

"You have to hide it. Don't let anyone take it, do you hear me?" She wrung her hands as she wavered, her unseeing eyes rolling wildly in every direction. "I promised that man. I promised him I'd keep it safe until he came back for it. 'Until I can come back,' he said. So, I did. I hid it. And I waited and waited and waited. But he never came back."

"The man? The bloody man who gave you the envelope? That man?"

Her gaze sharpened, and, for an instant, surprise widened her eyes. Then she nodded warily. "Yes, that man. How do you know about that man, Melly?"

I ignored her question. We didn't have time to get into a lengthy explanation about magic. The bottom half of her body had already faded entirely, and the rest of her was almost gone.

"Do you remember anything about him? Anything at all?"

She focused inward a moment, then nodded. "The envelope…" She looked me in the eye. "I threw it out. It was covered in blood. That's okay, right? You don't think he wanted the envelope back, right?"

"I'm sure he didn't, Mama. What about the envelope?" I nudged, my heart rate spiking as another three inches of her torso vanished.

"It had the same logo as his jacket. No words, just two crossed light sabers or flashlights or something. Never could find them in the phone book. And I looked. Until I got too tired. Why did I get so tired, Melly-boo?"

I didn't have the heart to tell her. "Can you think of anything else?"

She shook her head sadly. "No, baby. I'm sorry. He gave me the envelope. Said he'd be back and to keep it safe for him until he did. Said I couldn't give it to anyone who came asking for it other than him. I put the pretty necklace on. Figured it was safest on me, where I could keep an eye on it all the time. And I put the money in the closet. Who was going to look for it in an old box of tampons? Isn't it incredible that so much money can fit into such a little box? And then I guess I forgot all about it. I'm not really sure how. It was an awful lot of money, wasn't it?"

I nodded sadly. "It was, Mama. A whole lot of money." *Money that could have transformed our lives, maybe even prolonged yours,* I thought to myself. No use upsetting her further. It was too late, anyway. "Why?"

"Why?" she echoed, looking confused. "Why what?"

"Why did you help him?" Of all the questions I could have asked as her head started to fade, I don't know why I picked that one, but it suddenly seemed important.

She frowned as though disappointed in me for even asking. "That's what we do, Melody. If we're in a place to help when someone needs it, we help them. It's what makes us who we are. You know that."

"Even if it slowly kills us?" I whispered almost to myself as the edges of her face melted away.

"Silly boo, being kind and good doesn't hurt you. It's what makes people love you."

"Oh, Mama," I sobbed, as the tip of her nose faded from view. "I love you."

I thought I was speaking to thin air, but a faint reply echoed around the room. "I love you too, Melly-boo. Take care of you."

TWENTY-FIVE

The third time my phone vibrated in my pocket, I finally tore my eyes away from the spot my mother's eyes had been when they'd faded away. She wasn't coming back. I knew it. Zabrina had confirmed it. Juliette had repeated it. And still, a tiny, stubborn part of me refused to move. Because what if?

But it had been well over twenty minutes since she'd uttered her last words, and a few minutes longer since we'd seen the last remnants of her ghostly figure. It was time to admit she was truly gone.

I swiped an errant tear away with the back of my hand and yanked my phone out. But before I glanced down to see who was so desperate to get hold of me, I found Juliette's concerned gaze.

"Can we…" Words failed me, but she understood what I was asking, anyway.

"Of course. It'll be a while before she replenishes her energy, but we can try contacting her again in a few months."

Even though it wasn't a definitive promise that I'd see my mother again, it was better than knowing for sure that I wouldn't. The looming wave of grief receded enough for me to check my phone's notifications.

"Oh, no. No. No. No," I muttered, scrolling through the dozen messages and voicemails Momo had sent, first asking nicely when I was coming back, then getting progressively more terse. Rightfully so. "I have to go. I'm sorry. I'm so, so late. Thank you. Bye."

I waved in the trio's general direction and bolted for the store entrance.

Stepping out into the early dusk spurred me on. At least it wasn't meatloaf night, I reasoned as I hurried up the street to the well-lit diner beckoning in the growing dark, the arrow on its massive ancient neon sign helpfully pointing it out to anyone driving by in town and the nearby highway.

Maggie's Magic. It was a pun, Aggie explained. A combination of her husband's name and hers. Mitch + Aggie. Maggie. Together, they'd been pure magic. He cooked like he was born with a spatula in one hand and a pan in the other, and she could charm anyone into becoming a frequent regular.

When he'd passed away, she'd seen no reason to change the name of the diner. Especially when Momo had taken Mitch's place in the kitchen. Together, they still added up to Maggie, even though their partnership wasn't powered by the love that had kept Mitch and Aggie slow dancing around the diner every night after closing for close to five decades.

Mitch had been long gone by the time I washed up on Aggie's doorstep, but she'd shared enough stories to bring him to life. Momo and I had discussed keeping the name to honor Aggie and Mitch. We also couldn't think of a name we liked any better. A pang of regret shot through me as I hurried up the street.

I wanted the diner to be entirely mine and Momo's. Not just a hand-me-down that didn't quite fit. At first, I'd balked at changing the name. Loath to admit I was falling in love with having a diner of my own, I'd convinced myself I was buying the diner to save Momo's job and give myself something to do while I figured out my life. But I adored having my finger on the pulse of a cozy beach town—and even possibly being its beating heart.

"We need a new name," I called to Momo, bursting into the diner and rushing to the back to grab my apron and order pad. "Also, I'm so sorry for being late again. I owe you big, big time."

"No, we don't. And yes, you do," Momo replied without even looking up from the mushrooms he was sauteing next to three fat sizzling hamburgers covered with melted slabs of cheese. "Table three is on their third basket of bottomless fries." At that, he glanced up long enough to shoot me a disapproving look. "And Table five wants to know why we can't have meatloaf on the menu every night. I told them I'd also like to know why."

"We can discuss the name later," I said, tying my apron and throwing my unruly hair back into a ponytail. "I'm still not convinced I was wrong about the bottomless fries. As for the meatloaf, I've already explained. It's all about supply and demand. If we offer it every night, it won't be special anymore. People think, 'Eh, let's get pizza, we can always have meatloaf tomorrow,' and they end up never coming. But if we only offer it on Tuesdays, they get into the habit of coming every Tuesday, so they don't miss out." I tapped my temple with my index finger.

Momo rolled his eyes and shooed me out of his kitchen just as a party of three teens came in. "Is it true you've got bottomless fries?" the tallest of the three asked, his eyes gleaming with anticipation. I grimaced as I nodded, taking in his 6-foot-4-inch-tall, 3-foot-wide body clad in a football letterman jacket.

"Yo. Text Max. I'll text Cody," the linebacker called as he followed his friends to the booth at the far end of the diner. "Fries for days, yo!"

Fine. Momo was right. Bottomless Fries-day had some inherent flaws I probably should have anticipated, I thought, making a mental note to call the produce supplier first thing in the morning to request an extra delivery of potatoes.

By the time the last of the football team, lacrosse team, swim team, and cheerleaders had made their way out to the parking lot, where they showed zero intent to get in their cars and leave, I had a pounding headache that stretched from the back of my neck to my forehead.

My last four tables were happily enjoying various slices of pie with their after-dinner coffees, so I took advantage of the momentary lull to perch myself on an open counter stool. Digging the heels of my palms into my eye sockets relieved just enough of the mounting pressure to give me some respite. Unfortunately, it also allowed me to grasp why I'd spent the last two hours feeling like a jackhammer was attempting to cleave my head in two.

"What are you doing?" I cried at Demi, who was rhythmically kicking the small green door in my head. *"That hurts! Stop it."*

"Nope," it replied, shaking its head. *"Can't."*

"What do you mean, can't? Stop that right now!"

The tiny daemon shrugged and stepped back, leveling a smug look at me like anything that happened next was entirely my fault, and it wasn't about to accept any of the blame. The relief of having my throbbing headache vanish only lasted as long as it took me to wonder why it had been kicking the door in the first place.

"What's going on? Why did you say you couldn't stop?"

Demi shrugged in response without uncrossing its arms, looking pointedly at the green door, which was now bowing out alarmingly and looked like it might either fly open any second or, worse, explode.

"And the kicking helps how, exactly?"

It shrugged again, but when it resumed kicking the door with its steel-capped boots, the bulging door flattened into a more typical shape. My pounding headache came roaring back.

Digging my index and middle fingers into my temples, I rubbed utterly ineffective circles into the sides of my head.

"My choices are crippling headache or an explosion of magic? Fantastic. And do we know why I only have these two options?"

The only answer I got was an exasperated eye roll, followed by a few extra-hard kicks that resonated to the bottom of my stomach.

"And what happened to the little window?" I asked, noticing the missing peep door.

Demi shrugged.

If my unhelpful magical gatekeeping daemon wouldn't help me, I'd have to find someone who would. Squinting to block out the worst of the diner's halogen lights, I yanked out my phone and shot Cassie a quick text.

Awful headache. Help. Think it's magic related.

Three dots danced at the bottom of the screen, then vanished. They reappeared for a little longer before going away again. Finally, a text popped up under mine.

Have you accessed your magic at all today?

I don't think so.

Yesterday?

I thought back. When had the agents last been in the diner? The day before last?

Maybe?

That's your problem.

What's my problem?

**Magic build-up. Think pressure cooker.
Gotta release some of the pressure or...**

Kaboom?

Kaboom.

Not even wanting to imagine how a mental magic explosion might look, I glared down at my personal torturer.

"Stop."

Foot hanging in mid-air, Demi stopped, arching its eyebrow as it waited for further instructions.

The instant the throbbing ceased, the door bulged again.

"Cassie says we have to open the door."

The daemon looked back and forth between me and the door with an expression that clearly detailed what it thought of that plan.

"How about this? You grab the handle, turn it, then jump back, holding the door between the magic and you. It should keep you safe." At least I hoped it would. Demi's dubious expression didn't instill much confidence.

"Do you really think you can handle that much at once?" it asked, sounding a little more excited at the prospect than I would have preferred.

"Do I have a choice? Can you siphon some of the magic out or something?"

It shook its head.

"Okay then," I replied with a sigh. *"Ready?"*

Demi nodded, scrunched up its face in preparation for the worst, and grabbed the doorknob.

"Hold on." I held up a finger as I scanned the diner to make sure no one needed anything from me. The four parties all still seemed content, so I closed my eyes and nodded at the small daemon.

It grinned impishly and opened the door.

The magic hit me like a firehose on a scorching day, cool, refreshing, and about as pleasant as being punched in the gut by a freight train. The air burst out of my lungs with an audible *whoomp*, and I snapped forward, curling my body around my stomach. Spots danced in front of my eyes counterclockwise to the diner spinning around me.

Breathe, kid. Focus on one spot and breathe. It was what my eighth-grade basketball coach had told me when I'd gotten the wind knocked out of me by a girl who'd been held back twice. The instant she'd been assigned to block me and had grinned hungrily at me from a solid foot and a half above me, I'd known it wouldn't end well. It had taken her barely five minutes to prove me right.

Sucking a trickle of air in through my nose, I forced my eyes open and ignored the roiling in my stomach. The tips of my once-white canvas sneakers wavered into focus. *Focus on one spot and breathe.* My coach probably hadn't meant a literal spot, but the one on my big toe would do. Tomato sauce. Or maybe raspberry pie filling. Tabasco? Nah, too red. Is that a seed? Raspberry, then. Or olallieberry? Had Christina ever brought one of those?

The next breath didn't trigger as big a wave of nausea. Neither did the ones that followed. Soon enough, I was breathing somewhat normally and able to unclench my fingers. *That wasn't too bad, right? We can do this. Once in a while, I'll open the door, take a few deep breaths, and slam it shut again. No harm, no foul.*

Only the door wasn't open a bit, it was cracked down the center. A huge gaping crack that was being widened by the swirling tornado of glittering, shimmering colors forcing its way through. The shock hit me at the same time as the unfiltered and unrestrained thought of every person within a two-mile radius of the diner.

Groaning, I shoved my hands against my ears and sank to the ground, burying my face between my knees.

Is she gonna puke? Saaaa-weet. Dinner's not a total loss. Is he going to finish that last bite? Should I? Would that be rude? Will he think I'm a pig? Maybe he already does. I should never have eaten so much. That pie was damn tasty. Too bad I'm too full to eat the last bite. Why is she looking at me like that? Do I have something in my teeth? What if I don't want to go to the beach? What if I want to stay home and read all day? Huh? Why do we always have to do what he wants? When's it my turn? Would anyone hear me if I just got in my car and started yelling? That'd be weird, right? Probably. That guy on the other side of the street would think it was weird. New name? What's next, new sign? New booths? New menu? Nope. Not happenin'. No new menu. And no more of this endless-fries baloney. Might as well pour money right down the... Might be nice to have a new name. Make the place really ours. Still can't quite believe we bought it. That girl is not right in the head. What if she leaves? Don't think that, Mo. Nope. A new name could be a good sign. Like she's planning on stayin'. First thing? I'm getting fired. I shouldn't even bother going in.

Nothing good ever comes from a first-thing-in-the-morning meeting. Bet the kids are still up when we get home. Wish the good babysitter was there. Guess who's gonna have to put the kids to bed? And clean the kitchen? And prepare their lunches for tomorrow? Then clean the bathroom? All while   Mr. I-took-her-on-a-date-so-I'm-getting-lucky-tonight lounges in bed like the king he thinks he is. Did she really have to get the mushroom burger? Hate it when her mouth tastes like dirt. T-minus 45 minutes! All that planning and it's finally here. Why'd I agree to this? What was I thinking? Kidnapping? I've lost it. I should just go home. Tell her I have a headache. No! A stomachache! It's noro. Or E. coli. Or dysentery. Do people still get that? Would she even know what that was? Probably not. Look at her. She doesn't know anything. Why did I ever agree? I'm going to pay for this for the rest of my life.

Thoughts came at me from every direction. I fought the deluge back as long as I could, but I was no match for the overwhelming vortex of noise, chaos, and so many awful emotions. With one last gasp, I stopped fighting and everything went dark.

TWENTY-SIX

"**M**el? Melly? Are you okay?"

A girl in one of my college classes had once told me that not everyone had a constantly running internal commentary. The concept had blown my mind. I couldn't imagine not having the constant narration that kept me company no matter what I was doing. On the other hand, having fifty thousand trains of thought was unbearable. So was the low-pitched hum rumbling beneath the cacophony.

I clutched my head with my hands, shoving my palms harder against my ears, but the thoughts of those around me came louder and faster, hitting me from all sides, worming their way around each other, until I worried my head might explode from the mounting pressure.

Why is the laundry pink? That dog has got to stop whining. I can't believe I forgot the milk.

I'm useless. He's late! Dinner's cold again. I'm late! Is he here yet? Pregnant! What? Wine! Bed! We're going to be late. Where'd I put my book? Finally alone! So lonely. Just why? I hate everything about this. Can it be next week already? Not pregnant! Again? Too much. It's all too much. I can't take it.

I whimpered and squeezed my eyes shut and beat my hands against my head, but it didn't stop the thoughts from coming. There were so many, I could barely make out more than words here and there, but the overwhelming angst pouring into me had me in its increasingly tight grip.

"So sad. Everyone's so sad. And angry. And scared," I moaned.

"What did you say?"

Startled to hear a voice outside my head, I peered up at the worried face squinting down at me. The woman's features swam into focus, and I grabbed at Cassie's arm like a drowning woman reaching for a lifeline.

"Can't," I gasped. "Too many. So loud. Help."

"I'm here. You're okay," Cassie murmured, kneeling in front of me and gently prying one hand from her arm and the other from the side of my head. "How did you stop it the last time we talked?"

"Door. In head," I forced the words through the maelstrom of noise in my head, struggling to pick them from the chaos of thoughts and feelings.

"Okay, that's great. Can you close that door again?" Cassie cajoled.

Her head's going to explode. What happens if I can't help? Why am I helping? I don't know anything. If she dies, it'll be my fault!

"Gonna? Die?" I gasped. Maybe that wasn't such a bad thing. Then the pain and hurt would end.

"You are not going to die! You hear me?" Cassie's hands tightened around mine as her voice broke.

To appease her, I tried nodding, but it only jostled the voices in my head and made the world spin alarmingly. Groaning, I stopped moving.

"Melly, the door? Can you see the door?"

I almost shook my head and reconsidered at the last second. "No. Gone. Broken."

"What do you mean, the door is broken? What happened?"

"Too much. Magic." It was getting harder to speak. My words were coming out softly enough that she had to lean in to hear me clearly. At least she'd blocked me again, so I didn't have to hear the thoughts that went with her panicked expression.

"Okay. Forget that door for a moment. Have you ever seen one of those movies where there's a vault? And the thieves trigger the alarm system? And thick metal doors and walls come down all around the super expensive diamond they're trying to steal and traps them inside?"

Without the energy to nod, the best I could muster was a slow blink.

"This is it. The alarm has been tripped, and the diamond is in your head. I need you to drop the metal doors and walls. But you also need the ceiling and the floor. Bring them crashing down all around your mind. Now, Melly. Right now," Cassie urged.

With a clang that had to be imaginary, thick metal walls came down, locking into place with a satisfying *schick*. The sound almost echoed in the heady silence that followed. My left ear popped, then the right, and I dropped my head to my knees with a shuddering sob.

"Thank you," I whispered hoarsely.

"You okay?" Cassie asked, lowering herself next to me and leaning her shoulder against mine.

Having just my voice inside my head was a luxury I'd never appreciated before, and I savored it for a moment before nodding. "I think so. That was..." I shuddered again. "Awful. I never want to go through that again."

"I can imagine."

"It wasn't just the thoughts," I said, turning my head so I could look at her. "I could feel the despair that came with them. There must have been some good thoughts too, but the bad ones drowned them out." I blinked away the tears that flooded my eyes and let them drop onto my apron. "So much sadness and anxiety."

"When my shields are down, I can taste all of that. The angry and sad feelings always overpower the good ones. I've never understood why."

Her smile held more than a trace of weariness, and for a moment, I was grateful that at least I couldn't taste people's feelings. Even imagining the mixed flavors of the chaos I'd just weathered turned my stomach.

"You'll find the balance between keeping your shields up and venting the magic occasionally. I know it's hard to believe, but it won't always be like this. You'll learn how to manage it. I promise." Her words tickled something deep in my head that eluded me when I chased after it.

Something small. Red. Snarky.

Like a rubber band snapping into place, the thought connected, sending me into a panicked run through my head. Where was the daemon? Last I'd seen it, it'd been standing in front of the bulging green door, about to say something. Its eyes flying wide with shock had been the first sign that something terribly wrong was happening.

An instant later, the door had exploded and unleashed chaos.

"Where is it? Where is it? Where is it?" I muttered to myself, running through the tightly locked-down space inside my head.

"Where's what?" Cassie asked. If I hadn't been so panicked, the flummoxed look on her face might have been funny.

What if the walls crushed it? Can a figment of my imagination even die?

"Not a figment of your imagination," a voice grumbled off to the left, and I pivoted and ran in its direction. A large slab of green wood rested at an angle on something. If it hadn't been for the ornate design etched onto the door, and the fact that there was only one reason for a stray piece of green wood to be lying around in my head, I wouldn't have recognized the door without magic giving it its glowy shimmer.

"Hang in there," I muttered, grabbing hold of the edge of the door and heaving it off the small being.

"'Bout time. Thought you were going to leave me there forever," it grumbled, twisting itself onto its knees, then grabbing hold of my arm to haul itself to its feet. Other than a nasty bump on the side of its forehead, it didn't look too injured.

"Are you okay?" I asked, giving it a more thorough once-over to be sure.

"I'm fine," Demi snapped. *"And for the last time, I'm not a figment of your imagination. You conjured me when you asked for help to control your magic. So here I am. Not a figment of your imagination. A figment of your magic."*

"Uh." I had questions, and the sense that asking them might upset it further.

"I can't do everything, can I?" Demi snapped, correctly interpreting my silence. *"I tried to tell you something was wrong. This is your own darn fault for ignoring me."* As if to prove a point, it kicked me hard and stormed off.

"Ow! Little brat," I muttered to myself. "Next time, maybe you could use words rather than just kicking me." I rubbed my leg. Figuring out how getting kicked in my head could make my actual leg hurt was going to have to wait. Some of the thoughts I'd heard when the magic burst free had finally filtered through the chaos.

"Who's a brat?" Cassie asked, looking around to see if someone had miraculously materialized next to me.

"Miss? Miss? Can we please have the check?" a voice called from the other side of the counter.

"Do not go anywhere. We have a situation, and I think I need help," I hissed as I pulled myself to my feet using the countertop for leverage.

If the first thoughts I'd heard before pandemonium had broken out had belonged to the people closest to me, then the people who'd been plotting a kidnapping a few days earlier were back. And whatever they'd planned was happening soon.

TWENTY-SEVEN

When I returned from checking out a harried-looking father and his young son, Cassie was bustling around behind the counter like she'd always worked there. She topped off a coffee mug for an older man sitting at the end of the counter and replaced the pot with a grin.

"I've always wanted to do that. Oh, and he wants his check."

I arched an eyebrow dubiously as I pulled out my order pad. "You have? Don't you own a bakery with a full coffee bar?"

Cassie shrugged. "That's different, somehow."

I laughed. "Well, you're welcome to work here anytime. Here you go, Harry," I said to the man she'd pointed out. "Tell Jackie I hope she feels better soon. You sure you don't want to bring her back some soup? You know the FDA is sniffing around, asking for Momo's soup recipe.

Rumor says it could single-handedly wipe out the flu and the common cold!"

Harry dutifully laughed at my terrible joke as he placed a twenty on his tab and wished us both a pleasant evening. I waited until he'd left before turning to Cassie.

"Someone in here is planning a kidnapping. I'm just not sure who," I whispered, glancing over at the three occupied booths. On one end of the diner, two women in their early-ish twenties were half-heartedly stabbing their salads with their forks. Neither looked all that thrilled to be eating together. In the booth next to theirs was a couple wrapping up their dinner. The woman looked like she might pass out on the table before the guy popped the last bite of his burger into his mouth. At the other end of the diner, two more women, closer to their mid-thirties, were picking at the remains of an endless basket of fries.

If we ever did the bottomless fries thing again, we needed a one basket per person rule.

"What? What are you talking about? How do you know?" Cassie hissed, tugging on my sleeve to draw my attention back to her.

Tipping my head, I rolled my eyes and pointed at my forehead. "I heard it."

"Right," she said sheepishly. "That makes sense. But you've talked to all these people. Didn't you recognize the voices?"

"You know how your voice sounds different in your head than it does on a recording?" I asked. She nodded. "I think I hear the voice people hear in their heads. I can't match them at all."

"Well, that's annoying. A kidnapping, though? Are you sure? What exactly did you hear?"

I grimaced. "They didn't just think it tonight. They also thought it the other day. Thing is, I can't remember who was here that day. All these people have been here at least once in the last week, but I've been so distracted, I can't remember who was here when."

"And why do you think it's tonight?"

"One of them is super excited about something. The other thinks they're going to get in a ton of trouble over it."

"And, really, no clue who?" Cassie ran her eyes over the three tables, studying each couple. "I don't think it's the man and woman. She looks too tired to *get* kidnapped, let alone do it to someone else."

"I agree. Plus, I'm pretty sure both voices are female."

"So that leaves blonde and blonder over there." She gestured to the salad-eating duo, one of whom was giggling at something on her phone while the other stared at her plate with no expression on her face. "And grumpy/sunshine over there."

"Grumpy/sunshine?" I echoed.

"It fits! Look at them!"

Cassie wasn't wrong. One woman, who looked maybe twenty years younger than the other, scowled at the two packets of artificial sugar in her hand. Oblivious to her mood, the woman sitting across from her happily munched on fries. Mother and daughter? Out for a forced dinner? Hard to tell. Unlike the regulars who sat at the counter and chatted with me as I worked, I didn't know the booth regulars very well.

"So, what do we do? Question them?" Cassie whispered, her eyes gleaming with excitement. "Are you listening to their thoughts?"

"No, I'm not listening to their thoughts! Did you not see what just happened to me?"

Cassie shrugged. "You're going to have to access the magic again. Why not now?"

I shuddered. My head was still ringing with the echoes of all those thoughts. No doubt she was right, but I wasn't ready to expose myself to that level of assault quite yet. "Possibly, but not now. I need an hour-long shower and a pint of ice cream before I go there."

"Fine, but you're doing it. And no later than tomorrow. You hear me?"

I snorted a laugh at her stern expression. "Yes, Mommy. I promise I'll be good tomorrow. Should I also eat my veggies and make my bed?"

"Now who's being a brat?" Cassie laughed, elbowing me in the side. Her expression grew serious. "I'm not kidding, though. I've heard that magical burnout isn't fun. I'd hate for that to happen to you."

Before I could respond, the cheerful woman of the grumpy/sunshine duo got to her feet and dropped a stack of bills on the edge of the table, then made her way to the restroom at the back of the diner.

"Oh! They're moving. What do we do?" Cassie cried softly.

"Well, to start, I'm going to see if she left enough to cover her bill before they skedaddle."

"Skedaddle?" Cassie laughed.

Ignoring the teasing, I pushed past her and hurried to the table. "Hi, hon! All set? What're you up to tonight with your...mom?" Quirking my eyebrow, I emphasized the last word. The sullen young-adult woman glowered in response.

"I dunno. Some dumb thing she's been planning forever. I wanted to go to a concert, but..." Instead of finishing her thought, she bit her lip and shook her head. "Whatever. Doesn't matter, anyway."

I was about to ask her to clarify when the clip-clop of her mother's heels announced her arrival. "I hope I left enough to cover the tab?" she asked as she approached. "Everything was delicious, as always." The warm smile she turned on me froze in place when she turned to her daughter. "Let's go, Callie. We're going to be late."

"I asked you not to call me that," the younger woman groused as she wriggled herself out of the booth. "It's Calliope."

"And yet," the mother said through her forced smile, "that's not what is listed on your birth certificate."

"Only because you're a cruel woman who named me Calista. What kind of name is Calista? It sounds like a toilet cleaner or medication for a yeast infection."

The door closed on their argument, sadly cutting off the mother's reply.

"Follow them," I hissed at Cassie. "Go, go, go! I'll wait and follow these two."

Cassie frowned. "Split up? Follow potential criminals on our own? That does not seem like a great idea."

"Text Juliette and tell her to meet you. Or, even better, text Sam!" I whispered, suddenly remembering who Cassie was dating as I pushed her toward the door. On the other side of the plate window, Callie had just climbed into the passenger seat of what had to be her mother's shiny white Lexus. The mother in question was reapplying her lipstick in the rearview mirror. "Text me where they end up. I'll let you know where I am."

Cassie's protest died on her lips, and she darted through the door as the mother adjusted her mirror and prepared to pull out of her spot.

A moment later, the last table waved me over.

Help me nab a kidnapper? I typed quickly, then hit send and hurried over to my final customers.

"All set? Hope everything was to your liking. What are you two up to tonight?" I asked, collecting their cutlery and dropping it into an empty glass as they gathered their things.

"It's a surprise!" the taller of the two girls said, clapping her hands happily.

"Sounds fun," I replied, smiling at her obvious excitement.

"That's one word for it," the other girl muttered, sliding out of the booth and brushing a few crumbs off her jeans onto the floor.

Thanks for that, I muttered to myself.

"Well, you two have fun out there. Don't do anything I wouldn't do!" I called after them as they headed to the door.

I might have been hearing things, but the high-pitched laugh I got in reply sounded a little off to my ear.

I yanked my apron off as I tossed the few bills they'd left for me into the cash register.

"Momo! I have to run. I'm sorry. Leave everything. I'll be back in a bit to tidy up and get everything ready for tomorrow. Don't forget to lock up!" I called back to him as I darted out of the diner, eyes scouring the parking lot for the two young women.

There! They were arguing over the top of a beat-up burgundy Yaris that had seen many better days.

Taking advantage of their momentary distraction, I yanked the keys to my ancient Subaru out of my pocket, sending up a silent prayer to whatever entity looked over crumbling cars that it would start on the first try.

The car rumbled to life.

"I'm sorry I doubted you," I whispered to it, patting the steering wheel affectionately. "It won't happen again. Okay, it might, but not because I don't love you," I amended.

Slowly, I counted to twenty before inching the car out onto the street, looking in the direction the two women had headed, then floored the gas as I realized how far they'd already gotten.

"Whoops. Twenty seconds might have been a little too long," I muttered, as I rushed past a very ripe yellow light at the next intersection. Hopefully, Sam was busy following the other two women with Cassie, and his coworkers had better things to worry about than a mildly illegal traffic violation.

The beat-up Yaris turned right two blocks down, then left, then right again before going straight for another three blocks. Slipping my car into a spot on the other side of the street a few cars down from where the women parked, I texted a location pin and got out as quietly as my heap of junk allowed.

The door clunked as I shut it, but the two women still locked in a heated debate paid me no attention.

"...fine! I swear! I've done this at least a half-dozen times. I know what I'm doing!" the perky blonde was telling her friend, who looked even more reluctant than she had in the diner.

"But... what if it isn't fine? What if she calls the cops? I'll lose my scholarship! I can't afford college without it!" The anxious pitch of her voice didn't stem the other woman's determination to move forward with the plan.

"We're doing this! Stop being such a wet blanket already! I do not know what Allie sees in you. I really don't," she said, grabbing the other woman's arm and pulling her up the dark drive.

"Well, that makes two of us," the woman getting dragged muttered back.

"What's happening?"

"Why are we lurking behind a light pole?"

I'd been so focused on the two women that I hadn't heard Juliette and Amy sidle up to me. Startled, I cried out and grabbed at my hammering chest.

The woman spearheading whatever was unfolding in front of us stopped to scan her surroundings. I grabbed Amy and Juliette's arms and yanked them down with me behind the compact sedan in front of us.

"What is going on?" Amy whispered.

"Shhhh," I hissed, peering through the car's windows to see if we'd been made.

My shoulders sagged with relief when the woman shrugged and turned back around.

"I think we're witnessing a kidnapping," I explained, standing up.

"What?" Juliette gasped. "Why aren't we calling the police?"

"I'm not one hundred percent sure yet," I replied, ducking around the car and hurrying across the street.

"Where are you going?" Amy hissed, hot on my heels.

"Making sure," I replied, eyeing the distance from the sidewalk to the porch steps the two women were climbing. If we ran quietly, we could be hidden behind the bushes in two seconds with the potential kidnappers none the wiser. "Let's go!" I said, darting toward the shadows I hoped would be dark enough to hide us from sight. If I got caught by hardened criminals and didn't make it back to the diner to clean up, the cops would have another crime to solve after Momo got his hands on me.

TWENTY-EIGHT

I'd misjudged the gap between the bushes and the flimsy lattice walling off the underside of the porch. It was far smaller than I'd expected. Pricklier, too.

"Ow!" Amy complained when I pushed her deeper into the narrow opening.

"Sorry," I whispered, squeezing in closer to pull Juliette into our hiding spot.

Above us, I tracked the hollow footsteps of the two women as they approached the door. I relaxed my hold on Amy's and Juliette's arms once I was fairly certain we were out of their line of sight.

"What's the plan?" Juliette breathed. She made a face when I shrugged helplessly. I'd been so focused on following the would-be kidnappers, I hadn't thought past witnessing the crime.

"What do you mean, 'What's the plan?' Obviously, we tackle them and hold them in place until the cops arrive," Amy whispered back.

"Have you lost your mind?" Juliette hissed, leaning in. "Do you have any idea how many ways that could backfire?"

"What do you suggest?" Amy replied, moving her face closer so she could keep her voice down. Their noses were almost touching as they argued, keeping their voices just above audible. Given that I was standing between them and that our hiding place was already not big enough for three people, their faces were so close to mine that I could have reached out and licked their chins without moving my head.

"That's nasty." Demi sounded equal parts disgusted and delighted.

"I didn't say I would do it, just that I could."

"Whatever."

Conjuring a figment of magic to help me control my new abilities was cool, but did it have to be a being with the snark and attitude of an angsty teen?

"I heard that."

One who could hear all of my thoughts, no less.

"Should we ring the bell?" one of the women asked when they got to the door.

"No. I texted Jimmy that we're here. He says that if we wake the baby, we're bringing her, too."

Jimmy? Baby? Was the husband in on this kidnapping? What kind of monster arranges to have his wife kidnapped?

My phone vibrated, distracting me from coming up with a plausible answer. I pulled it out of my pocket and angled my body away from Juliette and Amy so I could read the messages hitting my screen in rapid succession.

This is Deputy Sheriff Griffin.
Where are you?
Do not do anything rash.
Actually, don't do anything at all.
Just tell me where you are. Then sit tight
until I get there.

"Sugar," I muttered under my breath.

"What?" Juliette and Amy's heads swiveled to look at me.

"The sheriff texted. I think we're in trouble."

Color drained from Juliette's face, and Amy grabbed her arm and squeezed. "We are not in trouble. It's Sam. He loves us."

Juliette only looked slightly mollified by this assertion, but she didn't have a chance to respond before the door to the house opened.

"Why would there be a package outside for me, Jimmy? I didn't order anything. Did you?" a woman called as the screen door screeched open. "Wait. What's happening? Why are the two of you here? Why are the two of you together?" She didn't sound scared, just confused. Maybe she had no clue what these women were capable of.

As quickly as possible, I texted the sheriff our location and slipped the phone into my pocket.

"Amy's right," I whispered. "If they grab her and drag her down the stairs to their car, we jump them. Sit on them until the sheriff arrives."

"What? No!" Juliette protested as Amy nodded enthusiastically.

"SURPRISE!" the two women on the porch shouted, one leading the cry and the other following a fraction of a second after, as if she hadn't been told the plan.

"What is going on?" the woman who'd opened the door asked in a bewildered but happy voice.

"I..." one woman started, then hesitated as the other corrected her. "Fine, *we* are here to kidnap you. We are taking you to The Oasis Spa for the weekend! Surprise!"

"What? No! That's so sweet! But..." The excitement melted from her voice. "I can't go. The baby... Jimmy..." My chest ached from the weariness dragging at her words.

"It was my idea," a deeper voice that presumably belonged to Jimmy cut in.

"What? Honey?" Her wary hope almost hurt more than her hopelessness.

"You are an incredible mom who does so much for the little guy and me, and who hasn't had a good night of sleep in over eight months. You're no longer nursing, and you are in dire need of a break," Jimmy said.

Juliette and Amy sighed wistfully in tandem.

"But... I have so many things I need to do! And there's no food in the house! What would you eat?"

Jimmy's answering chuckle was full of warmth.

"This might come as a shock to you, but I survived on my own for years before we met. I think I can feed myself for two days."

Our kidnapping victim muttered something about frozen ravioli not being food, which made Jimmy laugh again.

"Don't worry about me. I've got this. Take these, and go have some serious fun." The screen door screeched, and two heavy things dropped onto the porch. "I'm serious! No calling, no texting, no nothing other than whatever it is women do when they're being pampered at spas for forty-eight hours."

"But... the baby... I can't..." the young mom protested.

"I know you think I don't know my head from my armpit, but I can mix a bottle and change a diaper, and he doesn't mind my terrible singing voice too, too much.

Trust me. I've got this. Stormy and I are going to be just fine. And if you really want, send me a list of everything you were hoping to accomplish this weekend. I'll take care of it all. And if anything goes wrong, I can always call your mom."

"Don't call him that," she said, in a tone that gave me the impression it wasn't the first time she'd said it. "Why not *your* mom?" she tacked on.

"Because that's not what you would do, and this weekend, I'm doing things exactly how you'd do them so you can relax without worrying about a thing."

"Thank you." Her words came out more muffled as though her face was pressed into something soft, and I realized she must have hugged him.

"I love you." His murmured response brought tears to my eyes that I swiped away as surreptitiously as possible, feeling a little less sappy for my moment of weakness when I caught Amy's eyes glittering with unshed tears.

"I need to pack!" the young mom cried.

"All taken care of!" Jimmy replied, sounding very pleased with himself. "Everything you could possibly need is in those bags."

"Even my..."

"Everything. Trust me."

After another muffled exchange, the screen door screamed again, and three sets of footsteps headed our way. We ducked, biting back curses as the bushes snagged our clothes and scratched our arms. The phone digging into my hip vibrated just as I was repositioning it. If Amy hadn't grabbed my arm to steady me as I maneuvered it out, I would have fallen face-first into the bushes.

I'm 5 minutes out. Please tell me you're staying put.

Stand down, I replied to the sheriff's text as the three women piled into the car, chatting excitedly about the weekend's plans.

False alarm.

Heading home.

TWENTY-NINE

I was still laughing at myself for assuming the worst and going overboard when I rounded the dark diner and stepped into my yard. I wasn't reneging on my promise to Momo to get the place ready for the morning. But before I headed over to the diner to sweep and prep, I needed a moment to collect myself and pluck twigs out of my hair.

What exactly would I have done if we'd witnessed a real kidnapping attempt rather than a sweet gesture from a loving husband to his tired wife?

I was trying to picture myself and Juliette each sitting on a woman while Amy held their heads up with fistfuls of their hair when something large and black landed at my feet with a whoosh of wind and a series of soft clicking sounds. My heart jumped into my throat, and I stumbled back, freezing in place when a quiet rattling noise added itself to the clicking. I didn't need to speak crow to know something was wrong.

Willing my heart to stop beating so loudly, I looked around for what had freaked out the crow. My breath hitched when I spotted a light bouncing around inside the camper and the door hanging open. I never left the door open.

"Thank you," I whispered to my feathery friend. The crow preened and hopped around.

Despite the soft glow of light coming from the trailer and the solar-powered lights I'd sprinkled along the path to the entrance, it was hard to distinguish his dark feathers from the shadows surrounding him. However, his open wings beating me back when I took a step toward the camper were impossible to miss.

"Okay! Okay. Message received."

A loud crash, followed by a series of smaller ones, sent my heart into overdrive and made the crow do a few flying hops to move me farther back from the camper. If it hadn't been for the bird, I probably would have been running for the door, if only to see what was being destroyed.

"Yes, because your sad possessions are worth risking your life over," Demi quipped.

"They are when you have nothing else!" I snapped back, hoping the thief wasn't taking his rage out on anything I'd already refinished.

I shrank back into the shadows when a hulking form passed in front of the window. Time slowed as the reality of the moment crystallized. A massive man who looked entirely built of muscle was tearing my trailer apart.

Hands shaking, I fumbled for my phone and promptly dropped it onto the pebbles at my feet. Thankfully for me, not so much for my kitchen, the clatter of pots being thrown on the ground muffled the dull thud.

The crow jumped back two feet to give me room to pick up my phone with its new network of cracks spidering across the screen. Between the tiny shards of glass stabbing me, the dark, and the fear clogging up my brain and making my hands shake, it took me longer to pull up the text thread with the sheriff than it should have. And it distracted me enough from what was happening in my camper that I didn't notice the door swing open or the thief step out.

Panic turned me to stone, like a deer in headlights. If I moved, he'd see me. But if I stayed where I was, he'd run into me on his way out. There was only one path from the Airstream to the parking lot, and I was standing on it. I could run, but fit as he looked, he'd probably catch up to me in three strides. My brain was proposing and discarding options at breakneck speed when a large hand landed on my mouth, and a beefy arm wrapped itself around my midriff. Before I had time to even process what was happening, my feet were off the ground, and I was being hauled backward into the shadows of the diner.

My heart pounded hard enough to burst as every single self-defense tip I'd ever known vanished, leaving me only Sandra Bullock dressed in a ridiculously impractical milkmaid dress telling a rapt beauty pageant audience how to S.I.N.G. Not that I could remember what the self-defense acronym stood for.

Instep? Groin? Was I supposed to stomp or kick? Elbow? Elbow to the stomach, right? That had to be right.

Neither of my arms moved an inch.

"Shh. You're safe. I've got you. Don't move," a deep voice I faintly recognized whispered into my ear as the colossus stomped down the camper's stairs and into the yard, clenching his fists and muttering to himself.

"Let's go!" the large man barked toward the trailer, and I jerked in my captor's arms. I'd assumed that the man tearing my home apart had been alone, but a thinner, shorter figure filled the doorframe and took the three steps down in one.

"Freeze!" someone shouted from the parking lot.

The giant man laughed. "Who's gonna stop me? Where's your army, little lady?"

Little lady. The pieces fell into place, and I sagged in my rescuer's arms in relief, faintly surprised his hands didn't smell like pie.

"You know what I love?" Agent Sterling asked.

"What?" The colossus sounded surprised that he'd answered.

"Being underestimated." Agent Sterling tossed something in the air, and I flinched as whatever she threw burst into bright flames.

"So hot," Agent Thorne murmured under his breath.

"Oooooooh, a fireball. So scary," the thief drawled.

When Agent Sterling waved her hand again, something glinted at the tip of her index finger, and the massive man floated into the air as if he weighed less than a feather. She pinched her finger and thumb together, and his back arched until his head and hands were touching his feet. For his sake, I hoped he was a regular at his local yoga studio. Even though his mouth was open and his face was turning rage red, he wasn't making a sound. With a lazy flip of her hand, Agent Sterling sent him spinning, then waved him toward herself. As he hovered a foot or so away from her, still spinning slowly, she tossed a rope at him and twirled her hand. My jaw dropped as the rope wrapped itself tightly around his ankles and wrists.

She flicked her fingers as though flicking off a bit of dirt, and the ground shuddered when he dropped like a tightly trussed boulder.

Another wave of her hand removed whatever nifty bit of magic had silenced him, and his howls of rage suddenly filled my small yard.

"You're unhinged, lady. I'm just doing my job! I'll get you for this. Just you wait. You'll regret this every day of your miserable life. You... you... I'll get you. Just you wait."

"Oh, yeah, Brutus? You and what army?" Agent Sterling replied, walking over to him and casually resting the hottest three-inch heeled boot I'd ever seen on his rump and leaning her elbow on her knee. In any other situation, the strangled whimper Agent Thorne let out would have made me chuckle. The giant's furious thrashing made no impression on Agent Sterling as she directed her attention toward the camper. "You're next. I'm counting to two, then I'm coming to get you," she called out conversationally.

She was far enough from the trailer that her threat shouldn't have been audible to the smaller man who had darted back inside at the first sign of trouble. Still, the accomplice reappeared in the doorway, quickly followed by a third person. The two goons tripped down the stairs in their haste to comply with Agent Sterling's request.

As they approached their trussed-up partner-in-crime and the light from the fireball illuminated their features, I gasped.

"What?" Agent Thorne asked, suddenly releasing me as if he'd forgotten his arms were wrapped around me.

"That woman," I said, gesturing toward the woman wearing a dark turtleneck that camouflaged the long black braid hanging down her back. "She's been in the diner every morning this week. Said she was a drug rep treating herself to a little vacation after clinching a successful deal in Boston."

"That tracks," Agent Thorne replied.

"Who are these people? This isn't a random break-in, is it?" I asked, glancing at him over my shoulder. He had the courtesy to hold in the laugh I saw dancing in his eyes. "Hey! You don't know me. I could own nice things."

He sobered up and tipped his head apologetically. "You're right. It was rude of me to presume. Do you?"

"Do I what?"

"Own nice things that three thieves would break in to steal?" I didn't buy his butter-wouldn't-melt-in-his-mouth guileless expression.

"No," I replied, lifting my chin, "but you didn't know that for sure."

The left side of his lips quirked up into an impish grin, and he winked. "I didn't, you're right. But she probably did." He tipped his head at the woman, fuming as Agent Sterling zip-tied her hands together.

My jaw dropped. "You mean..."

He shrugged. "She probably cased the joint one day while you were working."

"In that case, why bother breaking in? She'd have known instantly there was nothing to steal. Unless they have a thing for upcycled trash and outdated clothing covered in grease stains."

Agent Thorne barked a laugh loud enough to earn him a glare from his partner.

"Good question, Just Melly. What could she have been looking for if there's nothing worth stealing in there?" he mused. "Could it be she knew that you have something in your possession that you've repeatedly claimed you don't?"

My mouth snapped shut. The amulet. Of course, they were all after the *amulet*. Which I'd stashed less than fifty feet away in the small safe under Aggie's desk.

Don't look toward the diner. Don't look toward the diner. Don't look toward the diner. I kept chanting, even as my eyes darted toward the diner.

"That's what I thought," Agent Thorne said. "Maybe we should take a little walk."

He prodded me in the back with something hard and pointy, and my stomach dropped to my feet.

They were *all* after the amulet. So much for my good guy radar.

THIRTY

Agent Sterling made short work of hog-tying the other two would-be thieves. Just as the rope had tied itself into one last knot, the fireball lighting the yard blipped out of existence, plunging us back into darkness.

The glint of a shiny black eye gleaming in the dark pulled my attention from the weapon urging me forward long enough to make me stumble over a rock. The crow tilted its head to the side and silently watched me flail. Agent Thorne grabbed my arm to stabilize me.

"Thank you," I muttered reflexively, glaring at the crow, who still didn't seem alarmed that I was being roughly handled by someone pressing a gun into my back. Except that when I straightened up, I didn't feel anything other than Agent Thorne's left hand splayed supportively against my lower back and his right cupping my elbow.

I twisted sharply out of his grasp and narrowed my eyes at him as he held his hands up defensively.

"Sorry! Just trying to help. You looked like you were heading down."

"Where's your gun?" I demanded, frowning at his empty hands.

"My gun?" he asked, looking confused. "Where it always is." He lifted the flap of his jacket to reveal a gun tucked snugly into a shoulder holster. "It's regulation. Have to carry it." He leaned forward conspiratorially and opened the other side of his jacket to show me a row of magazines. "Don't tell anyone, but even though I carry ammo, I never load it. Hate the thing. And have you seen who I travel with?" He arched an eyebrow at his partner, who'd single-handedly apprehended three armed robbers, tied them up, and was now murmuring instructions into her cell phone.

I didn't believe for a second that he couldn't load that gun and point it at me faster than he could say, "hands up," but there was no way he'd holstered it in time to grab my arm and keep me from falling.

"You weren't just holding it against me?"

Surprise widened Agent Thorne's eyes. "What? No! That would be a terrible idea. For so many reasons. Not the least of which is that crow over there giving me the stink-eye. Or the fact that you'd never serve me another slice of pie. Which would be an absolute tragedy." He shuddered and shook his head. "Why would I pull a gun on you, anyway?"

Because you want the amulet. Just like those guys. And the people who probably killed the guy who gave it to my mother! I yelled inside my head. Out loud, I said, "Then what was all that growly 'let's take a walk' stuff?"

Agent Thorne's eyes widened even further. "I thought this stuff was upsetting you and I wanted to get you to safety!" he cried. "Why does everyone always think I'm up to no good?" he muttered to himself, running a hand through his hair.

"My apologies," I said, trying to keep my tone as snark-free as possible. "It was unfair of me to accuse you. I'm not exactly myself. It's not every night you come home and find people ransacking your house. Speaking of which, can we go see the damage?" I widened my eyes to make myself appear extra innocent and overwhelmed. Twisting my ankle on the rock had wrenched my nearly healed shoulder painfully enough that I didn't have to force tears into my eyes.

Agent Thorne looked over at the diner, and I saw the moment he was going to argue. I widened my eyes a little further and rubbed my arm for good measure. If I could lead him away from the amulet, I might have time to come up with a plan of some sort.

"I may have pie. If they didn't trash it," I said, glancing at the three prone figures that had either stopped struggling and accepted their fate or been magically walloped into submission.

As expected, the mention of pie did the trick, and he let me lead the way to the Airstream camper.

Nothing could have prepared me for the devastation that awaited me inside.

Shards of plates and cups were smashed into the carpet and covered in the food they'd dumped all over the floor. Every article of clothing I owned had been tossed from the closet, every box opened and emptied.

My breath caught when my eyes landed on my bed. My pillows had been eviscerated, and they'd slashed my mattress to ribbons. More upsetting, the bench cushions I'd so lovingly re-upholstered had also been gutted. Foam chunks littered the small table and the floor.

Nothing had been spared. Not even my nearly full bottles of shampoo and conditioner, which had been squeezed out onto the mess on the floor. The only thing that had been spared the search and destroy treatment was my tiny fridge. Only three of the half-dozen eggs nestled next to four untouched yogurt cups had been cracked and dumped on top of the rest of the mess.

"Oh." My breath whooshed out of me, leaving me hollow and numb as I tried not to think about having to start over again.

"Whoa," Agent Thorne breathed, coming to a stop right behind me. He placed a hand on my shoulder and squeezed.

My eyes darted around the small space, revealing more damage every time they landed on something new.

"I know it seems bad," Agent Thorne said, breaking the silence after a few moments. "But it looks mostly superficial. It won't take long to set things right again."

I rounded on him, hands fisted at my side, rage bubbling up from deep inside me. "Mostly. Superficial?" I ground out through gritted teeth. If I opened my mouth fully, there was no telling what I was going to let loose.

Agent Thorne held his hands up defensively again. "I know. I know. I'm sorry. But look?" He gestured behind me. "They didn't kick in the cabinet doors. Or destroy any furniture. Or the windows. You can get new dishes and groceries. You're probably due for a new mattress, anyway. Aren't we all?"

I looked where he pointed. He was right. The cabinets were empty, but intact. So were the closet and the table. Still, the thought of having to do a second major clean-up so soon after the first was more than I could bear. Brushing away the tears that overflowed, I pushed past Agent Thorne and stepped outside to escape the chaos.

"Can we go to the diner?" Agent Thorne asked, following me out. "Not for pie! Just to sit and talk," he added when I glared at him.

"We might as well," I said, exhaustion making the distance between the camper and the diner appear three times as far as usual. I still had to do all the prep I'd promised Momo. And now I had to figure out where to spend the night.

But at least some poor, terrified woman wasn't sitting with her hands tied behind her back, wondering if she was going to die. That had to count for something, even if the risk hadn't been real.

"If you hadn't been meddling in things that were none of your business, you would have been home when these creeps came calling," Demi said, sounding unbothered by the implication. I shuddered and shook my head, rubbing my hands over the hairs suddenly standing on end on my arms. If I hadn't been trying to thwart an attempted kidnapping, I could have been the terrified woman tied to a chair.

"Would you like some coffee?" I asked Agent Thorne, eyeing the machines lined up behind the counter.

"It wouldn't be reasonable. It being after eleven p.m. and all."

"Not reasonable at all. How would we ever get any sleep?"

"Although it is going to take transport a while to come pick up those dirtbags."

"And it's not like I have anywhere to sleep, anyway."

"Plus, I have all that paperwork I'm going to have to submit before I can call it a night."

"So, that's a yes?" I asked, already heading toward the bank of coffee pots. While I was at it, I could prep everything for the next morning.

"Make it a double, please," Agent Thorne replied.

The familiar routine settled my nerves enough to still my shaky hands and the thoughts bouncing around in my head. By the time I handed Agent Thorne a steaming mug of coffee and busied myself doctoring mine with cream and sugar, I almost felt in control of my life again.

Agent Thorne stared silently at me over his mug for an uncomfortably long time, the amused glint that typically lit his eyes as conspicuously absent as his usual impudent grin. Just as I was about to squirm under his intense scrutiny, he let out a long sigh and put his mug down.

"Melly, I hope you see that it's time for you to stop messing around and give us the amulet." Agent Thorne's stern, no-nonsense expression would have made his partner proud. "These guys were amateurs; the next ones won't be. You're in real danger, and you're out of options."

My hand jerked and resumed trembling, sending overly sweetened coffee flying all over the counter.

So much for feeling in control.

THIRTY-ONE

"Listen. I know we've given you no reason to trust us, but you need to believe me when I tell you we're your best option here." No trace of the goofy sidekick agent fixated on pie remained as he met and held my gaze. I wanted to believe he only wanted to protect me, but I hesitated. His earnest expression and his intense tone screamed, "trust me," a little too loudly. For all I knew, he wanted to help, but if so, it wasn't purely out of the goodness of his heart.

Tension ratcheted between us as I stared into his eyes, trying to discern any hint of an ulterior motive, but he gave away nothing. I was almost convinced his concern was genuine and that I could trust him when his phone vibrated.

While he glanced at his phone and back at me, I reined in the impulse to give in and hand over the amulet. I pulled away from the counter, leaned against the bank of coffee machines, and crossed my arms.

His expression darkened as he instantly assessed how my mood had shifted, and I glimpsed the sharp intelligence he masked with his playful, good-guy persona. "Please, Melly. Let me help you," he said.

"I've told you again and again, I don't know anything about that amulet," I replied, my throat tightening around the lie.

Agent Thorne let out a disappointed sigh that stabbed me in the gut. He just wanted to help. And it wasn't like I wanted the amulet. I could hand it over and wash my hands of the whole thing.

"Can I tell you what I know, since you're reluctant to tell me your part?" the agent asked, arching an eyebrow at me as he shifted into a more comfortable position on his bar stool.

I relaxed my stance and nodded, picking up my mug. As long as he was talking, my secret remained safe.

"Once upon a time," he started and grinned when I laughed at his cheesy opening line. "A power-hungry, ambitious ruler hired a wizard to make him an artifact that would grant him absolute power over his subjects."

"Oh, really? Is that how the story goes?" I teased.

The corner of his lip twitched into a grin that reminded me why I so badly wanted him to be one of the good guys.

"More or less," he answered with a laugh of his own. "The wizard did as he was ordered and created a magical pendant that he named the Allmacht Amulett—the All-powerful Amulet. However, having a good grasp of history and sensing the extent of the king's depravity, he sneakily added a spell to limit the amulet's abilities. Unfortunately for him, the evil ruler immediately discovered the wizard's duplicity and ordered him to remove the guardrail spells. The king tested the altered amulet by forcing the wizard to wall himself off in a cave."

Agent Thorne's eyes glittered with laughter when I let out a strangled gasp.

"Don't worry," he added with a wink. "The lore says that the wizard was immune to his own magic, but he let himself be entombed because he knew of a secret exit from the cave. No one heard from him ever again, so anything is possible. Not that anyone ever checked the cave for remains."

"And the amulet?" I asked to get the story back on track.

"Well, at first, the evil king was content to rule over his people with an iron fist and unrestrained power. But it didn't take him long to realize that he craved more. So, wielding the amulet's magic, he commanded his army to conquer the closest neighboring domain, then the next, so on and so forth. Before long, war had broken out all over the world, and thousands of people were dying every day.

The war didn't end until a well-trained team of witches, heavily protected by wards crafted to counter the amulet's influence, broke into the king's rooms and stole the amulet in the dark of night while he slept."

Agent Thorne was telling the story as if it were a fairytale, but I had the sinking suspicion that he was relating a genuine part of our collective history.

"When he awoke to find the amulet gone, the king ordered his personal guard to find the perpetrators. But without magic compelling them, the men who'd been forced to protect him for years discovered that they no longer had to obey his orders. Many have speculated about what happened next, but the long and short of it is that the king's reign of terror came to a brutal end that day."

"And the amulet?" I repeated hoarsely.

"The amulet was smuggled out of the king's country and locked away for safekeeping. But years of being wielded by a tyrannical megalomaniac had fundamentally altered it. Some even claimed that it gained a semblance of sentience."

Agent Thorne's eyes softened at my distressed moan.

"After decades of being locked up, the Allmacht Amulett took control of a guard tasked with ensuring it remained neutralized. His coworkers found him insensible, lying in the bushes outside their headquarters the next morning, the amulet nowhere to be found. He never fully regained consciousness. The next person they found was more coherent, but she didn't know how she'd ended up in a dumpster two towns away from hers. Over the next few weeks, four more people were found in similar situations with few or no memories of their ordeals."

"Are you saying the amulet possessed them, then discarded them when it found someone more suitable to control?" An icy finger ran down my back as goosebumps erupted along my arms.

Agent Thorne nodded grimly. "Something like that. Though the amulet's influence seemed to wane as it jumped from person to person."

"It was running out of power?" I asked.

"We don't know. All we know is that we found one last man we believe had been under the amulet's influence, nearly dead, a block from the diner your mother worked at for six months." My eyes widened in alarm. "We had our people dig a little into your story. Funny coincidence, don't you think?"

"But..." I stammered. "I never gave you my name." Even to my ears, I sounded absurd. Agent Thorne shot me a look that confirmed that I should have known better.

"Wait. Did you say nearly dead?" The words came out higher-pitched than usual. Agent Thorne cocked his head and looked deep into my eyes.

"Nearly dead. He was never the same after, but he lived a long life following the incident."

"But he's..." I couldn't bring myself to ask the question. I knew the answer. Juliette had seen his ghost.

"Agent Mullins passed away in his sleep three years ago, surrounded by his family."

A tight knot loosened in my chest. "That's nice."

"Yes. We don't all get that luxury," Agent Thorne replied. "Do you see why we need to find and contain the amulet, Melly? In the wrong hands, there's no telling what might happen."

"I do. But I'm still not sure why you're so convinced I have it." We both knew I was wasting my breath, but despite understanding the direness of the situation, something in my gut stopped me from revealing that the amulet was only ten feet away.

Agent Thorne huffed a frustrated sigh and ran his hand through his hair to the back of his neck, which he rubbed absentmindedly as he narrowed his eyes at me.

"Let me recap. Six months ago, just around when your mother passed away from a mysterious wasting illness, the amulet's magical signature tripped our sensors. According to her neighbor—lovely lady who assures me she's taking great care of your mother's plants—you left shortly after."

"How nice of her," I murmured when he paused.

"Fast forward to earlier this week. The amulet's magical signature trips our sensors again, this time in this charming little beach town. Where, surprise, surprise, the daughter of the woman suspected of being the last person to come into contact with Agent Mullins before he was discovered clinging to life just happens to reside."

"Coincidence?" I offered hesitantly. My stomach churned as I remembered the electric shock I'd felt when touching the amulet's bag at the bank. I'd chalked it up to a static electricity build-up. Had it been testing me? I shuddered. Despite having no recollection of putting the small pouch in my pocket, it had hitched a ride home with me from the bank. Had that shock been the amulet taking control of me?

Before I could spin out, I firmly stopped myself from wondering what else the amulet could have made me do. Nausea crawled up my throat as I forced my attention back to the present.

Agent Thorne's usual grin was nowhere to be seen in the deadpan stare he leveled on me. I pressed my hands down on the counter so he wouldn't see them tremble.

"Melly, this is not a joke. We believe that your mother's wasting illness was caused by the amulet draining her of her life force to recharge its core energy." His expression softened when I inhaled sharply. "I'm so sorry."

He leaned forward expectantly when I opened my mouth. I snapped my mouth shut at the last second, picturing him snapping magical cuffs on me after hearing that the amulet had already taken control of me once. Glowering, he shook his head.

"Our people have hypothesized that it needs to absorb a witch's life force to regain full power. What we don't know is why it's trying so hard. To what end? Whatever the reason, it won't lead to anything good."

My chest tightened, squeezing my heart uncomfortably as I squirmed under Agent Thorne's intense stare.

"It's obvious that you know far more than you've let on, Melly. No matter how I twist things, I can only come up with three reasons you'd keep the amulet from us. One, you're protecting someone being controlled by the amulet. Two, despite everything I've just told you, you still think we're the bad guys and are determined to keep it out of our hands. Or three, the amulet already has its claws in you, and we're too late."

His phone vibrated, so he didn't glance my way as my jaw dropped, but I assumed he noticed and filed my reaction away.

He looked up from his phone and stared right into my eyes. If I hadn't already been a puddle of shaky nerves and on the verge of losing the meager contents of my stomach, the heaviness of his gaze would have wrecked me.

"I'll be right back. Think about what I said. I suggest you don't try to run or do anything stupid. You've seen what my partner can do. Believe me when I tell you that you don't want to get on her bad side."

Without another word, he got to his feet and strode out of the diner, leaving me struggling to breathe as he walked away.

My hands shook as I fumbled for my phone. I barely managed to tap out a quick text and hit send before my legs gave out and I sank to the floor.

THIRTY-TWO

"**M**elly? Melly? Where are you?"

A short but intense crying jag had drained me too much to do more than feebly call out, "back here."

As devastating as it had been to learn that an evil, sentient magical artifact had drained my mother of her life force, it was nothing compared to imagining how much worse things could have been. I didn't even want to imagine what might have happened if the amulet had been at full strength when Agent Miller handed it to her. Or if I'd been alone in the camper when the amulet had grabbed hold of my magic.

"Hey! What's going on? Your text just said 911." Juliette rounded the counter and lowered herself to my level. "I came as fast as I could and brought Cassie and Amy. I hope that's okay."

"Are you okay? Did you hurt yourself during our heroic rescue?" Amy asked.

"Heroic rescue?" I asked, finally lifting my head to frown at her.

Instead of squeezing herself into the small space with her friend and cousin, Cassie draped herself over the counter to peer down at me. "Remember? When you almost rescued a poor woman from a fate worse than death, a girls' trip to a spa?"

"Oh. That heroic rescue." My voice sounded flat, even to me. The three women glanced at each other, communicating silently.

Juliette lowered herself next to me and bumped my shoulder with hers. Amy sat across from her on my other side and placed a hand on my knee.

"What happened?" Amy asked softly. "You were fine when we split up."

I took a deep breath and shook my head. "There was a break-in. The Airstream is trashed. Agents Thorne and Sterling carried out an actual heroic rescue."

"What?" Juliette cried.

Cassie echoed Amy's earlier question. "Are you okay?"

The answer took a moment to come to me. Was I okay? Physically, yes. Emotionally? Not in the least.

"I don't really know how to answer that," I replied with a shrug.

"Did they take anything valuable?" Juliette asked. "Did they take the…" She let her voice trail away.

I shook my head. "No. There was nothing valuable in there. The amulet was in the safe here. Though that is what they were after."

"They were?" Amy exclaimed. "How?"

I shrugged again. "Agent Thorne didn't say how, but he assured me that's what they were after. And that others would be coming."

"Wait. Hold up. I need someone to catch me up," Cassie said, holding up a hand.

Glancing at me for permission, Amy summarized what she knew about the situation.

"So, you have an ancient, magical amulet that a stranger handed to your mom before, what, dying?" Cassie looked horrified.

"I don't think it's all that ancient, and he didn't die," I corrected. My body grew heavy in anticipation of relating Agent Thorne's part of the tale. I took a shuddering breath and told them everything he'd shared with me.

"Oh," Amy said, looking shell-shocked.

"Wow," Juliette added.

Cassie just stared at me, her eyes wider than I'd ever seen them. "That is...quite a story." I nodded grimly. "Did you give him the amulet?" She jerked upright when I shook my head. "What? Why not?"

I grimaced. "It's complicated. My mother made me promise to keep it safe. I don't know what to do."

"Didn't you just say that man died a few years ago?" Cassie asked.

I nodded. "Yes, but…"

"And didn't Agent Thorne say they worked for the same agency?" she continued.

I shook my head. "Maybe? Their whole thing is a little nebulous."

"Ah." Cassie nodded slowly, her index finger in front of her pursed lips.

As the women argued about what to do next, I tried to think of a way to tell them that the amulet had already controlled me once. A sharp kick pulled my attention inward, where Demi was stomping around, waving a short sword menacingly, muttering, *"Let it try. Let it try again. It won't even know what hit it."*

"What's going on?" I asked hesitantly.

Demi glowered at me. *"No amulet claws in here. I took care of that thing once, and I'm ready to do it as many times as it takes."*

"You've taken care of it once? What are you talking about?"

Demi rolled its eyes in perfect imitation of the teen protesting her mother's use of her given name and waited for me to connect the dots.

"You showed up when the amulet tried to force itself into me. You're the reason it failed?" Demi strutted proudly and

preened as I blinked disbelievingly. *And I'm safe. Thank you.*"

"*Just doin' my job,*" it drawled in what I suspected was an attempted imitation of Momo. Without waiting for a response, the daemon swung its sword onto its shoulder and resumed stomping around my head.

I winced as the jackhammering resumed, but kept my mouth shut. If the little daemon wanted to march around my head trying on different personas, it was more than welcome to do so as long as it meant I was safe from evil, sentient, human-controlling amulets.

Cassie threw her hands in the air and cried, "We are sitting ten feet from a very dangerous, sentient, magical artifact! We are not equipped to handle that! Juliette, we have to call the Witch Council. They can send the team that took the grimoire away!"

"What council?" I asked, frowning.

"There's a special council of witches who oversee exactly this type of thing!" Cassie exclaimed.

I shook my head. "No. No. There are already too many people involved. Plus, Agent Thorne already accused me of keeping the amulet to use it myself!"

"He what?" Juliette asked, blanching.

"He said it was one of the three possible reasons I was hiding it from them." The weight of his accusations and everything they implied hit me, and I dropped my head into my hand to rub my forehead wearily. "As if I'd want anything to do with the thing that killed my mother." I blinked back the tears that filled my eyes and swallowed the lump in my throat. There would be plenty of time to have a good, long cry after I avoided getting arrested by a secret government agency.

"Melly, what does your gut say?" Amy asked softly, placing a hand on my knee.

"About?" I asked, lifting my head to meet her gaze.

"Agent Thorne and Agent Sterling. Do you trust them? I understand that you know relatively little about them, but in your gut, do you believe you can trust them?" she elaborated.

I hesitated before replying. Did I trust them? I wanted to. I liked them. Both of them, surprisingly. But was that enough?

"I think you can trust them. Not that you asked," Demi piped up, coming to a standstill for a moment.

"You do? Why?" I asked, glancing inward at the little daemon.

It flopped down on a green loveseat it had conjured from somewhere and shrugged. *"Can't explain it. The people in your camper didn't feel trustworthy. Those two do."*

As unscientific or irrational as it was, I understood what Demi was saying. I nodded slowly. "I think I do," I said out loud. "They've given me no real reason to, but it's what my gut says."

"The crow agrees," Demi added, pointing out what I'd missed.

"The crow agrees," I echoed aloud, ignoring Demi's grumble about stealing credit.

"What crow?" Cassie asked, glancing at the other two women to see if they knew what I was talking about. Juliette and Amy both shrugged.

I dismissed their curiosity with a wave of my hand. "I have a crow buddy. It protected me from the intruders, but it let Agent Thorne get me out of the way." It had even looked on approvingly.

"Ah," Cassie said, looking not the least bit surprised at an animal getting involved in human matters. "So, what are you going to do?" she asked, cocking her head quizzically.

"Wing it," I replied as the diner door opened with a swoosh. With a sigh, I got to my feet and brushed off the back of my pants before holding out my hands to help Juliette and Amy to their feet.

"Melly? Are you ready to talk?" Agent Thorne asked as he stepped into the diner, a few feet ahead of Agent Sterling. Had that thread of steel always run under his jocular tone?

I squared my shoulders and nodded once. "We should sit."

THIRTY-THREE

The deputy sheriff arrived as I settled myself across from the two agents.

Cassie and Amy met him at the door to quietly catch him up, leaving Juliette to ask me if I wanted her to stay or go.

A flutter of panic made my voice shake. "Can you stay?" I asked, hating how much I wanted her by my side.

She smiled encouragingly at me with none of the irritation I expected to see. "Of course!" she said, moving to slide into the booth next to me. "I'll stay as long as you need me."

"Hold on," I said, holding a hand up before she could sit and wiggling myself out of the booth. "I might as well..." I arched my eyebrows at her and tipped my head toward the office.

Juliette nodded and stepped out of my way. "Good idea."

When I returned, she was sitting across from the two agents, and all three were looking at each other warily. Amy, Cassie, and Sam were nowhere to be seen.

"Where'd they go?" I asked, glancing around.

"They'll be back," Juliette said as I sat next to her. "They had something to do."

Assuming that her vagueness had more to do with the two strangers sitting across from us than intentionally keeping me out of the loop, I didn't press for more details. Instead, I apologized for not offering coffee and asked if anyone wanted a cup. I directed the question mostly at Agent Sterling, who shook her head after a moment's hesitation.

"It's late," the agent explained. "And it's time to get to the point. Agent Thorne here tells me he's caught you up, but he's unclear on why you won't hand over the amulet." She fixed her gaze on me and waited for me to speak. As interrogation techniques went, it was a good one. Thirty seconds in, and I was ready to tell her anything she wanted to know just to fill the silence. It was a good thing I'd already decided to talk.

"I do have the amulet," I said.

"I knew it!" Agent Thorne cried, pumping his fist in the air. "Told you so," he crowed to his partner, looking so smug that even I wanted to hit him. I got the impression

Agent Sterling was using every ounce of her restraint not to do so herself.

She focused on me, ignoring her partner's small victory dance. I held up my hand when she opened her mouth to speak.

"I have some questions first."

Agent Sterling took a long breath through her nose and nodded impatiently.

"I would like to know how those people knew to come looking for the amulet. They didn't seem very government agent-y. I also want to know what you're going to do with the amulet if I give it to you. I'd hate to be responsible for letting it fall into the hands of another megalomaniac dead set on world domination."

"When you give us the amulet," Agent Sterling said, putting heavy emphasis on the when and shooting me a pointed look, "we will put it in a special pouch designed to neutralize magic. That pouch will be put into a box reinforced with more protective wards and flown to our headquarters, where it will be stored in a vault far, far underground with more fail-safes and wards than you could possibly fathom. Only people with the very highest level of clearance will know it's there or what it can do."

I squirmed, wrestling in my head with what she said until I figured out why it made me so uncomfortable. Juliette got there before I did.

"Aren't the people with the highest level of clearance usually the people at the top of the chain of command?" she asked, her gaze darting back and forth between the two agents.

"Yes! Wouldn't those people be the most likely to be tempted by an amulet that can grant them absolute power?" I added, leaning forward in my seat.

The agents glanced at each other, then at us. Agent Sterling squeezed her lips together and nodded once. "Indeed. But..." She hesitated. "Rest assured that precautions are being put into place to ensure that this artifact never sees the light of day again. I'm afraid I can't tell you more. You're just going to have to trust us." She met my eyes and let down her guard enough for me to see the depths of her resolve.

"I would just like some sort of assurances that I'm not giving the amulet to some underground network of evil masterminds."

Agent Thorne grinned sideways at me, his eyes twinkling with laughter. "I solemnly swear that we are not Hydra or any other evil organization. As we told you the day we met, I work for the DAE, a very legitimate sub-branch of the Federal Bureau of Investigation. My partner over here works for the equivalent branch of the FBI's paranormal counterpart. It's all very aboveboard if a little secretive for obvious reasons. We can arrange to have you talk to our bosses if that would set your mind at ease…Though if we're evil, it would be hard to prove they aren't also," he teased.

"He's telling the truth," Demi said.

"How do you know?"

"Beats me." Demi shrugged. *"Just do."*

I'd be hard pressed to explain that the daemon in my head was the reason I was confident I was making the right decision, but its assurance was comforting.

"And the thieves knew because?…" I prompted.

Agent Sterling's face twisted into a sneer of disgust. "A leak."

"A leak?" I asked, my eyebrows climbing my forehead.

"A bounty hunting organization placed a man on the inside and had him infest our computer system with a worm that granted them access to our database. They have since…" He paused, searching for the right words. "Been taken care of. The hole in the system has been patched, and the security strengthened. But not before a significant amount of data was stolen, including the information gathered by the sensors that picked up the amulet's magical signature flare."

My eyes widened as my imagination ran rampant. "Are there many other artifacts like mine?"

Agent Thorne smiled reassuringly. "Not quite like yours, no. Thankfully. In any case, we will make sure the news of its capture is also leaked. I doubt any other bounty hunters will come after it once word spreads."

"That's reassuring. Thank you," I said, doing my best to pull my thoughts from imagining the worst as I reached behind me to maneuver the small food container out of my bag. It clunked quietly when I placed it on the table between us.

"Is that..." Agent Sterling breathed.

Juliette answered. "Yes. We neutralized it to the best of our abilities."

"Salt?" Agent Sterling asked, tearing her gaze from the small glass container.

Juliette nodded. "Probably not enough, but we used all we had on hand."

"I have more here if you'd like," I added, kicking myself for not thinking to add more sooner.

Agent Thorne shook his head. "No, thank you. That won't be necessary. We have everything we need to keep it, and us, safe." My head swam when he tucked the container into a shimmery silver bag that he pulled out of his jacket pocket, and relief flooded my senses.

"Oh, wow. I didn't realize how tense I was," I murmured, slumping back in my seat.

It wasn't you. It was them, Demi said, sounding smug.

What? How? I asked, glancing inward, expecting to see the steel fortress I'd dropped into place earlier. Instead, an opalescent wall stretched from one end of my head to the other. *"What...?"* I stammered.

Demi beamed proudly. *"I made it. I call it the Opalescence. Catchy, no?"*

"Eh," I replied absentmindedly, running my hand over the glistening surface. Unlike its namesake, the wall wasn't as hard as a rock; it was springy, like a thick rubber membrane. *"How does it work?"*

Demi stopped scowling at my criticism of its naming skills long enough to answer. *"It's a porous surface, which means your magic will never build up to dangerous levels again."*

"Doesn't porous mean thoughts can get through?" I asked, listening for the agents' and Juliette's thoughts. All I got was a deep sense of relief and satisfaction, along with a touch of pride.

"That's the beauty of this!" Demi cried, jumping up and down, clapping its hands. *"It should be thick enough to block complete thoughts, but thin enough to let enough of the magic through to keep it from building up. Genius, right?"*

"Uh-huh," I replied out loud, distracted enough by the wall that I forgot to keep my response in my head.

"Did you say something?" Agent Sterling asked, glancing up from feverishly writing in her small notepad.

"No, sorry," I replied.

A small bubble of joy burst inside me, and it was all I could do to keep myself from humming.

"Feelings! I get their feelings rather than their thoughts!" I cried to Demi, who nodded proudly, grinning from ear to ear. *"That is..."* I laughed internally. *"You're right. That's genius. You're a genius. Thank you."*

"'Bout time you realized it," the daemon grumbled. It did a terrible job of masking how pleased it was at the compliment.

"Wait! What if I want to hear full thoughts?" My face warmed. *"Uh... for safety reasons or something,"* I hurried to add.

"Easy." Demi touched the wall, and a small opening formed under its hand. *"You tell it what you want."*

> *I hope she doesn't hate me for my part in all this. In her shoes, I'd never want to be friends with me now.*

Juliette's anguished thoughts hit me hard, and I grabbed her hand under the table and gave it a quick squeeze as I willed the hole in the wall to close. I grinned as, instead of hearing her next thoughts, a profound sense of relief washed over me.

"The amulet belongs with them," Juliette murmured when the two agents put their heads together to discuss something Agent Sterling was pointing at in her notebook.

"What do you mean?" I asked, keeping my voice low to match hers.

Juliette flexed her fingers with a contented smile. "It could be because he put it in that pouch, but I think the magic released me because the amulet is where it belongs."

The last shred of concern I was harboring about handing over the artifact melted away, and with it went the last of my energy. I tried to hide a jaw-cracking yawn behind my hand, but Agent Sterling noticed anyway.

"I think that's all we need," she said, nudging her partner to exit the booth. "You have my number. You can call me if you need anything, but you shouldn't."

The subtext of her words came through loud and clear, and I laughed in response. "Noted. Don't call."

Agent Thorne laughed. "She's just cranky because it's late and we have a long road ahead of us. Please call if you ever need us. Or if you have an especially yummy pie." He winked as he stepped back to let his partner lead the way.

They'd made it to the door when a thought struck me. "Wait!" I cried, hurrying to catch up.

They turned as one. Agent Sterling gave me a look of patient exasperation.

"The..." I gulped. "What about the money?"

Both of their foreheads creased with confusion.

"What money?" Agent Thorne asked, glancing at his partner, who shrugged.

"We don't know anything about any money," she added.

"But..." I protested.

Agent Sterling held up her hand to stop me. "Melly, please listen carefully when I say this. On the off chance that the amulet you just handed us was in any way linked to any amount of money, we have no knowledge of it. If we were to learn about money connected to this amulet, we'd be forced to open an investigation, which could take decades to resolve. During that time, any related evidence, like, say, money, would languish in an evidence locker somewhere until the case is either shelved in the cold case files or someone discovers something helpful. Do you understand what I'm saying?"

My mouth snapped shut, and I nodded.

"So, what is this money you're asking about?" she asked, leaning closer and arching an eyebrow.

I shook my head. "No money. I'm sorry. I was...ah... confused for a moment. Please forgive me for wasting your time."

Agent Sterling beamed at me as though I'd aced a tough test, then tipped an imaginary cap at me. "Wonderful. Please get some sleep. Your government thanks you for your assistance in this matter."

When their taillights vanished, I still wasn't sure if she'd been talking about helping them find the amulet or dropping the money issue.

THIRTY-FOUR

"It's far too late to make your camper livable. Would you like to spend the night at my place? I'll help you clean up tomorrow if you'd like," Juliette offered, seeing me swaying on my feet.

I opened my mouth to protest, then snapped it shut when I remembered just how badly my place was trashed. Even if the mound of food ground into the flooring wasn't too disgusting to contemplate sleeping next to, my bed was shredded.

"Thank you," I said instead. "I'd appreciate that."

"Come on." Juliette tucked her arm in mine and pulled me toward the door. "Let's see if they spared any of your pajamas. If not, I have some you can borrow."

"We should go out the other way." I flipped the lock to the front entrance closed and led her through the diner to the back.

The moon, which had risen while we were in the diner, was full and bright enough to light up my entire backyard and a team of people hard at work setting my home to rights. A half-sob, half-whimper worked its way up my tight throat, and Juliette caught my elbow just as my legs threatened to buckle.

Full trash bags were piled next to my eviscerated mattress and the remains of my bench cushions, and, through the window, I could see a few people moving back and forth inside. The joy that bubbled up inside me was just as overwhelming as the horror of watching thieves tear my home apart, but it was nothing compared to the gratitude turning my insides to mush.

"What is happening?" I whispered hoarsely to Juliette, clutching her hand for support.

"Looks to me like a subsection of the Portney Main Street Merchants' Association is at it again," she replied with a smile in her voice. "Or it's just the Brewhahas doing what they do best."

"Which is?"

"Showing up for their friends," Juliette replied, squeezing my elbow gently and tugging me forward.

THIRTY-FIVE

Despite the late hour and the cramped quarters, the Brewhahas had cleared every surface and removed everything too damaged to clean up and put away. They'd also miraculously found a mattress that fit perfectly in the nook carved out of the Airstream's limited space.

Between the relief of finally having handed over the amulet, knowing the money was well and truly mine, and my unbelievably squishy and cozy new bed, I'd slept harder than I could ever remember.

I stretched lazily, savoring the lack of tension cramping my muscles or clutching at my chest, and sat up in a blind panic when my eyes landed on the microwave and noticed the time.

The red 12:12 blinked at me lazily, completely oblivious to the fact that Momo had to be flipping out in the diner, wondering why I had missed the breakfast service and was missing the start of the lunch rush.

It wasn't until I was flailing around looking for my phone that I realized he should have come looking for me when I hadn't responded to the dozens of texts he'd presumably sent.

A clang followed by a string of muffled swear words froze me in place, bent over the edge of the bed at an awkward angle, one hand on my discarded jeans, the other clutching the side of the new mattress for dear life. Cold sweat pooled on my lower back as I strained to hear what was happening outside.

"This would be one of those times you should poke a little hole in your beautiful new protective barrier," Demi drawled.

I let out a sound that was a cross between a sob and a chuckle, and did as it suggested. Nothing came through the tiny hole I opened with the gentlest of touches, so I pressed harder against the rubbery membrane. Unfamiliar thoughts poured in as the opening grew.

> *I should never have let anyone help me. There's no way she could sleep through this racket.*
> *I love a party.*
> *We have thirty hamburgers and at least twenty-five hot dogs. Seventy buns should be plenty, right? Maybe I should ask Christina to pull some out of the freezer. Did I remember to*

tell her to invite Raph?

This is the best idea I've had all year. Why
didn't I think of it sooner?

A happy whistle broke through the hush, and I grinned as I let myself drop to the ground. If Momo was whistling, then he couldn't be mad at me.

"What exactly is happening out here?" I called out from the camper's doorway once I found my voice. While I'd been fast asleep, a festive wonderland had been blooming in my yard. Lanterns hung from trees that three children were darting around, stringing with crepe paper. Bouquets of helium-filled balloons bobbed from the backs of folding chairs I'd never seen, and a massive "Welcome to Portney!" sign had been so haphazardly attached to two tree branches that it took me a moment to decipher the crooked words. Half a dozen dismayed faces turned my way, and, almost as an afterthought, Crystal cried, "Surprise!" and blew into one of the noisemakers she was putting in a bucket at the center of a table.

Her outburst shook everyone out of their disappointment, and they joined in with a belated chorus of echoes.

"Welcome to Portney!" Crystal cried, tossing streamers at me and laughing.

"I've been here for six months." I laughed.

Juliette approached and pulled me into a hug. "Yeah, but we weren't one hundred percent sure you were staying. Now we know."

"Oh, you do, do you?" It was easy to tease, because I knew in my gut that she was right.

"Oh, I do," she replied with a laugh and tapped the side of her nose. "Witchy intuition is never wrong."

The Opalescence thrummed with her delight.

"Thank you for this. It's beyond lovely," I whispered to her when she tucked her arm in mine, squeezing affectionately as she drew me into the fray.

"Anything for a friend," she whispered back.

Crystal approached with a party hat in her outstretched hand. She gave me a quick hug after putting it on my head and tucking the elastic under my chin. "Gorgeous!" she declared, inspecting her handiwork. "Sit! You're the guest of honor! Someone get this woman a beer!"

"Whoa," I cried, throwing my hands up as I lowered myself onto a bench. "Can I maybe start with a cup of coffee? We can see where the party goes after."

A warm buzz of joy spread through my abdomen and chest as laughter broke out, and friends stopped by one by one to hug me and officially welcome me to town. The scent of coffee reached me before I spotted Momo cutting through the throng, a steaming mug in each hand.

"So, that's it? I oversleep one day, and everything goes to pot?" I teased, taking a proffered mug with a grateful smile.

He chuckled as he lowered himself to the bench on the other side of the table from mine, his eyes glittering with delight in a way I'd never seen before. "Figured you needed a day off after the night you had. Then decided maybe we need a day off every week. Whaddaya say? We close every Monday? Do what we can to stave off burnout?"

I took a long sip of my coffee as I considered his suggestion. Every day we were closed, we lost money, but we'd lose a lot more if one of us got sick from never taking any time to rest. I was about to propose we alternate Mondays off until we figured out how to get our earnings back to where they'd been when we worked for Aggie. When the tail end of the previous night came back to me, I grinned at him.

"I think we can afford to close one day a week," I said, holding up my mug. "And maybe hire some help."

"Now we're talking." He grinned at me as he clinked his mug against mine.

"What we talking about?" My end of the bench jumped when Remi dropped himself onto the other end. His bright grin fell when hot coffee sloshed out of my mug, and I yelped. "I hurt you! I sorry!"

"It's okay, Remi," I said, wiping my hand on my jeans. "I'm not hurt. I was just surprised. Are you having fun?"

He nodded his head enthusiastically, momentary angst instantly forgotten. I'd seen him running around the yard with Cassie's daughter Aurie and her friends, all three of whom had been far sweeter about letting him galumph after them than I would have expected. They'd patiently coached him on how to hang garlands until they'd all realized he was far better suited to holding the ladder for them.

Spotting his new friends across the yard, Remi jumped to his feet and trundled off. "Back later!" he called to us over his shoulder.

"We'll be here!" I replied, my heart close to bursting with happiness. My whole life, I had longed to be part of this kind of casual, easy community where everyone was welcomed with smiles and hugs, and where people showed up for each other without being asked.

"You're good people, Melly," Momo said, like he'd given it a lot of thought and had finally come to that conclusion. "I'm glad you're my partner." He laughed at the goofy grin that spread across my face.

"I'm glad you're my partner, too," I replied quickly before I got too choked up to speak. Luckily for me, a black mass rapidly approaching the table distracted me long enough to stave off a gush of happy tears.

I focused on staying still as my crow buddy landed at the other end of the table with a small flap of his wings. As improbable as it sounded, I had the distinct impression the crow had made a point of keeping his movements small so I wouldn't be overwhelmed. The crow hopped across the table to drop a rock in front of me, then hopped back. Again, I was certain it knew exactly how far away to stay to avoid troubling me.

When I didn't pick the rock up right away, it bobbed its head up and down a few times.

"Would you pick up the darn rock already?" Demi grumbled. *"Put the poor thing out of its misery. And make sure you give it a nice, long look. Uh... just in case."*

"You know, you can just say you like pretty rocks. I won't judge you," I replied, scooping up the shiny stone.

"Did you know crows are messengers between this world and the spirit realm?" Aurie asked, approaching the table to stand near the crow, who sidled closer and tilted its head insistently until she got the message and ran two fingers down its glossy head. If it had been a cat, it would have purred.

"Oh, yeah?" I'd heard that crows were special, but not that. "You think this one has a message for me?" I asked, holding up the rock.

"He says it's a present from your mom. It reminded her of you." Aurie said matter-of-factly, without a hint of humor.

"He what? I don't understand."

The crow somehow managed to look down its beak at me without moving its head out from under Aurie's hand. Cassie's daughter rolled her eyes at me. "Magic. Duh. Didn't my mom tell you I can talk to animals?"

Momo chuckled. "Chil', I can talk to animals, too."

Aurie stuck her tongue out at him. "But can you understand what they say back?"

The large man burst into gales of laughter, and I stared at him with my jaw hanging open. In six months, I'd counted myself lucky if I saw Momo smile once or twice a week, but the man guffawing at her sass on the other side of the table seemed like a different person than the cook wracked with stress.

The crow nudged Aurie's hand with its beak, and she cocked her head as if listening to something no one else could hear. She nodded a few times as she listened, then finally looked at me.

"She told him to call you Melly-Boo so you'd know it was her. And if that didn't work, he was supposed to say you were his favorite melody."

My eyes filled with tears, and a sob burst loose. I clasped the stone in my fist and held it against my chest, covering my mouth with my other hand. "Mama?"

The crow bobbed up and down and skittered side to side in a strange little happy dance. Aurie and Momo laughed at its antics as I blinked back tears furiously.

"He wants to make sure you understand that he's not your mom, but he's keeping an eye on you for her."

I swiped at an escaped tear, shooting Aurie and the crow a tremulous smile. "Thank you," I mouthed, not trusting myself to speak. The crow bobbed its head up and down, then hopped away to launch itself into the sky. Without another word, Aurie scampered away to catch up with her friends.

People came and went all afternoon, drawn by the laughter and the sign on the diner telling people we were closed for the day, and inviting them to join us in the back. Far more than thirty hamburgers and twenty-five hot dogs were served, but somehow, we never ran out.

The crowd grew smaller as the sun went down, and by the time the lanterns and the surprise network of tiny fairy lights tucked among the trees' leaves had blinked on, the only people left were the Brewhahas. Momo had excused himself hours earlier when Remi had reached his meltdown point, and even Sam had been called away by a blurping radio hanging off his belt.

The women who'd become more than just passing acquaintances since Aggie had crashed her car into the diner and changed the trajectory of my life had pulled chairs up to a firepit I knew for sure hadn't been in the yard before that day. The fire crackled happily, bathing all of us in a warm, happy glow that matched the one warming me on the inside. I had enough money now to move into a house or an apartment, but I couldn't think of anywhere I'd rather be. I leaned back in my chair and let out a happy sigh that drew Juliette's attention.

"Everything okay?" she asked.

I smiled lazily back at her. "Everything is great. It's just nice to be home."

THIRTY-SIX

By the next evening, the only thing that remained of the previous day was Momo's good mood and a slightly persistent throbbing behind my left temple. Getting up for work after a long, lovely day off was almost harder than it would have been if we hadn't been closed for a day. It almost made me rethink our plan to take weekly breaks.

If I did the math properly, our latest meatloaf night had ten more customers than the previous week. Regulars we hadn't seen since Aggie's accident had stopped by to officially welcome me to town and had stayed for dinner, exclaiming that the place hadn't changed nearly as much as they'd feared.

That comment had been delivered with pointed looks at the fairy lights I'd brought in from the yard and hung around the restaurant. I liked the whimsical touch it lent to the vintage décor.

By the time I'd led the returning regulars to their favorite booth, all I could sense from them was excited anticipation. Any reservations they'd had about our ability to maintain Aggie's standards had vanished by the time I brought them their heaping platefuls of fragrant food.

"Just like I promised," I said, placing the last plate on the table. "Same food, same great service. Enjoy!"

I drifted away in a cloud of thank yous that faded to happy silence as they tucked in. Their delight twined itself around the other feelings I was picking up from the happy diners around me. In a minute, table four would need more water, and someone to my left was getting impatient. I hurried over to the customer raising his hand to catch my attention.

The man's confusion only lasted as long as it took me to pull the table's bill out and hand it to him with a wide smile. "Thank you for coming in tonight. We hope to see you again next week!"

It had been a long day after a long week. My feet and my lower back throbbed in concert with my head. Even so, I couldn't wipe the silly grin off my face.

I had felt painfully adrift since I'd lost my mother. She'd taken with her my sole purpose in life, and without it and her, I hadn't known what to do with myself. On the rare occasions when I'd given in to the grief and sadness, part of me had quaked with fear that I'd never again feel like I belonged or know what I was supposed to do with my life.

The fear lurking in the back of my head had vanished as the certainty that I was exactly where I was supposed to be, doing precisely what I needed to do, had taken root. Serving meatloaf and mashed potatoes was a different way of taking care of people, but I couldn't think of anything more worthwhile than serving comfort food to the people who made up the heart of this magical little town.

"Melly! Can we have the check, please?" Amy called from the end of the diner where the Brewhahas liked to sit.

"Nope," I replied, grinning at her. "Sorry. Boss man says your money's no good here, and I agree with him. Dinner's on the house tonight," I said to the whole table. "My way of saying thank you for seeing me through these challenging few days and for cleaning up my home."

"That is very sweet, and entirely unnecessary," Hattie, the Brewhaha I knew the least, chided me with a wide grin and twinkling eyes. "But we accept humbly."

The table burst into laughter.

"Hey! Do you two know what you're doing about the name? Is this place going to remain 'Maggie's Magic?'" Amy asked, leaning over to drop a few bills at the end of the table.

Her friends all followed suit until they'd deposited a stack of cash that far exceeded the value of the food they'd eaten.

I half shrugged and made a face. "I think we both agree we need a new name. We just haven't come up with the right one yet. Let me know if you have any suggestions!"

A pulse of distress drew my attention to the other side of the diner.

"Should I be listening?" I asked Demi as I hurried in that direction, tucking the generous tip from the Brewhahas into my apron pocket.

The daemon materialized inside my head, nodding grimly. *"I don't think they're upset about the meatloaf."*

"Funny," I replied.

With a gentle touch, a small opening formed in the Opalescence, and I sorted through the thoughts I picked up as I meandered from table to table, checking in with diners and keeping a mental ear out for the source of the distress I could still feel emanating off to my right, its intensity ebbing and flowing rhythmically.

They'll never believe it was an accident. I wouldn't. I'd call the cops so fast, their heads would spin. What am I supposed to do?

I strained, but the thoughts faded in and out of hearing in time with the waxing and waning general sensation of angsty malaise. None of the people still enjoying their meatloaves were moving, so the person I was sensing had to be... My eyes met hers as I glanced out the window. I recognized the car from the day after Aggie's crash, but the woman behind the wheel only bore a passing resemblance to the haughty daughter who'd whisked away my boss and friend without so much as a goodbye.

Heather glanced away, but not before a flood of guilt and shame hit me with the intensity of a sonic pulse. By the time I'd caught my breath and opened my eyes again, her car was nowhere to be seen. The only sign that I hadn't imagined the whole thing was a gnawing dread in the pit of my stomach and a nagging suspicion that I'd been right about her strange behavior the day we'd paid for the diner.

When Aggie had voiced her dislike of Heather's husband, I'd assumed it was knee-jerk motherly protectiveness. It had been clear to all of us that Heather's husband stressed her out. But what if there had been more to it? What if Heather was in real trouble and Aggie needed my help?

If you enjoyed The Magic of Meatloaf, **please take a moment to leave a rating or review** *to help other readers discover Melly, Juliette, and Cassie's magical world.*

Not quite ready to say goodbye to the Portney crew? Wondering what they'll name the diner?

Read about the Big Portney Diner Name Contest, where you, along with everyone in Portney, get a vote and Remi picks the winner. *(Yes, he is accepting bribes in the form of popcorn or screenings of 'The Muppet Movie.')* Download your free bonus chapter at https://bit.ly/TheMagicOfMeatloafBonus

Is this your first visit to Portney? If so, don't miss the

Baking Up a Magical Midlife series. **Read on** for a small taste of the magical hijinks that take place in Cassie's bakery, *La Baguette Magique!*

A nibble (excerpt) of Butter, Sugar, Magic

If you enjoyed the *The Magic of Meatloaf*, but haven't yet discovered the other series set in Portney, then more new friends are waiting to meet you! ☐

Read on for a small taste of <u>Butter, Sugar, Magic</u>, book 1 in Cassie's witchy *Baking Up a Magical Midlife* series.

"What are you looking at, Mom? We already had breakfast. Plus, it's closed," Aurie said, glancing up from her tablet.

I was too mesmerized by the bakery in front of me to answer. I rolled down the window to get a clearer look. Not a ruin. Not a hole in the wall. Not something made up to get me to hand over my personal information or however identity thieves operate. Just the most perfect bakery I could ever have imagined, smack dab in the middle of the most adorable downtown I'd ever seen.

La Baguette Magique!

The name was painted in a swirly font on a huge glass window framed in a pretty periwinkle blue. A loaf of French bread shooting sparks from the tip was stenciled under the name. Max would have hated everything about the place. The fantasy-loving child in me adored it. It was literally the bakery of my dreams, as in, I was pretty sure I had actually dreamed of this exact bakery at some point. And, if the lawyer was to be believed, it was mine. All mine. *My* pretty little bakery in the heart of a pretty little town.

"Aurie, pinch me."

She looked up from her game, scowl at the ready. "What?"

"Never mind." Shaking her head at the general absurdity of grown-ups, she went back to her screen.

Pinching my own arm did nothing to dispel the mirage in front of me.

When the lawyer said bakery, I heard Max snort dismissively in my head. *Foodservice! Ha! Total time and money suck.* I knew he was right. There was no way to get rich slinging coffee and croissants. Well, okay, a few people had, but they were making it near impossible for anyone else to do the same.

I tried to rein in my galloping imagination. It was all too easy to see myself in there, selling pastries and bread, chatting with regulars, loving every minute of it. But it simply wasn't a rational choice. Running a bakery wasn't a realistic career option for a single mom. And Aurie's dad lived a zillion miles from here. Not to mention the fact I knew exactly nothing about running a business of any kind, let alone something foodservice related.

I glanced down at Aurie. It had been a long two days and I absolutely had to deliver on my promise of lunch and fun, but first, I needed to set foot in the bakery. Just to see.

I mean, it was the responsible thing to do, right? We had nowhere to go after we explored Boston. The lawyer had mentioned a fully furnished move-in-ready apartment. If this place was livable, it would be smart to use it as our home base until I figured out what came next.

The rationale was flimsy at best, but I clung to it for dear life. I just wanted to see it. Walk around. Imagine myself living there. Indulge my inner child a little longer. After the last few weeks, I owed myself this tiny fleck of joy.

<u>Butter, Sugar, Magic</u> and the rest of the *Baking Up a Magical Midlife* series is available on KU, in eBook on Amazon, and in paperback and audio wherever books can be found online.

About The Author

Jessica Rosenberg is the queen of cozy witchy #FriendshipCore fiction that makes readers feel like they're having coffee with their best friends. She lives on the foggy Central Coast of California with her two wonderful teens, two playful dogs, and a mischievous orange cat named Persimmon for obvious reasons. When she's not weaving magical tales or getting lost in a good book, Jessica can probably be found strolling along the beach, searching for sea glass treasures even though she should probably be tidying her office.

Let's keep in touch

Sign up for my newsletter

at blueoctopuspress.com or by scanning the QR code for a fun, tasy treat.

Not a fan of newsletters? Find me on Facebook facebook.com/JessicaRosenbergFP or on Instagram instagram.com/kikarose for updates and fun.

Books by Jessica Rosenberg

Baking Up a Magical Midlife Series - Cassie's Story

Wyrd Words & Witchcraft Series - Juliette's Story

Midlife Magic on the Menu Series - Melly's Story

Stand Alone Books

www.ingramcontent.com/pod-product-compliance
Lightning Source LLC
Chambersburg PA
CBHW030731310726
48969CB00005B/1187